Cleveland took Freddie's hand in his. "Why are you trying to be so hard?"

Snatching her hands away from his, Freddie focused an intense glare on him. "Excuse me? So since I'm not throwing myself at you, I'm being hard?"

"That's not what I'm saying, but you could lighten up a bit since you're going to have the pleasure of spending the night with me."

Scoffing at his suggestion, Freddie folded her arms underneath her breasts. "As if that's some sort of prize. I don't want to spend all night here."

"I have a nice room at the Best Western."

Freddie raised her hand to slap him, but Cleveland was quick enough to block her blow. When he enclosed her hand in his, he whirled her around as if they were dancing, then pulled her against his chest. In one quick movement, he brought his lips down on top of hers. Surprisingly, she didn't resist him and she tasted even better than she looked.

Freddie didn't realize what was happening until her lips met his. Damn, he felt so good, so strong and warm. Why had her treacherous body responded to his soft lips and warm tongue? Why had she melted against the rigidness of his body? Before she'd gotten too heady from the passion of Cleveland's kiss, Freddie regained her senses and pushed him away. This time her smack made the connection with his jaw . . .

Also by Cheris Hodges

JUST CAN'T GET ENOUGH

LET'S GET IT ON

Published by Kensington Publishing Corp.

More Than
He Can Handle

CHERIS HODGES

Dafina
Books

Kensington Publishing Corp.

http://www.kensingtonbooks.com

DAFINA BOOKS are published by

Kensington Publishing Corp.
850 Third Avenue
New York, NY 10022

All Kensington Titles, Imprints, and Distributed Lines are available at special quantity discounts for bulk purchases for sales
promotions, premiums, fund-raising, and educational or insti-
tutional use. Special book excerpts or customized printings can
also be created to fit specific needs. For details, write or phone
the office of the Kensington special sales manager: Kensington
Publishing Corp., 850 Third Avenue, New York, NY 10022,
attn: Special Sales Department, Phone: 1-800-221-2647.

Dafina and the Dafina logo Reg. U.S. Pat. & TM Off.

ISBN-13: 978-0-7582-3151-2
ISBN-10: 0-7582-3151-2

First mass market printing: February 2009

10 9 8 7 6 5 4 3 2 1

Printed in the United States of America

This book is dedicated to my fans who loved Cleveland so much that they wanted to see his story told in his own book.

To Louise Brown, thank you for staying in my ear about Cleveland.

To Amesia Brewton, thank you for all of your support.

To the members of the Cheris Hodges Book Club (groups.yahoo.com/group/cheris_f_hodgesbookclub), thank you for being there for me and encouraging me when I have writer's block.

Acknowledgments

Without the help and support of my parents, Doris and Freddie Hodges, I wouldn't be doing this. So, thanks for that first word processor and laptop computer. I also know that I couldn't do this without my sister, Adrienne Dease. Thank you for listening and reading my e-mails and giving me advice about life and writing.

To all of the book clubs who have read my work, SBS Book Club, NC Piedmont-Triad RAWSISTAZ, Sista-friends Book Club, Sistas Unlimited Book Club, Akili Essence Bookclub and APOOO Books, thank you.

To my agent, Sha-Shana Crichton, thank you for all of your hard work. To my editor, Selena James, thank you for helping me craft a better story. To the reader holding this book, I appreciate you picking up this story and I hope you have as much fun reading it as I did writing it.

Chapter 1

Every head turned when Cleveland Alexander walked
into the dining hall of First Baptist Church in Covington,
Georgia. Groups of women huddled together and whispered
about the caramel God who had entered the building and all
the wanton things that his chiseled body made them want to
do. As he walked, their eyes followed him like he was the
flame and they were the moths, only they wouldn't mind
getting some of his fire.

One bridesmaid wanted to stare into his slate gray eyes
and run her fingers through his long, black Nubian locks
while he kissed her senseless, because despite the frown
on his thick lips, they looked so kissable and delicious.
Another bridesmaid leaned into her friend and told her that
if she had the chance, she'd turn that frown on his face into
the biggest smile because a man like that needed a woman
who could work her hips. The only thing that stopped her
from giving a demonstration was a stern look from the
reverend who'd overheard their conversation.

But there was one woman who didn't give a damn if he
smiled or not. The only thing that Winfred Barker cared
about was seeing him turn around and walk out the door so

that he could get to the Atlanta Falcons pep rally that he couldn't stop talking about. Unfortunately, she was the only woman who was going to know the feel of Cleveland's big hands. He was the best man and she was the maid of honor and they had to walk down the aisle together. While there was a table full of bridesmaids who would've switched places with her in a heartbeat, Freddie was dreading spending time with Cleveland Alexander. Sure part of it had to do with the fact the she was tired of hearing him complain. Cleveland had told everyone in earshot that the only reason he'd been a part of the wedding party was because his brother, Darren Alexander, was expecting his first child and at the last minute he'd graciously stepped up and stepped in for him. But she couldn't deny his sex appeal, either. Freddie glanced at Cleveland as he took a seat at the table with the groomsmen. She rolled her eyes when she heard him start with that damned Falcons pep rally story—again. Part of her wanted to walk over there and ask him why he was even here. The best man was supposed to be the friend of the groom and if this is how he treated his friends, she would hate to be one of his enemies.

The bride, Lillian Thomas, walked over to the table where the bridesmaids sat. "Ladies, thanks for a great rehearsal." She ran her fingers through her shoulder-length raven hair for dramatic effect. Freddie smirked as she watched her friend. Lillian had always had a flair for the dramatic, but this wedding had turned her into an actress worthy of an Oscar. "I appreciate all of your hard work, and I really enjoyed last night's bridal shower. Give yourselves a hand," Lillian said, then she turned to Freddie. "Now, if I can borrow the maid of honor for a moment."

Looking at her best friend and seeing the look of drama in her eyes, Freddie figured that she wasn't going to be eating her plate of spaghetti and marinara sauce tonight.

Rising to her feet, she headed to a quiet corner with Lillian. "What's up Lil?" she asked, ignoring the rumbling in her stomach. Lillian had been keeping her so busy that she hadn't had a bite to eat since breakfast, which had been more than twelve hours ago.

"I need you to find out what Cleveland and those groomsmen have planned for tonight. See, if Darren had been the best man, I wouldn't be worried about a bachelor party, you know? He's married and wouldn't do anything too wild. But Cleveland . . ." Lillian cut her eyes in his direction and a dark shadow seemed to cover her face. "He's a bachelor and I'm sure he's planned something wicked. The last thing I want is to have my future husband spending the night before our wedding with some greasy, silicone-enhanced stripper. You remember what happened with Mario Lopez and that pretty B-list actress he was going to marry. He cheated on her the night before their wedding. It's okay if they have a party planned, but do strippers have to be involved?"

"Lil, you know your future husband loves you more than anything in the world. Besides, you're not a pretty B-list actress," Freddie joked. Lillian slapped her friend on the shoulder.

"Freddie," Lillian said. "I'm serious. I don't want to be up all night worrying about what my future husband is doing."

"It's Louis's last night as a free man, let him have his fun." Honestly, Freddie didn't want to talk to Cleveland. Though she thought that Cleveland was beyond arrogant and a total jerk, he embodied everything that made her knees quiver. Maybe that's why she kept looking for reasons not to like him. If she didn't like him, she could play down the attraction that had been building since the moment their eyes met. She didn't want to admit it, but she felt a jolt when he closed his hand around hers as they walked down the aisle during the rehearsal.

"Louis will always be a Freeman."

"You're corny, I know the man's last name is *Freeman,* but you know what I mean."

Crocodile tears welled up in Lillian's eyes and Freddie knew that her friend was about to start with the theatrics. *Here it comes,* she thought.

"When you get married, you will understand what I'm feeling. I don't want my future husband to spend the night before our wedding with some hootchie on his lap."

Freddie rolled her eyes. "Umm, you got a lap dance at your bridal shower and you still want to marry him. I don't think a stripper is going to change his mind about marrying you."

Lillian sighed, placed her hands on her hips and pouted at her best friend. "I don't think he's going to cheat on me or run off with the stripper. I just want to know what's going on."

Slapping her hand against her forehead, Freddie expelled a loud breath. "Whatever."

"Just ask Cleveland. No one is near him now, you could get it over with right now." Lillian practically pushed Freddie in Cleveland's direction.

Rolling her eyes, Freddie slowly walked over to him. Each step she took toward him made her heart race. *Calm down,* she thought. *He's just a man, no matter how good he looks.*

"Excuse me," Freddie said as she sat in the empty chair to his right. "Can we talk for a moment?"

Cleveland fought back his smile when Freddie asked him if they could talk. Hell yes, they could talk. His excitement was tempered, though. From the moment he arrived in Covington, every bridesmaid had hit on him. He was flattered, as any man would be, but Cleveland liked a challenge. And she was the only one who hadn't hit on him, but he'd be willing to hear her out if that's what she wanted to talk about. He studied her face as she sat down. She was a beauty—rich brown skin like ebony wood and the darkest brown eyes that he'd ever seen. Her hair, which was naturally curly, looked to be softer than cotton. With it pulled back off her face, her striking beauty shone like the sun in the sky.

"Yes?" he said, keeping his voice cool. The last thing he wanted was to reveal the lusty fantasy he'd been having about her since he held her hand walking down the aisle.

Sighing, she rolled her eyes, "Look, Lillian's a little worried about what you're planning for Louis's bachelor party tonight."

"Really?"

"Do you even speak in sentences? Or do you have to be complaining about how much you don't want to be here to do that? If you could just not keep Louis out too late, Lillian would appreciate it."

Cleveland snarled at her. "It's Winfred, right?"

"Freddie to my friends. But you can call me Miss Barker," she said, her voice tinged with indignation.

"Well, Miss Barker, tell Lillian that I have no plans to keep her husband out at all tonight. I'm a stand in, I'm getting him to the church on time and I'm holding the rings. Other than that I'm doing nothing else. If I had my choice . . ."

"You'd be in Atlanta at the Falcons' pep rally," Freddie finished. "I know, you've been saying it for a day and a half. You're not there so I wish you would get over it."

"You women like stuff like this? A big production for

nothing? Instead of going into debt to declare your undying love, why not go to a Justice of the Peace?"

"But this isn't your wedding, so show a little respect to your friend and shut up." Freddie rose to her feet, casting a sidelong glance at Cleveland. Even though she was scowling, she had the prettiest lips he'd ever seen. He was ready to write her off, though. She was obviously one of those stuck up sisters who thought her role as maid of honor made her an extension of the bride. Lillian was a bridezilla, if he'd ever seen one, and her friend *Miss Barker* was one in training.

"Listen, lady," Cleveland said, "I'm showing respect, as you say, just by being here as the best man. My brother has an obligation to his wife and I came in off the bench to walk you down the aisle. Where's the gratitude? All I'm getting from you is attitude."

Whirling around, Freddie focused her dark glare on him and Cleveland thought for a second that she might take a swing at him. And even though she had an evil glint in her eyes, her lips looked delectable, and he had to fight the urge to kiss her in a way that he was certain she hadn't been kissed in a long time—if ever.

"You have a high opinion of yourself that I just don't share," she said as she turned and walked away.

Roland Hamilton, one of the groomsmen, walked over to the table with his third helping of spaghetti. "She shot you down, huh?"

Cleveland waved his hand as if he were swatting annoying gnats. "Lillian said not to keep her future husband out too long tonight. While you fools are out spending money you don't have at some strip club, I'll be in my hotel room."

"What do you have against strip clubs? Besides, we got to help this man remember what he's giving up," Roland said in between bites of pasta.

"This is a waste of my time. I'll bet you these two won't last a year," Cleveland said snidely as he watched Lillian straighten Louis's shirt.

Roland wiped his mouth. "Shit, I don't give them six months. But I've been wrong before too. Look at Darren and Jill, hell, who thought they would still be together. When's the baby coming? I still can't believe that they're married and about to be parents."

"Darren said Jill was having severe labor pains last night. The doctor thought she was losing embryonic fluid, so she's been in the hospital for the last few days. Her pregnancy was high risk from the beginning," Cleveland said.

Roland nodded as he twirled spaghetti around his fork. "Chief has been on pins and needles lately," he said of Darren.

"He really wants to be a father and will do anything to make sure his wife and unborn child are all right," Cleveland said as he glanced down at his food.

Roland ripped into a piece of garlic bread before saying, "I can't believe that rich woman wanted Darren. Hell, I should've worked that night and I could be Mr. Jill Atkinson." He wiped a spot of sauce from his lips with the back of his hand. Cleveland looked at his friend in disgust and laughed.

"Only if she would've gone blind that night."

An excited Louis walked over to the table. "All right, where's the bachelor party and when are we leaving?" He glanced over his shoulder a few times as if he was checking to make sure Lillian wasn't in earshot. "I love Lillian and all, but if I don't get out of here soon, we're going to elope. Who knew weddings were this stressful? Let's hit it, guys."

Yawning, Cleveland rose to his feet. "That's on y'all.

But before you get too drunk and up to your eyes in strippers, make my reservations for Mardi Gras."

Louis shook his head. "I can't believe I had to bribe you to step up and be my best man. That's real foul, man."

"You're lucky it's only costing you a trip to New Orleans. After all the Falcons went through to make it to the playoffs, you got me down here in Newton County when I could be partying and making use of my sister-in-law's sky box in the Dome. Besides, you know the future Mrs. Freeman doesn't like me."

"Well," Roland said, "the way these women are throwing themselves at you, you should be paying Louis. I'll give Lillian credit, she has some fine friends. There is nothing like banging a bridesmaid."

Louis laughed hysterically, "Too bad you won't be finding out what that's like. Lil said the women are talking and they want you to leave them alone."

"All these fine women around here, it's like being in a candy shop. They need to stop acting so stuck up and get with this good thing. I'm going to say it again, your future wife got fine friends."

Cleveland's eyes sought out Freddie and he silently agreed.

Chapter 2

Just as Freddie was about to take a bite of her cold dinner, Lillian pulled her away from the table again. *Damn it,* she thought as Lillian dragged her back to the corner.

"What did Cleveland say?" she demanded.

"Nothing. He said there isn't a party, or at least he isn't involved in it."

Lillian folded her arms across her chest. "Whatever. Why does he keep staring at you?"

"Who?"

"Cleveland. I like his brother a lot better than him. Cleveland is so blah. He's one of those guys who's good to look at, but once you talk to him, he is so arrogant."

Tell me about it, Freddie thought. Her eyes collided with Cleveland's and he smiled, well it was more like a smirk. She knew he was the kind of man that her mother, Loraine, had warned her about. A man like her father, Jacques Babineaux. He probably thought the sun didn't rise until he got out of bed.

She rolled her eyes in repugnance at the thought of Cleveland getting out of bed, shirtless with his hair spilling over his shoulders while some bimbo lounged in his bed.

She could almost hear him softly telling his booty-du-jour that it was time for her to leave. Surely, a man like that didn't sleep alone often. Turning her head, Freddie cast a sidelong glance at Cleveland as he laughed it up with his friends. As infuriating as he was, she couldn't deny that this man had sex appeal beyond description. Maybe it was the way his light eyes twinkled when he laughed or the curve of his lips when he smiled. And what lips they were, thick and luscious, reminding her of juicy strawberries. Their eyes met again and her hormones betrayed her by heating her up like a summer's day in the desert. How she wanted to tear her eyes away from him, but she couldn't. And it seemed that he knew it and liked it. Licking his lips, he winked at her and held up his glass in a mock salute.

Lillian looked from Freddie to Cleveland. "So what's that all about?" she asked.

Shrugging, Freddie pretended that she didn't know what Lillian meant. "Who knows? Do you know all he's been talking about is the Atlanta Falcons? Why would he agree to stand in for his brother if he was only going to complain?"

"That's just who he is . . ." Lillian stopped talking as she saw the florist walk into the reception hall. "What is this? These are not the silk flowers that I ordered. I wanted pink, this is mauve." Her voice rose several octaves as she stalked over to the florist. The few people who were left in the reception hall started making their way to the door, as if they could feel the storm brewing. Lillian didn't handle stress well, she just screamed at whoever was around, whether they deserved it or not.

Freddie stuck her finger in her right ear as the shrill from her friend's voice seemed to split her eardrum. Ah, there it was, the maid of honor migraine. She knew it wasn't going to be long before it flared up. *Why did I agree to do this? I should've stayed in New Orleans and sent a gift. These big weddings are a waste of time anyway.* She ran her hand down her face and closed her eyes. When she opened them, Cleveland was standing inches away from her.

"What do you want?" she asked.

"I couldn't help but notice you staring at me, which I found kind of odd, because moments ago, you were chewing me out," he said, with a smile plastered on his face.

Freddie didn't like the way his silky voice made heat rush to her cheeks and her groin catch fire. And she couldn't stand the fact that her heart was doing flip-flops at the sight of his smile. "First of all," she said, hoping her voice didn't waver or crack, "you flatter yourself, I wasn't looking at you."

Stepping closer to her, Cleveland laughed, his breath tickling the tip of her nose. "I know you were staring. But that's okay, because I was doing the same thing."

"Don't you have a gentleman's club to go to?"

"Nope."

"Well, excuse me, but I need to go check on Lillian. At least I'm doing my duties with a smile," Freddie said, needing to escape Cleveland. When she inhaled, his masculine scent filled her nostrils and if she didn't turn away now, she'd fantasize about what it would feel like to be held in those strong arms and have his lips pressed against hers.

Watching Freddie walk away made all types of thoughts dance through his head and most of them had her walking straight into his bedroom. It had been a long time since he'd had to chase a woman. The thrill of the chase was much better than just having everything handed to him on a platter. Freddie definitely wasn't trying to hand him anything and that made him want everything she had to offer. Louis walked up to his friend, forcing him to tear his eyes away from Freddie's shapely backside. "You're never going to get any of that, so don't even try it."

"I can get whatever I want," Cleveland said confidently.

"That's a hot-blooded Louisiana babe. She and Lillian grew up together and went to Xavier. When Lil and I were dating in college, Freddie was always around. She was pretty cool, and I thought she'd make a brother a great girl-friend and give us some space. Then I made the mistake of trying to hook her up with my cousin who was at Dillard. Well, he said something that she didn't like and she ripped him a new one. I think she made him cry. Ever seen *Deliver Us From Eva?* She's the Eva prototype."

Shrugging him off, Cleveland said, "She can't be that bad. If anyone can break her, you're looking at him."

Louis shook his head as he laughed hysterically. "She's not a stallion. Oh, my bad, this is your MO."

"What are you talking about?" Cleveland asked.

"You go after that unattainable woman so you don't have to commit, but can say 'I tried.' Aren't you tired of serial dating? Countless encounters that lead to nothing?"

Cleveland placed his hand underneath his chin and pretended to be deep in thought. "No. Don't think that because you're getting married that it's your job to marry everyone else off. Darren is doing a good job of trying, but it's not going to work. Marriage and misery seem to go hand in hand. So, while I'm still young and fly, I'm going to enjoy myself. There are too many single women in Atlanta to be tied down to just one."

"Who did a number on your heart?" Louis asked.

Looking away from his friend, Cleveland didn't answer him. He didn't have a snappy comeback because he'd never been brave enough to fall in love. He'd had relationships, entanglements and the like, but he'd never met a woman he felt he could trust with his heart. Unlike Darren, his older brother, Cleveland didn't love easily—hastily rushing into marriage and relationships. When things got too deep, Cleveland would walk away because he didn't want to care too much and end up hurt. He'd seen Darren's devastation after his first marriage ended because of the lies his first wife told. He'd seen how even women with good intentions had caused hurt. His second wife, Jill, nearly destroyed Darren when she'd lied about her identity and that newspaper blasted her, making it seem as if she was a man-eating CEO who was only using him.

Cleveland knew he'd never be able to handle anything like that, so if he was a serial dater, then so be it. Women, he reasoned, say they want one thing and turn around and go for the exact opposite. Deep inside, he wanted a love like his parents or even like his brother's marriage to Jill. But he didn't think he'd find that with a woman in Atlanta since they all seemed to want men with huge bank accounts and prestige. As a firefighter, he was far from rich, but he was comfortable and could take care of himself and a family, if he ever had one.

Cleveland turned to Louis. "Listen, I bet you Freddie and I will be leaving your reception together."

"You don't stand a chance. But hey, it's going to be fun to watch. I'm out of here. Roland is salivating to see some naked women. You sure you don't want to come?"

Nodding as his cell phone rang, Cleveland waved goodbye to his friend and answered the call.

"Yeah."

"How's it going?" Darren asked.

"How do you think? Overbearing bridesmaids, the bride is tripping, Roland is taking the groomsmen to some strip club, and I have a room at some hotel that I think Norman Bates built. Your wife had better have given birth by the time I get back."

"Well, I don't think that's going to happen. Jill's lying in bed mad," he said.

"What happened to the contractions and 'I think my baby is coming early'?" Cleveland asked.

"Well, thankfully, she's not leaking any fluids as the doctor thought, but her blood pressure is higher than the doctor would like so he put her on bed rest. I had to hide that damned laptop from her."

Cleveland laughed at his sister-in-law's unnatural attachment to that machine. She'd been the talk of the fire station when Darren pulled her from her burning high rise apartment and she wouldn't let go of it. At that time, no one knew she was one of the richest women in Atlanta and the future Mrs. Darren Alexander.

"So, how is she coping without it?" Cleveland asked.

"I had to distract her with the NFL Network's coverage of the Falcons' pep rally. You know Jill loves football more than the average man and the Falcons are her favorite team."

Cleveland chuckled. "Yeah, she has some prime seats in the Georgia Dome. I hope someone took those tickets off her hands."

"Well," Darren said, "you know she was holding those tickets for you. There was even going to be a meet and greet with the new quarterback."

"Shut up! I should've been there."

"Come on, with all the single women in that wedding party, you should be thanking us for having a baby."

Cleveland's eyes sought out Freddie again and found her standing at the door trying to hold Lillian back from the florist. If things worked out with the fiery Miss Barker, then maybe he would be thanking his brother. "We'll see about that," he said. "It looks as if some of these ladies are losing their minds in here, so let me go and offer my assistance." After hanging up with Darren, Cleveland walked over to the bickering women. "Ladies, is there a problem?"

Freddie rolled her eyes. "No."

Lillian waved her hands frantically. "There is a problem and I'm not going to have these ugly mauve roses at my ceremony."

"Ma'am," said the flustered florist. "These roses are pink. This is what you ordered, we went over your order three times. I showed you these very same roses two days ago."

Stomping her foot, Lillian shrieked, "I know what I ordered, this isn't it. The live ones better look like what I ordered."

Cleveland stepped between Lillian and the florist, calmly placed his hand on Lillian's shoulder and smiled. "Calm down, beautiful. Now, these roses are very pretty, but the lighting in here isn't. I'm sure that when the candles are lit and the sun is beaming in through the windows, you're going to see how beautiful these roses really are. Then again, when people see you in your wedding dress, they aren't going to care what these roses look like."

Casting her eyes upward, Lillian seemed to calm down. "You really think so?"

"Yes," Cleveland said. "Right Miss Barker?"

Freddie nodded. "It really is the lighting, Lil." She shot an apologetic glance at the frazzled florist.

"So, may I unload the rest of these flowers?" the florist asked, refusing to look at Lillian.

"Yes," Freddie said, "unload them and set everything up. Lillian, go home, run a bath and relax."

Running her hand over her face, Lillian nodded. "Fine, I think I need to relax, but you two had better stay here and supervise."

"I don't think so," Freddie said. "I have a million . . ."

Cleveland cut her off, "Come on, Miss Barker, you're not trying to get out of your duties are you? I mean, your little speech earlier inspired me and if we have to stay here all night, to make this wedding perfect, then that's what we have to do."

She folded her arms underneath her breasts and glared at him. "If you think I'm staying anywhere with you . . ."

"Freddie," Lillian interrupted, "you're doing this for me, not him, and you did tell me to go home. If you want me to stay and do these floral arrangements, then I will."

Sighing, Freddie placed her hand on Lillian's shoulder. "No, you go home, *Mr. Alexander,* and I will handle your flowers," she said.

Lillian hugged her friend tightly then turned to Cleveland. "Please, be nice," she warned. "I know if you had it your way, you wouldn't be here."

"We all know that," Freddie mumbled with a smile on her face. "Lil, let me walk you out."

"No," Lillian said. "Stay here and please make sure this woman doesn't ruin my arrangements because she's too busy staring at Cleveland."

He waved at the women, letting them know that he was listening to their conversation. Freddie rolled her eyes, alerting him to her annoyance. Cleveland returned her gesture with a bright smile. Once Lillian was out the door, Cleveland turned to Freddie, watching her every move. He didn't realize he was smiling until she walked over to him with a deep frown on her face.

"Is there a reason why you're standing here with your mouth agape looking at me when you told Lil that we would get her flowers ready for tomorrow?"

Cleveland took Freddie's hand in his. "Why are you trying to be so hard?"

Snatching her hand away from his, she focused an intense glare on him. "Excuse me? So, since I'm not throwing myself at you, I'm being hard?"

"That's not what I'm saying, but you could lighten up a bit, since you're going to have the pleasure of spending the night with me."

Scoffing at his suggestion, Freddie folded her arms underneath her breasts. "As if that's some sort of prize. I don't want to spend all night here."

"I have a nice room at the Best Western."

Freddie raised her hand to slap him, but Cleveland was quick enough to block her blow. When he enclosed her hand in his, he whirled her around as if they were dancing then pulled her against his chest. In one quick movement, he brought his lips down on top of hers. Surprisingly, she didn't resist him and she tasted even better than she looked.

Freddie didn't realize what was happening until she parted her lips to allow his tongue entry into her awaiting mouth. Damn, he felt so good, so strong and warm. Why had her treacherous body responded to his soft lips and warm tongue? Why had she melted against the rigidness of his body? Before she'd gotten too heady from the passion of Cleveland's kiss, she regained her senses and pushed him away. This time her smack made the connection with his jaw.

"You cocky son of a . . ."

"Excuse me," the florist said timidly. "I have a question about the archway for the church."

Freddie plastered a smile on her face and followed the woman into the kitchen where she had the roses laid out. Much to her chagrin, Cleveland followed them. *Ignore him,* she told herself as she tried to focus on what the florist was saying to her. But Cleveland's masculine scent filled her nostrils, making him impossible to disregard. Plus, she couldn't get the taste of his lips out of her mind. As much as she wanted to just get through this evening, she couldn't help but wonder if she was going to want more of Cleveland. *No, this man probably has a stable of willing women to do whatever he wants them to do and there's no reason for you to join in.* Turning to the florist, Freddie tried to direct her as to how she was to form the archway.

"I have a suggestion," Cleveland said, his voice sending a shiver down her spine. "If you're building this grand archway, shouldn't you do it at the entrance of the church, that way when you move it, you won't lose so many petals?"

The florist nodded. "Yes, but this is too heavy for me to move on my own."

Cleveland lifted the arch as if it weighed less than a pound and headed for the front of the church. Freddie, for the first time since his lips left hers, took a deep breath as he walked away. There was no way she'd allow him to place her under his spell.

Chapter 3

It had taken half the night to get the flowers arranged at the church as Lillian had instructed. By the time Cleveland, Freddie and the florist were finished, the place looked like a spring garden. Freddie was surprised that Cleveland worked as hard as he had and he was kind to the florist, who had more than once gotten frustrated by Lillian's constant phone calls and demands for photos to be sent to her cell phone.

But just as she was about to count Cleveland as an okay guy, he'd say something smug that reinforced her initial thoughts of him. As the florist was packing up to leave, Cleveland turned to Freddie and said in a low voice, "Was it everything you dreamed it would be?"

"What?" she asked, furrowing her brows.

"Spending the night with me."

"You're so crass and we're in a church for God's sake."

"You need to lighten up. Smiling every now and then would do wonders for you."

Clicking her tongue against her teeth, she said, "If I had something or someone to smile at then I would. What, did you think I would jump into bed with you because you stuck a few flowers in the right places and you finally stopped complaining every five minutes about being here?"

"No," he said as he rocked back on his heels. "I thought you'd hop into bed with me because you find me incredibly sexy and you want to have the time of your life."

"Not if you were the last man on the face of the earth."

Closing the space between them, he stroked her cheek gently. "If that's the case, then why did you kiss me? There was a spark and I know you felt it just as much as I did."

Rolling her eyes, she was about to deny everything he said, but Cleveland quickly brought his lips down on hers again. She was expecting another passionate and fiery kiss, instead he pecked her gently and pulled back. Despite herself, she moaned and Cleveland smiled knowingly.

"Stop fighting it, Freddie," he growled. "You want me and you know it."

"I want no such thing," she said weakly.

"Save a dance for me tomorrow," he said as he headed for the door. "Are you coming, or are you going to stay here and pray that you won't dream about me when your head hits the pillow?"

Straightening her back, Freddie marched out the door, then turned to face Cleveland. "You flatter yourself, you know. You're not a prize and I'm not some empty-headed bridesmaid who believes in the magic of weddings. If I did sleep with you, you'd be the one who couldn't handle it and would be begging me to be with you every night. So, dream of that as you go to sleep hot and bothered. And one more thing, touch me again and I'll make certain that you'll regret it."

"Or will you regret it if I don't kiss you again and make you quiver all over. When's the last time you had . . ."

Freddie pushed away from him. "That's all it's about to you, isn't it? Sex."

"I never said anything about sex, you keep going there. If that's what you want, it can be arranged and trust me— you'd love it."

She fought the urge to flip him off, instead she walked to her car and ignored him. But she couldn't help wondering if Cleveland was right about how good it would be to lie in his strong arms and feel the heat of his breath against her neck as they wrapped themselves around each other and got lost in a wave of passion and ecstasy. "Stop it," she whispered to herself. "That man is just like all the rest, he's just a little smoother."

"Only crazy people talk to themselves," Cleveland said as he walked up behind her.

"Are you following me?"

Cleveland rolled his eyes as he watched her fumble with the lock on her door. "Most women would just say 'Thank you.'"

"For what? Stalking me? You flatter yourself too much."

"No, for seeing you to your car in this dark parking lot, making sure no harm came to you. I could've just gotten in my car and sped off."

"I don't need a man to take care of me. I've done a fine job of keeping the boogeyman at bay without your help."

"Forget it, you're so damned bitter that you wouldn't un- derstand someone being nice to you if he kissed you dizzy. Which, I might add, I did a few minutes ago, even if you try to pretend that it didn't happen." Cleveland stormed away from her and Freddie slid into her car. Placing the key in the ignition, she turned the key, but nothing happened. Banging her hand against the steering wheel, she cursed herself for not getting her vintage Mustang serviced before making the trip to Georgia. The candy apple red car was the only thing of value that she had of her father, a faceless man whom she had only fleeting memories of. What she did remember was her mother, Loraine, telling her how men like her father were not to be trusted. They only wanted one thing and once they got it, they'd move on. Just like her father did. Just like the boy she loved in college did and just like Cleveland would if she gave him a chance.

Freddie wasn't bitter, she was a realist. And in her reality, love didn't last and didn't exist. She had too much going on, running her business and trying to rebuild her life after the devastation of Hurricane Katrina. The last thing she needed was to be worried about some man and his comings and goings. Her childhood home had been destroyed and she wasn't sure if she wanted to rebuild it. On the other hand, the boutique hotel that she and her mother owned in the French Quarter was thriving. Though with tourism at a standstill in the Crescent City, it wasn't going to be long before they started feeling the economic pinch as well. Freddie wanted to start over like so many people in New Orleans had done following the storm, but her mother depended on her to run the place.

Since the storm, Loraine had been living in Houston at Freddie's expense. A part of her thought that her mother was happy that Hurricane Katrina had washed most of New Orleans away. It gave Loraine a chance to put her past behind her, a past that included Freddie's father, Jacques Babineaux. He was known around New Orleans because of the crime he'd committed, killing a man of God. While Freddie knew bits and pieces of the story, her mother never told her everything.

Freddie remembered the day when her father disappeared and the whole city started treating her and her mother as if they were criminals as well. While the whole city knew the story, no one ever told Freddie. As she grew up, she started to search through old newspapers and Internet articles about the 1986 murder, but she wanted the truth from her mother or her father, who was now an escaped convict.

Getting out of the car, she slammed the door and kicked the new tires. Sure the car was pretty, but right now it was pretty useless. Pulling her cell phone out of her purse, she started to dial AAA, but a car pulled alongside her. The driver got out without saying a word and took the phone from her hands.

"Do you need some help?" Cleveland asked softly.

Turning her eyes upward, Freddie realized that she was hardly in a position to turn him away. "My car won't start."

"Pop the hood and let me take a look," he said, rolling up his sleeves.

She did as he requested, surprised that he was willing to get his manicured hands dirty.

Cleveland released a low whistle. "Man, I would've given anything to have one of these back in the day. It looks as if you've kept it in good condition."

"This car has been nothing but a headache, much like its previous owner."

"What was that?"

"Nothing. Do you have any idea what's wrong?" she asked, biting her bottom lip.

He shook his head as he jiggled cables. "I think I found the problem," he said as he stepped back from the car. "Get in and try it again."

Freddie slid into the driver's seat and turned the key. The car started immediately. "What did you do?" she asked as she hopped out of the car, afraid to turn the ignition off.

Pulling a handkerchief from his pocket, Cleveland wiped the oil from his hands then smiled at Freddie. "Loose battery cable," he said. "You might want to get your battery cleaned. And you have some acid leaking from your battery. If you have a cola in your car, I could clean the built up crude on the battery. That's why your cables aren't connecting tightly."

"Thanks," she said. "I thought you'd left."

He shrugged. "I was going to, but I saw that you were having some issues with your car and being the gentleman that I am, I stopped to see if I could help you. Besides, I wondered who this car belonged to."

"I have to get to Lillian's mother's house before she thinks that I'm not coming home tonight."

"Let me follow you just in case your car conks out on you again. If you don't consider that stalking," he said.

"Cleveland," she said, her voice barely a whisper. "I don't mean to be hard, but you have to admit that you come off a little arrogant, and I don't find that attractive at all."

"And that shrew act you put on, it ages you ten years. Do you want me to see you home safely or what?"

Freddie chewed again on her bottom lip. She really didn't want to go to Lillian's tonight. She'd actually told her friend and her overbearing mother that she was going to check into a hotel. She couldn't deal with those drama queens and their wedding chatter all night. The last thing she wanted, as well, was to answer questions about her life in New Orleans and how she was dealing with the hurricane recovery. But the one decent place in town was booked.

However, there was no way she was going to let Lillian and her nosy mother see Cleveland following her to their house. She would be forced to answer too many questions and all she wanted to do was go to sleep. "I'll be fine," she said. "Thank you for helping me."

"You're welcome." Cleveland said, and got into his car and drove off.

Freddie watched as he drove away and wondered if she might be wrong about him.

* * *

    Alone in his hotel room, Cleveland had finally found something to think about other than the Atlanta Falcons' playoff berth. Freddie Barker. She wasn't the wicked witch that he thought she was. The way she kissed him was enough to make him want to bury himself inside her until the earth and sun became one and the same. Pacing back and forth in the dank room, he wondered what would've happened if she were in the room with him. Did she wear sexy, lacy underthings or nothing at all? Glancing over his shoulder, he imagined Freddie lying in his bed, inviting him to taste her all over.

    What in the hell is wrong with me? Cleveland thought as he threw himself on the bed, locking his hands behind his head and staring up at the ceiling.

    Sleep didn't come easy for Cleveland because Freddie haunted his dreams. He could smell her, taste her, and he damn near expected to feel her in the bed beside him. What was it about this woman that had made him painfully aware of how long it had been since he'd slept with a woman?

    After Darren and Jill got married, Cleveland didn't find the satisfaction in temporary entanglements that had gotten him through the last few years. He wanted something like what Darren and Jill had. A real connection, not just a physical one, but he wasn't going to admit it. With Freddie, he'd settle for a physical one because she was one sweet piece of—The telephone rang announcing his wake-up call and Cleveland rolled out of bed. He wasn't rested, but at least this wedding would be over soon.

    Freddie closed her eyes tightly as the alarm clock blared. Why in the world was she in Covington, Georgia? Oh, yeah,

Lillian's wedding. Today was the day and she couldn't wait for it to be over. Before she could force herself out of bed, the door to the guest room flung open and Lillian burst in as if it were noon and not six in the morning.

"Good morning, maid of honor. So, how did it go last night? You rushed in here and went straight to bed before I could ask you any questions." Lillian pounced on the bed and Freddie grunted. "That well, huh?"

Freddie flung the covers back and sat up in the bed. "First of all, things went fine last night. Secondly, why are you in here and how in the hell are you so damn perky?"

Lillian stretched her arms over her head. "It is my wedding day. I'm marrying the man of my dreams in twelve hours and there is so much to do. When are you going to settle down, Winnie?"

"Don't call me that. Settling down isn't in my future. I have to rebuild, remember? My home was blown away." Freddie gritted her teeth. "You could've brought me some coffee."

"I forgot, you're a caffeine addict. Why not leave New Orleans and start fresh? You could move here. It would be like old times at Xavier, except we wouldn't be roommates this time."

Freddie shook her head. "New Orleans is my home and let's not forget that my business is there. Thankfully the water didn't reach the French Quarter and my hotel is still standing. With Mardi Gras coming up, I've got to see if I can make enough money to get the ball rolling on rebuilding. The government isn't helping and my insurance company is a damned joke. This is going to be a do-it-yourself project."

Lillian pushed her hair behind her ears. "I couldn't do it. It was too horrible to watch New Orleans drown and the government do nothing to help. Then I couldn't find you . . . Freddie, you're like a sister to me and I'm scared for you. Look at all the crime and what about the levees? Are they fixed? I mean, hello, hurricane season is right around the corner and who's to say that another storm won't come and . . ."

"Lil, it's your wedding day, can we please talk about something else and get me a cup of coffee?" Freddie said as she swung her legs over the side of the bed.

"All right. Did you and Cleveland get my flowers arranged right? He didn't do anything sleazy, did he? He has a reputation, you know." Lillian rolled her eyes for effect. "I don't trust him as far as I can throw him."

Intrigued, Freddie turned around and faced her friend. "What kind of reputation?"

"A real ladies man. Did you see how those other women in my bridal party looked at him? He walks around like he's some kind of Greek god. Since Louis and I have been together, I don't think I've seen him with the same woman twice. And they're all the same airheads. So you can imagine what he wants them for, and it's not stimulating conversation. Ugh, and to think that he was the one who planned Louis's bachelor party."

"He didn't plan the party, remember," Freddie said, feeling as if she needed to defend Cleveland. She shook her head and tried to focus on what Lillian was saying. But her mind when back to the two kisses she and Cleveland had shared the night before.

"Are you listening to me?" Lillian asked when she noticed her friend's silence.

"Yes," she lied.

"Anyway, I don't even know why Louis and Cleveland are friends, aside from the fact that they are both firefighters in the same battalion. They are so different."

Freddie chewed the inside of her cheek to keep from

saying anything. Cleveland Alexander, the bane of her existence, the star of her erotic dreams last night and the man who made her engine purr and sent her heart into overdrive.

"Whatever," she said. "I guess women are dumb and fall for those eyes and that hair. Like he's a black Fabio or something." Lillian eyed her friend suspiciously.

"Nothing happened with you two last night, did it?"

"Hell no, Lil. I had some car trouble and he helped me out, but that is it."

Lillian nodded slowly. "I guess you're one of those dumb women. Was it the hair or the eyes that got you?" She giggled and shook her head. "I can't believe you! You fell for him too."

"Please! Cleveland Alexander is not, I repeat, not someone I am remotely interested in," Freddie protested.

Lillian smiled knowingly. "Is that so? The last time you got so upset about a 'man you weren't interested in' it was Marcus Thompson."

"Let's not go there." Freddie said, placing her hands over her ears. The last thing she wanted to hear was a rehashing of her failed relationship with Marcus, a controlling and arrogant man who used people to get what he wanted and wasn't above throwing out the L-word to get it.

"Whatever," Lillian said. "I recall you giving up meat for him, even though you really love steaks."

Freddie ran her hand over her face. "I was young and stupid. That's a mistake I'll never make again."

"You like those types of guys and Cleveland falls right in line with your type of man," she sang.

"Lillian, today is about you and your wedding, not about me and Cleveland or Marcus or any other ex."

Lillian rose from the bed in a flourish. "Whatever you say, sis. I'm going to take a long hot bath. My mom is cooking breakfast, so you can head downstairs and get your coffee." When Lillian left the room, Freddie lay back down and pulled the covers back over her head. She'd forgo her morning cup of coffee if it meant dealing with Michelle Thomas.

Before she could drift back to sleep, her bedroom door opened again and Michelle stood in the doorway. "Winfred, are you still in bed? You know there is a lot we need to accomplish this morning."

Freddie groaned. "I'm not the one getting married. Besides, Lillian is taking a bath."

Michelle put her hands on her hips and looked at Freddie, who was gripping the blanket tightly. "You're going to be in the wedding and from where I stand, getting you ready for that dress is going to be a chore. Your hair is a mess and let's not even talk about those nails of yours."

Freddie glanced down at her hands and rolled her eyes. "Fine," she said as she sat up and climbed out of bed. "I'm up. What do you need me to do for a wedding that's twelve hours away?"

Michelle sauntered out of the room. "Nothing much, just wanted to get you out of bed."

Freddie shook her head and held her tongue. Despite the fact that Michelle had pissed her off, she still had to respect the older woman, because that was how she was raised. And in spite of all her airs, Michelle was her best friend's mother.

"Can I at least get a cup of coffee?" Freddie said, as she followed Michelle downstairs to the kitchen.

Chapter 4

Morning bled into afternoon and finally it was time. Time for Cleveland to stand up for Louis and get the hell out of town. He arrived at the church at 4:30, dressed in his black tuxedo and silver accessories. His hair was hanging loose and tumbled down his shoulders. As he turned the corner to head into the room where the groomsmen were, he collided with Freddie. Cleveland wrapped his arms around her to break her fall. She looked beautiful. The silver strapless dress clung to her body in all the right places and made her breasts look ready to taste. With her hair pulled back in a chignon, Cleveland got a chance to look deeply into her expressive dark eyes. She drew him in with the way they sparkled, and he wondered if they also sparkled first thing in the morning.

"Where's the fire?" Cleveland asked when his breath returned to his chest.

"Could you get your hands off me?" she snapped. Cleveland could've sworn he felt her tremble against him.

"Next time, watch where you're going," he replied as he released her.

Freddie shook her head and leaned against the wall. "You know, for a pig, you clean up really well." She brushed a stray loc behind his ear and then moved her hand as if she had touched fire.

"And for a frowning spinster, you look nice too," Cleveland quipped. "Don't you have some duties to perform for the bride?"

Freddie rolled her eyes. "I love Lillian to death, but if she yells at me one more time, she isn't going to make it down the aisle, because I'm going to break her damned leg."

Cleveland laughed, because he believed that Freddie would fight her friend, even though they were all dressed to the nines. "I'd pay to see that. Throw in a little mud or Jell-O and I'd sell tickets and bootleg it on DVD."

She shook her head. "Just when I thought you were human, the pig comes out again."

"You painted the picture," Cleveland said, flashing a wily smile.

"I guess it's a good thing that I ran into you because Lillian wants to know if you have the rings," she said. "She also wants to know if you and Louis have gone over the checklist."

Cleveland felt his jacket pocket. "Well I'll be damned, I knew I forgot something. And what is the 'checklist'?"

Freddie's mouth fell wide open. "Please tell me you're not serious."

He pulled the rings out of his pocket. "Tell Lillian everything is under control, Louis has his vows memorized and he's going over them with Roland because I don't want to hear that mushiness."

"Thanks," she said as she started to walk away.

"Hey," Cleveland called out. Freddie turned around. "Don't forget to save me that dance at the reception. Remember you promised."

"Delusional much? I never agreed to that," she said with a slight smile on her lips and that mischievous sparkle in her eyes. Cleveland knew that by the end of the night, he'd be holding her naked body in his arms and tasting all of her secrets.

Freddie exhaled loudly as she entered Lillian's dressing room. "Where have you been?" Lillian asked. "I needed you."

"For what?"

"The rings. Did you find out if Cleveland has the rings? And I want you to give this note to Louis. I really missed him last night and . . ." She held out a piece of paper to Freddie.

"Lillian, please. In a few hours you and Louis will be husband and wife, why do I need to pass him a note?"

Lillian grabbed Freddie's hand and pressed the note inside. "Because I asked you to and as my maid of honor you have to do what I say."

Just breathe, because the next words that come out of your mouth aren't going to be nice. Freddie took the note, then took off her shoes, and slipped on a pair of satin slippers. "Fine, I'll take him the damned note."

"Temper, temper," Michelle said from the doorway. "You know that Lillian has to be calm so she will be a glowing bride for Louis."

"Uh-huh," Freddie said as she pushed past Michelle. The main reason she didn't want to take Louis the note was because she didn't want to see Cleveland again. When he touched her in the hallway earlier, she nearly lost it. Being that close to him short-circuited her system. He had a clean and masculine scent that drove her wild and seeing him dressed in that tux made her wonder how he looked underneath it all. And his hair. It was like an aphrodisiac, that's why she had to touch it.

Slowly, she walked into the groom's dressing room. "Are you all decent?" she asked through a small crack in the door.

"Yes," Louis and Cleveland said in unison. Freddie walked in and crossed over to Louis. She didn't look in Cleveland's direction, but she could feel his gaze on her as she moved.

"Lillian wanted you to have this," she said as she handed him the note.

"Aww, that's so sweet," Roland said. "She's passing notes like y'all in high school."

Freddie shot him a contemptuous glance. "Anyway, I trust that you all are ready for the ceremony and there are no hangovers?"

Cleveland smiled and strode over to Freddie. "You're not slick," he said in a whisper only she could hear.

"Excuse me?" she replied in a hushed tone.

"You just wanted to see me again. I'm flattered, but there are other and better ways for you to get my attention."

She sucked her teeth. "Pig."

Cleveland reached out and stroked her bare arm, causing Freddie to shiver inadvertently. What was it about this man that made her want to get naked and do all sorts of erotic things that would make her blush? Maybe that's why she was trying so hard not to like him.

"Don't forget what you owe me," Cleveland said softly; his voice had a sing-song quality as he spoke.

"I didn't promise you anything."

A weaker woman would've swooned and fallen into his arms. But not Freddie. She had to do something to deflate his swelling ego. So, she punched him in the shoulder. However, her dainty fist did little to hurt Cleveland, because his body was as hard as a rock. Still, he pretended to be hurt. "Hey," he said. "That's assault. Should I call the cops or take the law into my own hands?"

His friends laughed as they watched the pair. "How

about this," Freddie said. "Grow up." She turned on her heels and stormed out of the room. Once she was away from Cleveland, Freddie's breathing returned to normal and the sweat on her palms dried a bit. Still, her arm seemed to burn from where Cleveland's hand had been. Why was she allowing him to affect her in this way? After the wedding and reception, she knew that she'd never see him again. Freddie smiled as she thought of having a wedding fling with him. No one would ever know and she'd never have to see him again. There'd be no promises, no commitments, and no strings.

Freddie didn't want to think about the last man that elicited such freaky thoughts from her. She made the mistake of thinking that good sex with Marcus was love. But when she wanted to get serious with him, she found out that Marcus had been spreading his love all around the French Quarter. Still, that wasn't the ultimate betrayal. Heartbroken, she'd made the mistake of turning to her mother, who in typical Loraine fashion, told her to get over it.

"When are you going to learn that men are born to be disappointments?" she'd said coldly.

After that moment, Freddie vowed that she would never allow another man to hurt her. Then she found out about her father. Shaking her head, she headed into Lillian's dressing room. The moment she opened the door, Michelle pulled her inside. "Come on, I need you to help me with this veil. Where have you been and why am I doing your duties?"

Because you're a control freak, Freddie thought bitterly as she grabbed the end of Lillian's veil as Michelle placed the headdress on Lillian's head. *I can't wait for this day to be over!*

* * *

Cleveland glared at his friends. "Y'all are some juvenile assholes," he snapped.

Louis continued laughing as Roland walked over to Cleveland. "Give it up. That tight chick ain't giving you the time of day," Roland said.

"I tried to warn him, but he didn't listen. A woman that evil is not going to give you what you want."

"Please, she's fighting it," Cleveland said. "I know she wants me."

Roland smacked his lips. "And how do you know that?"

"I just know." Cleveland furrowed his brows. "Besides, have you ever known me to not get the woman that I want?"

Louis stood up and crossed over to his friend. "If Freddie is what you want, then there is a first time for everything. She's not going to give you anything."

"Well, I'm not going to have to take it," Cleveland said. "She might not know it, but Freddie is going to give me what I want, willingly."

Roland reached for his wallet. "How much do you bet you're going to see those panties?"

Cleveland waved his hand. "You need to grow up and then maybe you'd find a woman who you don't have to pay to sleep with you. Whatever happens between me and Freddie will be just that, between me and Freddie."

"In other words, you're too chicken to put your money where your . . ."

"Boys," Louis said, "this is my wedding day and that's my future wife's best friend you two are trying to wager on. Cleveland, give it up, dude. Freddie ain't going to give you anything, not a dance and definitely not the panties."

Cleveland stood silently, he knew there was a spark between him and Freddie and by the time the night was over, he knew where Freddie would be—in his bed.

Before anyone could say anything else, the minister walked into the room. "Gentlemen, it's time to begin the ceremony. If I can get you all to take your places at the altar," he said in a calm voice.

Roland walked over to Louis and said in a loud whisper, "This is your last chance to bail out."

Cleveland slapped Roland on the back of the head. "You can be so stupid. This man is getting married, because if anything happens to stop this wedding, Lillian is going to kill us."

The men followed the minister to the altar. Cleveland smiled because this wedding fiasco was nearly over. Why did people need all of this to get married anyway? If he ever met the right woman and decided to get married, it would be nothing like this. No big crowd at a church, no huge bridal party, and no big production like Lillian had planned. All he would need would be the Justice of the Peace and the woman who would be lucky enough to be his wife. And that would be one lucky broad, because Cleveland had yet to meet a woman who inspired thoughts of matrimony.

The soft notes of a flute filled the air as the bridal party marched in. As Freddie slowly glided down the aisle, Cleveland's breath caught in his chest. In the faint glow of the candlelight, she looked like an angel. He studied her frame as she walked. The erotic thoughts that he was having were sure to put him on the pathway to hell. His mouth went dry as she came closer to him. Maybe it was his imagination, but when she passed him, he smelled the faint scent of roses. Sure, it could've been her bouquet, but Cleveland could have sworn that the sweet smell radiated from Freddie's essence.

As the bride came down the aisle, Cleveland didn't turn away from Freddie. She didn't have the look of the other bridesmaids. There was no look of longing in her eyes, nor did she look as if she was interested in what was sure to be a long ceremony. Maybe she was different. The type of woman that Cleveland could see himself . . . *Wait, wait, what am I thinking? After tonight, I'm never going to see this woman again, and besides, who knows what she has going on at home? She may be a different woman in New Orleans than she is in Georgia.*

He forced himself to look away from Freddie, then leaned into Louis, who looked as if he was about to pass out at any moment. "Breathe man," he whispered. "This is what you wanted."

Louis nodded. "I love this woman with everything in me. Still, I hope this is the right thing."

Cleveland smiled; he still didn't give this union a year. The ceremony began and a small part of him wondered how Freddie would look in a wedding dress.

Freddie turned her head away from Cleveland and tried to focus on the ceremony. But she could feel his eyes roaming her body and it made her feel hot and bothered. *I'm in a church for God's sake,* she thought as the image of a naked Cleveland danced in her head.

"The rings, please," the minister said and looked pointedly at Freddie.

She smiled and pulled the wedding band from underneath her bouquet and handed it to Lillian. Though her friend was smiling, Freddie could tell that she was a little perturbed that her maid of honor was a little distracted. Lillian held the ring up, then kissed it.

"The wedding ring is a symbol of eternity. It is an outward sign of an inward and spiritual bond which unites two hearts in endless love. And now as a token of your love and of your deep desire to be forever united in heart and soul, Louis may place a ring on the finger of his bride," the minister said.

"I give you this ring as a symbol of my love and faithfulness to you. I give you this ring as a symbol of forever, a symbol that you are the only woman that I want to spend my life with," Louis said as he slid the ring onto Lillian's finger, then kissed her hand.

"And Lillian, by the same token, you have a ring to give to Louis. You may place the ring on his finger," the minister said.

Lillian smiled and tears fell from her eyes. To the crowd, it was a beautiful gesture, but Freddie knew that it was scripted. She'd seen Lillian practicing her tears earlier in the day. She rolled her eyes as Lillian began her vows.

Drama, Freddie thought. She glanced at Cleveland and he seemed to have the same thought judging by the look on his face.

"Louis, my love for you has grown like a seed planted in the earth. And it has blossomed into this beautiful flower. You are the man I want to spend the rest of my life with and the man whom I pledge my love to, willingly and without hesitation." She paused and wiped a crocodile tear from the corner of her eye. Louis gripped her hand and smiled at Lillian.

Hook, line and sinker, Freddie thought as she watched the couple. Though she didn't doubt Lillian's love for Louis, she knew her friend was performing right now. Lifting her head, Freddie's eyes collided with Cleveland's again. He was smirking, as if he were watching a cheesy chick flick and was going to spoil the ending for everyone.

Lillian continued her speech, "A love like ours only comes once in a lifetime and I'm going to spend my life with you, loving you and being the wife that God has called me to be."

The minister cleared his throat. Lillian flashed him a look of irritation. Today was her day and the minister and everybody else were going to have to deal with it and listen to her vows that she'd written and rewritten six times.

"I love you more than words can begin to describe," Lillian continued. "Thank you for allowing me to be your wife."

Freddie fought her laughter and only smiled. She had to hand it to Lillian. If this had been a Hollywood movie, she would've been up for Actress of the Year. Freddie knew that if she ever got married, she wouldn't need all of this. No long speeches and no big production. Just her and the man of her dreams standing on a beach at sunset with a few witnesses and the preacher. Lifting her head, she caught Cleveland's eye again. Had he been staring at her the entire time?

Cleveland hadn't taken his eyes off Freddie since the ceremony began and as the minister pronounced Lillian and Louis husband and wife, Cleveland found himself excited about the prospect of walking Freddie down the aisle, touching her arm and feeling her body against his. The music began to play and Lillian locked arms with her husband. Next, Cleveland and Freddie linked arms and headed down the aisle.

"Some show," he whispered in her ear.

"Tell me about it," she replied and tightened her grip on his arm. "Lillian and her mother really outdid themselves with the theatrics."

"And I thought I was the only one who felt that way. Lillian did get one thing right, though."

Freddie raised her eyebrow. "What's that?"

"This dress looks amazing on you."

She smiled uncomfortably but once they exited the church she dropped her arm from his. "One question. Why were you staring at me during the ceremony?"

"Because you were a lot more interesting to watch than Louis and Lillian," Cleveland said. "And you weren't crying like every other woman in the bridal party. You kept your makeup in tact."

"Whatever," she said, fighting the urge to smile.

"Is it time for the reception?" Roland asked as he walked up behind Freddie and Cleveland. "Or do we have to take a thousand pictures first?"

"No, we have to toss the rose petals at Lillian and Louis before they get in the limo," Freddie replied as she started walking down the steps to join the rest of the bridal party. The flower girl handed Freddie and Cleveland a small packet of rose petals. The little girl, with curly pigtails, smiled at them, then asked, "Are you married too?" Before either of them could reply, the little girl skipped away to the end of the line.

"I bet you want a few of those, huh?" Cleveland asked as he noticed Freddie smiling at the little girl.

"You really think you know me, don't you?"

"I know women. Weddings make you all think about babies and marriage, right?"

"You don't know as much as you think you do, so please shut up and toss the petals," she said as Lillian and Louis appeared at the top of the church's steps. A trumpet blared and everyone ripped open their packages. As Lillian and Louis descended the steps, they were showered with pink and white rose petals. Actually, mauve and white. It was Cleveland's idea to use the roses that were left over from the archway. Freddie was surprised that he had the where-withal to come up with the idea. It turned out to be beautiful and even Lillian would have to admit that despite her hysterics, the wedding came off without a hitch.

"Our duties are almost over," Cleveland said as he and Freddie headed to the limo earmarked for the bridal party. She slid in first and Cleveland inched in beside her. His knee brushed against hers as the other bridesmaids and groomsmen got into the car. He felt her shiver and he knew that he had an effect on her. Cleveland smiled at Freddie then slid his hand on top of hers. Freddie looked pointedly at him, but made no effort to move her hand.

Amid the din of the chattering bridesmaids and groomsmen, Freddie and Cleveland exchanged heated glances at one another as if they were in the limo all alone.

Chapter 5

"All right, single ladies," Lillian called out. The reception was in full swing and everyone had drank their share of expensive champagne and liquor. Even Michelle, who'd been uptight all day was loosened up and had tried to get the group to do the Electric Slide.

Freddie was going to keep her seat, because her feet were throbbing and her head was spinning. However, her intoxication wasn't coming from the three glasses of champagne she had downed in succession. It was the heated looks that Cleveland had been giving her from his end of the dais. The way his gray eyes roamed up and down her body made her feel as if he'd unzipped her dress, slowly removed her bra and kissed her breasts until her nipples hardened underneath his full lips.

It's the champagne, she thought as she pushed her glass away.

"Hello? Where is my maid of honor?" Lillian called out. "Freddie, get down here, now."

"She is working my last nerve," Freddie mumbled as she headed for the dance floor. Her steps in those three-inch heels were a little more wobbly than they had been marching down the aisle. She tried to stay in the back row of all the single women who actually believed that catching a bouquet would mean that they'd be the next person to get married. Freddie rolled her eyes; no bunch of flowers would bring a man into any woman's life and—

"Ready ladies?" Lillian said as she turned her back to the crowd. She tossed the bunch of roses over her shoulder and much to Freddie's dismay, they landed right in her arms.

Cleveland laughed at the look on Freddie's face when she caught the bouquet, but he also knew that if he was going to get a dance with her then he was going to have to be the one to catch Lillian's garter when Louis tossed it. Typically, the groomsmen and the other single men ran to avoid catching it, but Cleveland had to make sure he caught it.

"Hey man," he said to Louis. "I need that garter."

"What?" he replied, his voice filled with surprise. "Why do you . . . ah, Freddie caught the bouquet and you're determined to have that dance, huh?"

"And all this time that I've known you, I thought you rode the short bus to high school."

"Keep playing with me and I'll hand deliver the garter to Roland."

Cleveland rolled his eyes. "Just do it," he said.

Louis shook his head from side to side. "I'll do it, but I'm telling you, Freddie is one nut you won't crack."

Cleveland winked at his friend. *After tonight, you can call me the nutcracker.*

After the women cleared the dance floor, Louis headed off the dais and stood in the middle of the floor. "All right my brothers," he said. "Let's see who's going to be the next one to get married."

A rumbling of "not me" rippled through the single men

as they headed to the middle of the dance floor. Cleveland smiled knowingly as Lillian took a seat in the chair that Louis stood next to. He didn't watch his friend as he snaked his hand up his wife's dress and removed the blue garter from her thigh. He wanted him to go ahead and toss the damned thing.

If tradition held, the rest of the bachelors were going to back off when the garter went flying. Cleveland was just going to hold his hand out and catch it. Then again, unless the other groomsmen and single guys at this wedding were blind, for a chance to dance with Freddie, there might be a fight for that garter.

"All right, he who catches this is next on the matrimony train," Louis said as he blatantly tossed the garter at Cleveland. Easily, he caught the satin and lace garter on his index finger. He turned to Freddie, who had her hand wrapped around a champagne flute.

The DJ stepped up to the microphone, "All right, if we can have the lady who caught the bouquet and the gentleman who caught the garter to the middle of the floor so that they can have a dance with the bride and groom?" He began to play Keith Sweat's "Make It Last Forever."

Freddie didn't make a move toward Cleveland until the photographer prodded her. "Lillian wants a picture of this," the round man said.

Cleveland crossed over to her, his face split into a broad smile. "Come on, Miss Barker, it's tradition."

Freddie downed the remainder of her drink, then placed the glass on a tray held by a waiter who was walking past her. "Fine," she said. "But if your hands drop below my waist, I'm going to hurt you, badly."

Cleveland wrapped his arms around her waist and led her to the middle of the dance floor. As he pulled her against his body, her sweet smell filled his nostrils and she felt better than he could imagine. It took all of his strength to keep his hands on her waist and not slip down to feel the firmness of her round ass.

He had something he wanted her to feel though, and that was his manhood, which was pressing against his zipper. As Keith Sweat began singing "ooh, ooh, ooh," Cleveland pulled her closer and the gasp that escaped her throat let him know that she felt exactly what she'd done to him.

Cleveland half expected her to slap him and leave the dance floor. But she didn't. Instead, she leaned her head against his chest. Her move emboldened him and he slipped one hand down the small of her back. Cleveland waited for her to protest. When she didn't, he smiled. Slowly, he inched his hand down until he cupped her bottom.

Freddie pinched his side hard. "What did I tell you?" she whispered.

"Ouch," he said. "Why are you acting as if you didn't like it?"

Freddie stepped back from him and smirked. "You know what? I'm going to call your bluff, Mr. Alexander."

"Meaning?"

She licked her sexy lips and Cleveland felt as if he had gotten even harder. "It's obvious what you want from me," she said. "Let's go back to your hotel room."

Cleveland nearly choked on his tongue. "You're playing with me, right?"

She raised her eyebrow. "See, I knew you were full of it. If you're not the hunter, you're not interested. I'm offering myself to you on a silver platter. Are you going to turn me down?"

"How much champagne have you had tonight?" he asked. "I don't want to take advantage of a drunk woman."

"I'm not drunk," she said. "Far from it, so you're not taking advantage of me."

Holding her at arm's length, it took him all of two seconds to decide that he and Freddie were getting the hell out of the reception hall, best man duties be damned.

"Let me grab my jacket," he said, then headed for the dais.

Louis and Lillian were so caught up in kissing, that neither of them noticed the best man and the maid of honor slip away.

The hotel where Cleveland was staying was within walking distance of the reception hall, so the couple headed in that direction. Cleveland looked at Freddie as she walked, her painful shoes in her hand and a slight smile on her face; he wasn't going to wait until he got into the room to taste her lips. Whirling around, he pulled her into his arms and captured her lips, kissing her with all the built up tension that he'd felt since meeting her. Her lips parted and allowed his tongue entry into her mouth. She tasted sweet. But what was more surprising to Cleveland was that Freddie returned his kiss with even more intensity. Her tongue overpowered his as she took the lead in the kiss. Wantonly, she pressed her body against his and rotated her hips against him. For a moment, he forgot that they were in the middle of the street in rural Georgia. Before things went too far he broke off their kiss.

"Damn," he moaned. "Let's go."

They nearly ran down the street to the hotel, but once they got into the room, Cleveland decided it was time to slow the pace a bit. He pressed Freddie against the door and roamed her body, taking in the curves and contours of her body as he unzipped her dress and peeled it from her body.

Underneath, she wore the prettiest black lace strapless bra and matching panties. She looked amazing to him, her body was like a work of art, curved in all the right places. He ran his fingers down the valley of her breast, traveling down to her flat stomach and stopping above her panty line. Her skin was softer than the finest of silk. Freddie wrapped her arms around his neck and pulled Cleveland closer to her. "We're wasting time," she said in a commanding voice.

"You have me on a schedule? I was hoping we had all night," he said as he lifted her into his arms and walked backward to the bed. She wrapped her legs around his waist and kissed his neck softly and sensuously. Cleveland nearly dropped her when she began nibbling on his ear, which was the one spot that turned him on more than any other. Falling backwards, they landed on the bed. Freddie loosened Cleveland's tie and smiled. "Are you sure you can handle me all night?" she asked in a lust-filled tone as she unbuttoned his shirt.

"Oh yeah," he breathed as her fingers unbuckled his belt.

Maybe it was the champagne that made Freddie act this way, she surmised as she reached into Cleveland's pants and stroked him. Maybe she was just releasing years of frustration on a man that she would never see again. She'd never done anything like this before, but she'd never had this much fun either. Cleveland squirmed and moaned in delight as she slid down his hard body and took his manhood into her mouth. She took him deeper and deeper, her lips caressing his throbbing manhood and sending waves of pleasure through his body. He buried his hands in her hair as he felt himself reaching the point of no return. Freddie pulled back and locked eyes with him. The total look of bliss on his face made her smile. She pushed his pants and silk boxers down to his ankles. Cleveland propped up on his elbows, watching her as she stroked him. Then in a quick motion, he reached down and grabbed her wrist.

"It's my turn to taste you," he said, turning over on his side. Freddie was now on her back, looking up at Cleveland. She reached up and ran her fingers through his locks. He reminded her of a sexual warrior and she wondered if she was going to be able to handle what he had in store for her.

Cleveland parted her legs and kissed her inner thighs, making her shiver in anticipation of feeling his tongue buried between the wet folds of flesh hiding her pleasure point. She wanted him to rip her panties off and get on with the tasting, but Cleveland had other ideas. He was going to sample all of her treasures. Slipping his hand inside her panties, he lowered himself on top of her and kissed her neck, then traveled down to her breasts. He lifted her bra with his teeth and her bosom spilled forward. She had perfect breasts, nipples that looked as if they were designed for his lips. When his lips grazed one of her nipples, Freddie moaned and stroked the nape of his neck. Then he flicked his tongue across her nipples, alternating each breast he took into his mouth as she writhed underneath his kiss. When she thought his tormenting kiss couldn't get any more torturous, he slipped his finger inside her panties. She was so hot and wet that it was almost embarrassing. She didn't know this man well, but he'd found ways to turn her on like no other man who'd ever taken her to bed.

She groaned as his finger found her throbbing bud and caressed it, slow then faster and faster still. Freddie felt as if Cleveland was pouring gasoline on a fire that he'd built and now it was a raging inferno. There was only one way to put it out and his finger wasn't going to be enough. Still, she grasped his wrist, urging him deeper, harder, faster.

Cleveland was quick to oblige her silent demand as she arched her back. She was closer to a climax than she wanted to admit. Could he tell how love-starved her body was? He removed his finger, brought it to his lips and licked it.

"Mmm, sweet," he said. Then he pulled her panties down and buried his face between her thighs. The moment she felt the heat from his breath near her moist flesh, Freddie trembled as his tongue touched every place where his finger had been. Her legs quaked as he nibbled and sucked on her throbbing bud. She called out his name as she felt the waves of an orgasm ebb at her senses. Freddie attempted to push Cleveland away, but he deepened his kiss and she exploded from the inside out.

Reversing the direction of his kiss, Cleveland found his way back to her breasts, kissing and sucking them until Freddie cried out in lust. She wrapped her legs around his waist, pulling his sex against hers. Though part of her wanted him to take her right then, she was smart enough to know that they had to be protected before they could go any further. She loosened her grip on his waist. "You need to . . ."

"I know," he said as he reached underneath his pillow and retrieved a condom.

Part of her wanted to ask why he had a condom underneath his pillow? Maybe he planned to bring someone back to his hotel room after the wedding, then again, she was so far gone that it didn't matter. All she knew was she had to have Cleveland inside her and fast.

She took the condom from his hands. "Allow me," she said as she pushed him on his back.

"Miss Barker, you can do whatever you want to do," he said with a sly smile.

Freddie straddled Cleveland and rolled the sheath into place, then she guided him to where she needed him most. At first, it was a tight fit because it had been so long since she had been with a man and Cleveland was all man, thick and long. For a moment, it felt as if it was going to be too much for her to handle, but Cleveland shifted his hips and then it felt just right.

He groaned as Freddie rode him slowly. Her intensity was building as they ground against each other and then it was as if she were possessed. She bucked like a stallion, grasping his shoulders as he pressed deeper and deeper into her wetness.

"Oh, Freddie," he exclaimed. "Damn."

She felt as if she was about to climax, but Cleveland wasn't finished with her. He flipped her over on to her back, taking control of their rendezvous. Freddie arched her back, pressing her hips into his and matching him thrust for thrust until they were both spent from their love-making. Collapsing in each other's arms, they both exhaled. Freddie glanced at Cleveland, his eyes were half closed and he had a satisfied smile on his lips.

Despite herself, she thought about Marcus. He'd always turn his back to her and go to sleep. Yet Cleveland held her tightly as if they'd been lovers for years.

It's just one night, you can let him hold you and give you all the pleasure you can handle, but you will never see him again, she thought.

"What are you thinking?" he asked, when he noted her silence.

"Just wondering how long we're going to have to wait for round two," she said, leaning in to kiss him on the neck.

Cleveland looked down at his crotch area; he was erect

again. "We can get started right now," he said as he pulled her on top of him.

The next morning, Cleveland woke up marveling at Freddie's naked body. She was even more beautiful in the morning light. The sun cast a golden glow over her chocolate body and made her look almost edible. He knew how good she tasted because he'd sampled every inch of her the night before. Cleveland had to admit, he was shocked that he and Freddie ended up in bed. At the rehearsal, she made it known that she didn't like him. Last night, though, she showed him a different side of her. Gently, he stroked her arm, struggling with the fact that he wanted to wake her up and make love to her all over again.

Freddie's eyes fluttered open and her lips curved into a smile. "Good morning," Cleveland said.

"Morning."

"Do you want to get some breakfast or something?" he asked.

Freddie shook her head and rose from the bed. Modestly, she pulled a sheet from the bed and wrapped it around her body. "What time is it? My head is killing me," she said then dashed into the bathroom.

Cleveland furrowed his brows as he sat up in the bed. *What in the hell just happened here?* He walked over to the bathroom and knocked on the door.

"Are you all right?" he asked.

Freddie opened the door and stepped out of the bathroom, wrapped in a towel. "I'm fine, I just have to get out of here."

"What's wrong?" he asked. "I thought . . ."

"It was what it was," Freddie said as she picked her dress up off the floor. "Wedding sex."

"Wedding sex? I've never heard of that," Cleveland said.

"Whatever. You know that this was just a one time thing and don't pretend that there was more than sex between us. Besides, we're never going to see each other again," she said as she zipped her dress up. "I had a wonderful time."

Before Cleveland could say anything, Freddie was out the door. *What in the hell just happened?* he thought as he plopped down on the bed.

Once Freddie was outside of Cleveland's hotel room, she realized that she hadn't driven to the hotel and she needed a ride back to Lillian's mother's house. If she called Michelle, she knew she was going to have to do a lot of explaining and she didn't have money for a cab. The only thing she could do was hope that Cleveland would take her where she needed to go. Slowly she turned around and knocked on his room door.

Seconds later, a shirtless Cleveland opened the door. "This is a surprise. I thought we were never going to see each other again."

Freddie smiled, though she had a snappy comeback forming in her mind. "Well, last night when we came here, I didn't drive. Didn't bring any cab fare either."

"Now you need my help?" he said with a smirk. "Let me take a shower and I'll give you a ride."

She sucked in her bottom lip, thinking that one last ride with Cleveland wouldn't be such a bad idea. As he disappeared behind the bathroom door, part of her wanted to strip out of her dress and join him. But Freddie was the one who set the rule of one time only and she was going to have to abide by that, no matter how tempting it was to know that a naked Cleveland was inches away from her.

* * *

Twenty minutes later, Cleveland and Freddie were on their way to Lillian's mother's house. "Do you think you can let me out a few blocks away?" Freddie asked.

"What are you, sixteen?" Cleveland asked with a laugh.

"No, I just don't feel like answering a bunch of questions about you," she said.

"All right, whatever you wish," he said as he circled Michelle's house and stopped a block away.

As Freddie reached for the door handle, he locked the door. "Before you go, I have one question. How does this end? Do we shake hands and walk back to our corners?"

"Pretty much. You live in Atlanta, I have a lot going on at home and this is best. We gave in to the temptation and now it's over."

Cleveland unlocked the door, then handed Freddie one of his business cards. "Just in case you ever want to visit my corner again."

She looked at the card and shook her head. "I don't think so. Thanks for the memory, though." Freddie got out of the car and walked the block. She couldn't resist looking back at Cleveland as he drove away. The time she spent with him was a memory that she wasn't going to soon forget.

Chapter 6

Two days before Mardi Gras

Cleveland sat in his brother's office, twirling a loc around his finger. In the month since Louis's wedding, Cleveland had thought of nothing but his night with Freddie. She invaded his thoughts whenever a cold wind caressed his cheek or when he had a silent moment alone. She'd been the star of his dreams and the cause of several cold showers. Maybe he'd run into her in New Orleans. But she'd made it clear that what they'd shared was a one time thing.

"If weddings make her crazy like that, I wonder what Mardi Gras does to her," he mumbled.

"Talking to yourself is the first sign of insanity," Darren, his brother, said from the doorway. "And what are you doing in my office?"

"Waiting on you," Cleveland shot back. "I'm out of here in the morning."

Darren took his seat behind his desk and pushed his brother's feet off the top of it. "I can't believe that you are making Louis send you to New Orleans in exchange for being his best man. If anything, you should be paying him."

"When is the baby coming?" Cleveland said, changing the subject.

"Your guess is as good as mine. Jill is now two weeks overdue and it's killing her because her laptop won't fit on her lap. She wants to go into the office, but the doctor has her on total bed rest because of her blood pressure."

"I thought she'd given up control to that dude, Malik?" Cleveland said.

"When have you known my wife to ever give up control of anything? I can see her now when the baby comes, she'll be changing diapers and running her computer company from the baby's nursery. Malik's wife just had a baby about two months ago. It must be something in the water around here. So, you better watch your back, little bro and watch out for Lillian. Since Louis is picking up your hours this week, she's steaming. You were never one of her favorite people anyway."

"It doesn't matter, she'll get over it," Cleveland said. But he knew that she could hold a grudge. Lillian was still miffed that Cleveland and Freddie made a mad dash from the reception and didn't show up to take the final pictures.

"Yeah, but you will be hearing about it for a while. Was your romp with the maid of honor worth it?" Darren asked, folding his hands underneath his chin like a therapist.

"You're trying to live vicariously through me now since you're an old married man with a kid on the way?" Cleveland laughed. "Winfred Barker was the most amazing woman that I've ever seen naked."

Darren shook his head. "I still can't believe you slept with her."

"We didn't do much sleeping, if you know what I mean," Cleveland said as the image of Freddie straddling his body in the dingy hotel room flashed in his mind. Licking his lips, he relived the taste of her lips, nipples, and everything else he'd tasted that night.

"So, you have no problem having a one night stand? What are you, a college frat boy?" Darren asked.

"Just because you're an old married man doesn't mean I have to follow your lead," he said, feeling as if his brother was judging him. "We're adults, it happens."

"Still, when are you going to find something more meaningful?"

"When the time is right. And to be honest with you, there is something about Freddie that . . . Never mind. Just know that it was mind blowing sex." *But could it have been more than that?*

"Whatever. Your time off is approved and I hope you don't go to New Orleans and come back with another tale of casual sex. Isn't that chick Freddie from New Orleans?"

Cleveland smiled. "She sure is. Maybe I'll look her up."

Sitting in her office at The French Garden Inn, Freddie tried to focus on the reservations that were due in over the next few days. Then she came across his name.

Cleveland Alexander.

"This can't be right," she mumbled. Closing her eyes, she pressed her fingers into her temples. She was never supposed to see this man again. He wasn't supposed to come to New Orleans and stay at her boutique hotel for Mardi Gras. And because she'd lost her home to Hurricane Katrina, the hotel also happened to be her home.

Freddie had been living in the hotel since the storm while she decided if she wanted to rebuild her home or not. She'd thought about selling the hotel and relocating, but before she could decide, she had to find out what her mother had been hiding from her about her father.

All of her life, Freddie was under the impression that her father had abandoned the family at a time when they needed him most. Her mother had lost her job, the hotel that the family owned was in disrepair, and her dad just disappeared. Still, it didn't make sense that once Jacques Babineaux was out of their lives that things started looking up. Money appeared out of nowhere and Loraine didn't explain any of it. She said that her father was a selfish bastard and he was as good as dead.

But following Katrina, Freddie found out Jacques hadn't disappeared because he wanted to, he had been sent to federal prison. Freddie had to know why and why he'd never reached out to his only child when she needed him most.

Growing up, things weren't easy for Freddie, and her mother fed her a batch of lies about her father that eventually colored her relationship with men.

What she didn't need was to see Cleveland again. He had sparked a passionate fire inside her that she didn't want ignited again.

Of all the hotels in New Orleans, why had he chosen hers? She picked up the phone and called every hotel within a five mile radius, hoping she could reroute Cleveland, but the answer was the same. No vacancies.

Freddie bit her lip as she hung up the phone, there was no two ways about it—she was spending Mardi Gras with Cleveland Alexander. There was no way to avoid him. She was a very hands-on owner during Mardi Gras, helping her overwhelmed staff and handing beads to her guests as they entered. How was she going to handle seeing Cleveland walk through the entrance of the hotel and having to hand him a string of beads? What was going to happen when her hand grazed his skin or if his fingers touched hers, ever so gently? Would her body suffer a series of hormonal explosions, causing her to leap into his arms and kiss him as if they were the only two people left on the earth?

But what if he isn't alone? a voice whispered in the back of her head. Freddie figured that Cleveland was probably going to come to The Big Easy with a woman. He probably doesn't even think about what happened after Lillian's wedding, she surmised. Rising to her feet, Freddie decided that she wasn't going to let Cleveland's presence bother her. They were adults who shared a one time sexual experience and neither of them would cross that line ever again.

After Cleveland packed for his trip, he headed to Louis and Lillian's new house in Stone Mountain. Somehow he was going to have to charm Freddie's address out of Lillian Freeman.

Cleveland knew it wasn't going to be an easy task. Bounding up the steps, he rang the doorbell and waited for Lillian to answer.

Lillian opened the door with a scowl on her face. "What are you doing here? Louis is at the fire station, thanks to you."

Cleveland smiled. "Can't I come by and check on you?"

"In the five years I've known you, you've never done anything that didn't benefit yourself. Just like my wedding. Louis told me he had to bribe you. If he was really your friend, you would've done it with a smile." She folded her arms across her chest. "So, Cleveland, what do you really want?"

"Why are you so hard on a brother? May I come in?" he asked.

"Only because my mother taught me manners am I

going to invite you in," Lillian said as she stepped aside. "So, what do you want?"

Cleveland sighed and realized that charm wasn't going to work with Lillian. "I need a favor."

"Ha! You got some nerve." She flipped her hair and pursed her lips together in a tight line. "What do you want?"

"You know I'm going down to New Orleans," he began.

Lillian shook her head furiously. "I will not give you Winfred's number. See, I knew something was going to happen between you two. You kept looking at her like you wanted to rip her clothes off in the middle of the reception hall. Then you two stayed out all night. She doesn't need what you bring into her life."

"What are you talking about?" he asked. "You don't know anything about me. I mean, I don't want to do anything to Freddie that she doesn't want me to do. Besides, I've never been to New Orleans and I was hoping that she could show me around."

"Show you around? She's not going to have time for that being that she'll be running her business," Lillian snapped. "Why don't you get out of here? Freddie is like a sister to me and women are disposable to you. I'm not going to watch you do that to my friend."

"Whatever, Lillian. I don't know why you have this negative image of me built up in your head. All I want to do is tell the woman hello, since I'm going to be in her city."

Sighing, Lillian shook her head again. "That's not all you want and I'm not stupid. The two of you didn't spend my wedding night together just talking."

"You make it sound as if we did something wrong. We're grown-ups and guess what, she doesn't need your protection. What is she, a child?"

"I'm going to say it again. Freddie is my friend and I

wouldn't want my worst enemy to get involved with a man like you," Lillian said.

"A man like me?"

She nodded and pointed her finger at his chest. "Freddie is more than just someone to warm your bed. Just let it go, Cleveland. She has a lot going on and she doesn't need you to add to it."

"Okay, Lillian, you think that I'm this evil person and I'm out to hurt every woman I run across. So, that explains why you and I have never gotten along. Maybe you should get to know me, I might surprise you," he said as he turned and headed out the door.

Though he left empty-handed, Cleveland wondered if Freddie was as fragile as Lillian was making her out to be. Maybe he should just forget about her. What they shared was a one time thing and there was no need to try and recreate that night.

Driving home, Cleveland decided that it was best to not even try to find Freddie in New Orleans. He was going to enjoy Mardi Gras and not think about the woman who rocked his world.

Chapter 7

Mardi Gras begins

Cleveland arrived in New Orleans after a turbulent flight. He'd never prayed so much to land on solid ground. Flying didn't bother him, it was the crashing that got to him. As a firefighter, he'd cleaned up a plane crash at Hartsfield-Jackson Atlanta International Airport and there were no survivors. That day soured him on flying, since it was pilot error that caused the plane to skid off the runway and ram into a fuel truck.

"This is your captain speaking, we're making our final descent into the Crescent City. Please make sure that your seat and tray tables are in an upright and locked position. The weather here is a pleasant sixty-five degrees and the humidity is low," the pilot said.

"Thank God," Cleveland muttered as he fastened his seat belt.

Once everyone had deplaned, Cleveland headed for the baggage claim and looked for the car service that Louis said would be waiting for him. He pulled his reservation confirmation out of his back pocket. The French Garden

Inn was in the heart of the French Quarter and Cleveland had always heard that that was where he needed to be to enjoy the festival.

Cleveland smiled as he saw a man dressed in a black suit with a few dozen strings of Mardi Gras beads around his neck holding a sign with his name on it. This was definitely the greeting he was expecting.

"I'm Mr. Alexander," he said as he handed the man his garment bag.

"Yes, sir," the driver said, reaching out for Cleveland's bag. "The car is right this way."

Easing into the backseat of the car, Cleveland sank into the soft leather and closed his eyes. He was happy to be in the car and not in the air. Cleveland hadn't realized that he dozed off until the driver tapped him on the shoulder.

"Sir, we've arrived."

Cleveland wiped the side of his mouth checking for drool. "Thanks," he said as he stepped out of the car. He smoothed his tan slacks and absorbed the scene. People dressed in bright colors ran around the streets, women lifted their tops as men hanging out on the balconies of their hotel rooms tossed beads down to the street. Shaking his head, Cleveland realized that he was going to enjoy himself. As the driver took his bags to the door, a buxom blonde walked up to Cleveland and planted a wet kiss on his lips.

"You are so freaking hot!" she exclaimed as she took a strand of her beads from around her neck and placed them around his.

"Ah, thanks," he said as he pushed her away.

"Wanna come to my hotel room?"

"Baby, I just got here, let me check in and I'll find you," he said.

She waved her hand as if she knew that she wouldn't see

Cleveland again. "Whatever," she shot back as she skipped down the street.

He shook his head and laughed as he headed into the hotel. A crush of people stood near the desk trying to get checked in. Glancing around the room, Cleveland eyed the women, whose style of dress ranged from conservative to freaky. A woman dressed in a pair of shorts that looked like underwear winked at him.

Shaking his head, Cleveland didn't know what to think of all of these women who were just throwing themselves at him. It must have been the nature of the party. What he wouldn't give to have Freddie wanting him the way these strangers did. He knew that New Orleans was way too big to go chasing after her. And he wasn't going to. He came here to have fun and he wasn't going to . . .

"Welcome to the French Garden Inn," Freddie said.

Cleveland locked eyes with her. "Freddie," he stammered.

She inhaled sharply. "Enjoy your stay," she said as if she had no idea who he was. Cleveland nodded and headed to the front desk. He'd let her play this game now, but knowing that she worked in the hotel meant he would see her again. Cleveland walked up to the front desk and checked in. As he took his room key from the curvy brunette, he nodded toward Freddie. "What does she do here?" he asked.

"Miss Barker? She owns the place," she said. "You can't have a complaint already."

He shook his head. "Not at all. I think she's doing a wonderful job. Make sure you tell her I said so," he said.

She furrowed her brows and nodded. Cleveland figured that she wouldn't pass along the message, so he rushed up to his room and unpacked. Then he took a shower and changed into a pair of low slung blue jeans and a white button-down shirt that he left open to show off his sculpted chest. However, by the time he got downstairs, Freddie was gone.

No matter how prepared she thought she had been for Cleveland's arrival, seeing him did something to her.

Enjoy your stay. What in the hell was I thinking? I knew he was coming, so I should've been prepared.

Even though the lobby was still filled with people, Freddie retreated to her room. She had to pull herself together because after seeing him her knees went weak, her mouth went dry and her heart sped up. Yet, all she could say was "Enjoy your stay." She flung herself on the bed and stared up at the ceiling. She knew that she couldn't ignore him; she lived in the hotel and she would run into him. Freddie called down to the front desk.

"Yes, Miss Barker?" the front desk clerk asked.

"Cleveland Alexander, what room is he in?"

She could hear Jewel typing the information into the computer. "He's in suite 7218."

"What? Can you change his room?" Freddie exclaimed. Cleveland couldn't stay there, it was right across the hall from her suite.

"Miss Barker, we don't have any other rooms open. Is there a problem?"

"No, Jewel, I'm sorry I bothered you. I'll be down there in a little bit," Freddie said.

"All right," she replied, her voice filled with confusion. Freddie hung up the phone and groaned. How did this happen? Why hadn't she gone into the computer to see what room he'd been assigned when she saw that he had a reservation at her place? Sitting up, Freddie ran her hand over her face and decided that she couldn't put it off any longer, she had to go downstairs and help her staff. Besides, Cleveland was probably out enjoying the revelry of Mardi Gras. What man wouldn't be out roaming the streets and enjoying the sights and highlights of the festival? It had been years since Freddie had a chance to enjoy Mardi Gras. She would kill for a King Cake right about now and some pralines. With her stomach growling, Freddie left her room and headed downstairs. As the elevator opened, she ran, chest first, into Cleveland.

"Whoa," he said, "are you all right?" Instinctively, he wrapped his arms around Freddie's waist.

"I'm fine," she said as she pushed away from him. "Just a little distracted, it's busy here."

"I can see that. I had no idea you owned this place," he said.

"Uh-huh," she said. "Well, if you'll excuse me."

"Wait, do you think we can grab some dinner sometime this week?"

She stepped into the elevator as he stepped off. "I don't think so. I'm going to be so swamped that I'll barely have time to sleep."

Before Cleveland could say another word, Freddie pressed the button and the elevator doors closed.

Standing in the hallway, Cleveland shook his head. Freddie was acting as if nothing had happened between them and he knew that she'd enjoyed their night together just as much as he had. He knew that before the week was over, they would have an instant replay of the night of Lillian's wedding and when he was done with her this time, she wouldn't forget or be able to get enough of what they were going to share. However, he wasn't going to sit in his hotel room and pine away for her. He was going to check out the scene on Bourbon Street and hope that when he returned Freddie would still be in the hotel. He headed downstairs and when he reached the front desk, where Freddie and her clerk were, he winked at Freddie, but didn't say a word.

Once on Bourbon Street, Cleveland was swept up in the big party. Big brass bands played in the middle of the street, restaurants seemed more like clubs, and there were people everywhere. The smell of Po-Boys and sweet King Cakes wafted in the air. He found it hard to believe that this was the same city devastated by Hurricane Katrina. Cleveland decided that like New Orleans, he was going to go after Freddie with a renewed spirit. Though she tried to act as if she wasn't affected by seeing him, he knew that she was. The heat between them was the same as it had been the night of Louis and Lillian's wedding. Now that he knew he'd be seeing her, since she worked in the hotel, Cleveland started formulating a plan for the seduction of Freddie Barker. Seduction was a skill that he was well versed in and Winfred Barker was going to find out that he didn't take no for an answer. Hungry and excited about the prospect of tasting Freddie again, he stopped a man passing by.

"Hey, excuse me, where can I get a great Po-Boy?" Cleveland asked.

The man smiled, then tugged at his beatnik beard. "Whatcha wanna do is take the street car to St. Charles and head on down Robert Street and hang a right on Ammunition Street. You gonna see Domilise's Po-Boys. That place is amazing, but don'cha ask for extra gravy, you'll never get it out of your shirt."

Cleveland shook hands with the strange-looking man, thanked him and headed for the street car. The sights he saw caused him to wonder why it was taking so long for the Ninth Ward to be rebuilt when so many people were in town, dropping millions of dollars into the city's economy. If Katrina had ruined the French Quarter, he couldn't imagine that the state, the city and the federal government would've taken years to rebuild the place. The entire situation made him angry, helpless and distrustful of the people that were supposed to represent the citizens of New Orleans.

Days after Katrina, he and Darren had helped the city of Atlanta set up shelters for evacuees from New Orleans and they were also part of a convoy, sponsored by DVA, Jill's computer company, to take supplies to the victims who didn't have water, food or clean clothes for a full week after the levees broke. It was a harrowing experience, seeing the babies crying for help and parents standing around crying as well because they couldn't do anything to make their children feel better.

The street car came to a stop and Cleveland hopped off the trolley and walked to the restaurant. It was the kind of place that had grease stains on menus that were older than him. He knew the food was going to be good.

After ordering an oyster Po-Boy, dressed of course, he took his sandwich outside and soaked up the more subdued atmosphere. More families were walking around and unlike Bourbon Street, no one had to lift her shirt to get beads. He wondered if Freddie was still at the front desk and if he could catch her before she disappeared. But before he left, he was going to take her a Po-Boy. She had to eat some time.

Every time someone walked into the front door of the hotel, Freddie looked up and hoped it was Cleveland. She had a feeling of relief and disappointment each time it wasn't him. As much as she wanted to see him, she didn't want to. He stirred up a mess of trouble in her panties every time she saw him or heard his sexy baritone voice speak her name. Closing her eyes, she thought back to the motel room in Covington. The things they did that night opened her up to a different type of sexual satisfaction. It wasn't the champagne, it was the man that gave her multiple orgasms and made her feel as if . . .

"Miss Barker," Jewel said, breaking into her thoughts. "Are we going to be able to take a break for dinner soon? We have most of the reservations in."

"I'm sorry, I hadn't even thought about that. You go and get something to eat and I'll handle things here."

"Do you want me to bring you something back?"

Freddie smiled at her hard-working desk clerk. "You know what, go ahead and take the rest of the day off since most of the reservations are taken care of. I really appreciate you, that was good work today."

"Oh, thank you, Miss Barker," Jewel said as she grabbed her purse and sweater from underneath the desk. "By the way, 7218 said that you're doing a great job."

"I'll be sure to tell housekeeping to leave an extra mint on his pillow." She rolled her eyes when Jewel wasn't looking at her. Just how in the hell was she going to control her thoughts of Cleveland when every time she turned around . . .

"Freddie," he said as he walked up to the front desk. "I bet you haven't eaten all day."

"Cleveland, why don't you head up Bourbon Street and have a good time partying."

He placed the paper bag with the sandwich in it on the desk. "I've been doing that. But, I still wanted to make sure my favorite hotel operator had something to eat."

"What is this?"

"A Po-Boy, dressed," he said proud of the New Orleans lingo he'd picked up.

She giggled as she tore into the bag. "Been here one day and you think you're a native. Is this an oyster Po-Boy?" Freddie took a big bite of the sandwich. "This is my favorite."

Cleveland wiped a bit of mayonnaise from her chin with a paper napkin. "I can tell," he said. His fingers lingered on her face a little longer than they should have. Freddie turned her head away from him.

"Thank you for the sandwich," she said in between bites. "Now, I have to get back to work and . . ."

A short brown-skinned girl with bright red hair, dressed in a pair of black slacks and a white French Garden Inn shirt, walked in. "Hey Miss Barker," she said. "I'm ready to take over for you."

Celeste, you would pick today to come to work on time, Freddie thought through her tight smile.

"Looks like you have some time after all," Cleveland said.

"Looks can be deceiving because I have to go and check on the construction at my house and . . ."

"Miss Barker, chere, you know t'ain't nobody working on nothin' this week," Celeste said.

"Thanks, Celeste. Why don't you check on those reservations that have yet to get here," Freddie said, then turned to Cleveland. "I thought we had an agreement."

Cleveland leaned into her, their lips inches from one another's. "And I never thought I'd see you again. See, me ending up at your hotel was just fate's way of bring us back together again."

She wiggled her finger for him to walk around the corner. The last thing she wanted was for Celeste to hear their conversation.

"Yes," he said in a whisper.

"I don't know what you think is going to happen, but forget it. There are thousands of women in this city who you can make beautiful memories with. I just happen to not be one of them," she said.

"So, you admit we made beautiful memories," he said smugly. "And there could be a million women in this city, but you're the only one I want in my bed."

"Sorry, it was a one time lapse in judgment, flooded by alcohol and . . ."

Cleveland pulled Freddie against his body. "I don't want to hear that. I know you want the same thing that I want." Before she could pull away or protest, Cleveland kissed her until her knees went weak. She melted against him, wrapping her arms around his neck and pulling him deeper into the kiss. Cleveland's hands felt so good on her body and if she were honest with herself, she would admit that she didn't want him to stop. She would tell him all of the naughty things that she'd dreamed about since Lillian's wedding.

But Freddie was in no mood to be honest. Forcefully, she pushed Cleveland away. "Have you ever thought that I don't want you?"

"If I had any doubt, you erased it with that kiss." He licked his lips. "What are you afraid of?"

"Nothing," she said in a near whisper. "Cleveland, please, work your charm on someone else, all right?" Freddie stomped away from him, but in the back of her mind, she knew that she wouldn't have any peace until he was back in Atlanta where he belonged.

Chapter 8

Though the party was raging on the streets below, Cleveland couldn't think of anything but Freddie's lips and the curve of her body in his arms. Touching his lips, he thought about hers again. Walking over to the balcony, he looked down over the city. There were so many people clogging the streets that he wondered what would happen if an emergency vehicle had to get through that crowd. It reminded him of the days of Freaknik in Atlanta and how many calls they could barely get to because people were dancing in the streets and having impromptu car shows.

He should've been enjoying the party, drinking hurricanes and rum punch but the only thing he wanted to put in his mouth was Freddie. If he had to bring her Po-Boys every day for the rest of the week, then he would. He did need a drink and if he were lucky, he'd run into Freddie and they could pick up where they left off in the hallway. She wanted him and the minute she stopped denying it, the sooner they could have more fun together.

But Cleveland had a feeling that there was more to Freddie than just a few rolls in the hay, no matter how enjoyable they were. She had a lot going for herself, so why was she single and why did she feel the need to deny herself pleasure? He had six days and he'd do his damnedest to find that out. He crossed the room, tearing himself away from the excitement below him. Looking around the room, he could understand why the hotel was classified as a boutique. It had all the comforts of home, with an extra long king-sized bed and black-and-white décor. What he really loved was the mini bar, which was fully stocked with bourbon, gin, rum, and any other liquor you could want. Part of him had to wonder if this room was created for him.

Cleveland was about to pour himself a stiff drink when he realized that he didn't have any ice. Though he could've called the chambermaid and had her bring him some, Cleveland decided to explore the hotel and see what he could gleam about Freddie from the way she decorated and ran her business. Obviously she wasn't a horrible taskmaster because all of the employees he'd seen her come in contact with seemed to like her and have a friendly relationship with her.

Especially the chick that had shot down all of the excuses that Freddie tried to fly his way; she had to be friends with her boss. Grabbing the ice bucket, he headed out the door and saw Freddie walking into the room across the hall from him. The night was taking a definite turn for the better.

"Well, good evening," he said.

Freddie turned around with a startled look on her face. "Did you come to New Orleans to spend Mardi Gras inside a hotel room?"

"It's such a nice hotel, why wouldn't I spend at least one evening in here? Care to join me?" Cleveland asked with a smile.

"I'm very tired," Freddie said, "and remember what I said, we're so over."

Dropping his ice bucket on the floor, Cleveland closed the space between the two of them with the quickness of a cheetah, then he pressed her against the door and assaulted her lips with kisses that made her spine turn to jelly. Cleveland felt her let go as she wrapped her left leg around his waist. Though he tried to gently unbutton her blouse, he ended up ripping it open.

Freddie pressed her tongue deep into Cleveland's mouth, forgetting all of those promises she made to stay away from him. He tasted so good, his hands as they slipped underneath her skirt made her hot, wet, and filled with desire. She had to have him right now. Cleveland lifted her into his arms and pushed her room door open. It didn't matter that her bed hadn't been made and her running shoes were in the middle of the floor because all either of them saw was one another.

Cleveland laid her on the queen-sized bed and stripped her down to her pink lace bra and lace boy shorts. Slipping his hands between her thighs, he could feel her heat and he wanted to taste her wetness. Just as she'd taken the lead in their first rendezvous, Cleveland was going to be in control all night. He pulled her panties off and spread her legs apart, kissing her inner thigh and running his lips across the source of her desire. Freddie writhed underneath his faint touch with the anticipation of what was to come. When his tongue flicked across her throbbing bud of passion, she lost it—her legs shook, her body seemed to go limp and lustful cries died in the back of her throat.

Cleveland alternated his tongue and finger, bringing Freddie to climax in rapid succession. Still, he wasn't finished with her as he reversed his trail and kissed her navel, then snaked his tongue up to her breasts. All the while, he was kicking his shoes and pants off so that they could make their bodies one again. He'd longed for this moment since the wedding. He'd needed to taste, touch and feel Freddie again. She was the woman of his erotic dreams, and now she was in his arms.

"Cleveland," she moaned. "I need you."

Taking her nipple into his mouth, he ignored her request for the moment. He sucked her breast until her nipple hardened against his lips. "I got what you need," he said.

She placed her hand in the center of his chest. "Protection?"

He leaned down on the floor and pulled a gold package from his pocket. "Always prepared."

"What a Boy Scout you are," she teased.

Though he wanted to ask her why she ran hot and cold, his yearning for her was stronger than any question that was weighing on his mind. This was crazy, because this wasn't how Cleveland operated. No woman got under his skin, but Freddie had gotten under his skin and in his system. Looking down at her as he opened the condom package and slid the sheath in place, the only thing he could think about was melting with her.

Cleveland dove into Freddie's awaiting body, she was so wet and primed for him that he nearly climaxed with one thrust. Nothing had ever felt so good. It was as if he'd met his sexual match because as he pressed deeper and deeper, she matched him thrust for thrust. She even clutched his buttocks, silently begging for more. He didn't mind and gave her just what she wanted. Lifting her from the bed, he wrapped her legs around his waist as if they were ribbons, then backed her up against the wall. Cleveland raised her hands above her head as they continued their sensual dance so that he could feel the soft curve of her breasts. With her free hand, Freddie grabbed his shoulder as she tightened herself around him, alerting him to the fact that she was about to climax. Cleveland felt as if he could finally release what he'd been holding back and spent himself inside her. But he wouldn't let her go. For a few silent moments, they stood there looking at each other. Neither could deny the unyielding desire that had blossomed between them, and this time, Cleveland wasn't going to let her run away from it.

He carried her to the bed and laid her down. To his surprise, Freddie pulled on his arm so that he would join her. Holding her against his chest, Cleveland watched her as she fell asleep and wondered what other surprises Freddie had in store for him.

All she heard was water and wind crashing against the walls. "Mama!" Freddie called out. She reached out in the darkness and felt nothing. "Mama, don't leave me!"

She felt a hand grab her wrist. "Mama?"

"You have to do this on your own. I can't help you anymore," Loraine said coldly. "It's just going to break your heart."

"Please, Mama, don't do this. Just tell me the truth!"

A wall of water came crashing down on Loraine and she let go of Freddie's wrist.

Shooting up in the bed, she screamed. Sweat poured from her face and she shivered as a hand stroked her back.

"Freddie," Cleveland said, "are you all right?"

Hugging her knees to her chest, she shook her head. "It was just a bad dream, I guess."

He stroked her back gently, he said, "Do you want to talk about it?"

She pushed his hand away. "No, I don't." Tugging at the sheet, she covered herself with it. "What time is it?"

He looked at his wristwatch. "A little after two."

Freddie pushed her hair back from her forehead. "I need

to check on my night auditor. I can't believe that we've done this again."

Cleveland forced her to turn around and look at him. "Why do you do this?" he asked. "You run hot and cold. There is no middle ground with you, is there?"

"No, there isn't and you know what, there isn't room for you in my bed either," Freddie said as she leapt to her feet. Cleveland followed her lead, but instead of letting her force him out of the room, he pressed her against the door that she'd been trying to open.

"This is like déjà vu all over again," he said. "Why do you give yourself so freely and then when it's over, you act as if you're ashamed or someone forced you into doing something that you didn't want to do. What are you afraid of? That you're going to like it, that you're going to have to admit that . . ."

"Everything is not about you. The world doesn't revolve around Cleveland Alexander. I have my own stuff going on and this is too much," she exclaimed.

"What's going on?" he asked. "Are you just using me for sex, or what?"

She turned away from him and shook her head. "This is something I have to do on my own. Getting involved with you wasn't supposed to happen."

"What is the something?"

She sighed and rolled her eyes. "I have to find my father. I have to rebuild my life. And you're a distraction to me. You can't handle my life right now, because I can barely handle it myself."

Cleveland ran his hand across his forehead. "You know what? Let me decide that."

Freddie shook her head and pushed against his chest. "You're here for a week, Cleveland, and then what?"

"Then it's whatever we want it to be. But if you need my help, I'm not going to leave you hanging."

She turned her back to him and walked over to the window. "I don't want your help or anyone else's. I'm going to find my father and deal with the issues that we have. I'm going to rebuild my house and my life here in New Orleans. You, on the other hand, will be back in Atlanta doing whatever it is that you do."

Crossing over to her, Cleveland pulled her into his arms, forcing her to look into his eyes. "Do you know what I've been doing in Atlanta since the night we spent together?"

She shook her head, struggling to meet his intense gaze. "Thinking of you," Cleveland said. "The way you felt in my arms, the way you tasted, the way you moved. I don't know what kind of man you think I am, but this isn't something I normally do. I don't chase women. But I feel like I'd follow you to the ends of the Earth to unravel this mystery that you've become to me."

Closing her eyes, Freddie let his words sink in. She wanted to believe it all, but she'd heard it all before. A man who wanted to help her find her father, a man who wanted her, a man who was telling a lie. That's what Marcus had done, lied to her because he wanted the fortune that went along with finding Jacques Babineaux, an escaped federal prisoner. Freddie's father had a bounty of one million dollars on his head. Everyone in New Orleans knew about Babineaux and the crime he was accused of. But Freddie never knew the details of the murder.

Her mother wouldn't be honest with her about what happened. For years, she painted Babineaux as a deadbeat and even changed their last name to Barker.

"You don't understand," she said. "It's too much to get into it with you because . . ."

"Because what?" he asked.

Freddie looked up at Cleveland. He wasn't from New Orleans and he didn't know who Babineaux was. "Are you sure you want to give up your vacation to help me find my father?"

"I wouldn't have made the offer if I wasn't sure," he said as he stroked her cheek.

Freddie smiled tersely. "Then we're going to have to take a trip in the morning," she said. "It's taken me a month to get a strong lead on where he is."

Chapter 9

Cleveland would've been content to hold Freddie all night, but after what little she'd told him, he couldn't sleep. She wanted to find her father, but she made it seem as if they were about to embark on a deadly recon mission at the heart of a five alarm fire. Hopefully, he thought as he stared down at her slumbering frame, she'd be more talkative and tell him more about what they were really looking for.

By the time he drifted to sleep, Freddie was waking him up. "Cleveland," she said. Her voice had a soft sing-song quality. "Get up. We've got to go."

"What time is it?" he asked through a haze of sleep.

"Time to go. Come on, you've got fifteen minutes and then I'm gone. If you're going to be dragging me down, then I can do this on my own."

Sitting up, Cleveland noticed that Freddie was wrapped in a plush pink towel and her hair was pulled back in a ponytail. "How long have you been up?" he asked.

"Long enough to take a shower. We have an hour's drive and I want to try and get out of here before too many partiers wake up and before the parade starts," she said.

"All right, let me run across the hall and shower. Do you want me to meet you in the lobby?" he asked.

"No, no. The last thing I need is for my staff to see us together. There's no telling what Celeste has already told them. I have strict rules about my employees fraternizing with the guests. If they see you and me leaving together, I'm going to look like the biggest fraud. Meet me in the parking deck near my car, okay," she said.

"You're not trying to blow me off, are you?"

"I'd be lying if I said the thought didn't cross my mind," Freddie said honestly. "But maybe I need some new eyes. I'll be down there in fifteen minutes. Please don't keep me waiting."

After putting on his clothes, Cleveland dashed across to his room, took a quick shower, and dressed in a pair of jeans and a long-sleeved cotton shirt. He was ready in less than ten minutes, because in the back of his mind, he figured that Freddie would leave him. But when he reached the parking deck, her car was still there. Five minutes later, so was Freddie.

"Thanks for being on time," she said.

"I don't like to make people wait when they need me. So, where are we going?"

"Mississippi," Freddie said as they got in the car. "I think the last place I heard my father was seen was in Pass Christian right after Katrina."

"Pass what?"

Freddie laughed, "Pass Chris-chee-ann. It's an hour away from here. Robin Roberts from *Good Morning America* is from there. And something drew my father there."

"Okay, before we get started on the journey, tell me what you expect to find?" Cleveland said.

"Answers. My father isn't a nice guy. He's supposed to be serving a life sentence in Pollock, Louisiana. About seven years ago, he broke out, and before Katrina we were supposed to meet but . . ." Freddie stopped talking. She didn't want to say too much. Then again, there was so much that she didn't know. That's why she had to talk to her father and find out the whole story. Something she would not get in media reports or from her mother. "If I don't find him soon, I may never get the answers I need."

"Why didn't you meet him before the storm?" Cleveland asked.

"It wasn't safe," she replied, not getting into specifics. Again she fell silent.

"Freddie?"

"Just help me follow the lead that I have and don't ask too many questions. If what my mother says about him is true, Jacques isn't a nice man anyway. But I need to know that for myself."

Cleveland leaned back in the supple leather seats of the classic Mustang. "Does your father have family in Pass Christian?"

She shrugged and bit her bottom lip as if she was pondering whether she should tell him the entire story about her father, at least what she knew about him.

Noting her silence, he pressed on. "What's so important about finding your father?"

"Because, I have to know why he left us and let us struggle the way we did. What kind of man does that?" Her voice rose several octaves as she spoke. "Growing up was really hard for us. Half of the town treated us like we were pariahs. If it wasn't for Lillian and her family, there would've been days that my mother, Loraine and I wouldn't have eaten."

Cleveland nodded. He knew about hard times because after his father died things were hard in the Alexander household. Margaret became the breadwinner and he and

Darren had to grow up fast. They didn't give their mother a lot of trouble growing up. But unlike Freddie, they had a support system in place. The men in their father's battalion made sure Cleveland and Darren were taken care of, and they gave them those man speeches that Margaret couldn't provide.

"Why didn't people want to reach out to you and your mom?" he asked.

"I wish I knew," she said. "There are still some neighborhoods in New Orleans where you can't speak my father's name without someone shaking a gris-gris at you."

"A what?" Cleveland asked.

"A gris-gris is a charm that people believe can bring good luck or ward evil spirits away," she explained. "I don't believe in it."

"So, your dad's a bad guy?"

She shrugged her shoulders. "I don't know. I feel like he's an asshole for leaving me and my mom the way he did. We had so much debt and that hotel was like an albatross for so many years. But Mom would never sell it."

"It's a good thing that she didn't. Looks like you've made a go of it."

Freddie flipped the radio on and Cleveland got the feeling that she didn't want to talk anymore.

You're doing it again, Freddie thought as she merged on to Interstate 10. *You're letting someone in and you're going to end up paying for it.*

She was wishing that she hadn't told Cleveland anything. She should've left him sleeping in her bed. What was he going to do when he found out that her father could net him a million dollars? Her mind flashed to the last night she and Marcus had spent together. It was two days before the storm and she had talked to her father. They'd planned to meet in the hotel's restaurant before the evacuation. After hanging up with Babineaux, she'd rushed into the bedroom where Marcus was waiting.

Happily, she leapt into his arms. "Guess what! I found him."

"Found who?" he'd asked.

"My father. He's going to meet me at the hotel in the morning. Then we can get out of here before all hell breaks loose."

Marcus smiled and kissed her on the tip of her nose. "I'm happy for you. This is what you've wanted, right."

Freddie nodded. "Thank you so much for helping me find him."

"Of course. I'd do anything for you, baby."

Letting him go, she walked seductively to the bathroom. "Well, let me do something for you. I'll be right back."

Freddie was about to change into a sexy lace nightgown when she heard Marcus walk out of the bedroom. *Where is he going?* she thought as she stepped out of the bathroom. That's when she heard him talking in a hushed tone.

"Yes, at The French Garden Inn. I don't know what time, but his daughter just told me that she was meeting him there in the morning. When do I get my money?"

Money?

"Look, I've been with his daughter for the last six months, haven't I told you everything that she knew about him? It's not my fault that your men are slow."

Freddie burst out of the bedroom. "You slimy bastard. You set me up. You haven't been trying to help me find my father because you care about me!"

Marcus snapped his cell phone shut. "It's not what you think . . ."

Freddie punched him in the face, causing blood to spurt from his nose. "Get the hell out of my house!"

"Look," he said, "we can split the million."

She swung at him again, but missed. "You'd better hope that my father doesn't get caught because . . ."

"He's a criminal. I don't know why you want a relationship with him anyway. Everyone in New Orleans knows what he did and if you'd take your blinders off, you'd know that prison is where he belongs."

Once again, she swung at him and this time she connected with his eye. "Out!"

Marcus stalked out of her house and out of her life.

The next morning, Freddie didn't have a chance to meet with her father. He called her with a warning.

"Chere, I don't think this storm is one to play with. Get out of New Orleans," he warned.

"Jacques, when am I going to see you so we can talk?"

"After this water blows over, we'll talk. What I have to say has to be face to face. It's not going to be safe in New Orleans, so you get to high ground, okay?"

Sighing, she told her father that she would leave. Hours later, she and Loraine were on their way to Atlanta.

"Freddie!" Cleveland called out, breaking into her thoughts. "Watch that car."

She slammed the breaks as the car in front of her did the same. Swearing under her breath, she quickly changed lanes.

"Bit of road rage?" he asked with a tense laugh.

"Don't worry, I'm not going to kill you—today."

Cleveland sneered at her. "You're so funny. Where did you go?"

She ran her free hand over her ponytail. "I was listening to the radio."

"The toothpaste commercial?"

She sighed and stared straight ahead. "I'm focusing on

the road, okay? Open the glove box, the directions to where we're going are in there."

He opened the glove compartment and blanched when he picked up the map and saw the nine-millimeter handgun underneath it. "What in the hell have you gotten me into?" Cleveland demanded as he picked up the gun.

"Put that down," she said calmly.

He lowered the gun. "Why do you feel the need to have this? Are you going to kill your father?"

"No! What kind of person do you think I am? That gun is for protection, there have been a lot of robberies in the area and . . . Why am I explaining this to you? You're the one who said you wanted to help me. If you want to back out, then let me know now."

"That's what you want, isn't it? You want me to leave you high and dry, don't you, so that you can say, he's just like the rest of them?" Cleveland asked.

"Did I say that? Stop projecting your bullshit on me and trying to analyze me," Freddie said. "Do you have a hero complex or something?"

"Superhero actually," Cleveland said. "I save lives for a living."

Rolling her eyes, Freddie struggled not to smile. "You are a firefighter, I forgot. Still, I don't know why you think you know so much about me."

"I know I don't," he said. "But I'm willing to learn."

"Opening up about this is hard for me," she said. "So, can I trust you?"

Freddie glanced at Cleveland, sizing him up. Was he more trustworthy than Marcus had been? The best thing about Cleveland was that he wasn't from New Orleans and he didn't know who Babineaux was, that meant he wasn't after the money. But what was he going to do when he found out? A million dollars could change everything.

"My father is wanted by the FBI. I just want the truth, and he's the only person I can get it from."

"Why don't you just ask your mother?"

Her eyebrows shot up in frustration. "Damn, why didn't I think of that?"

"All right, stupid suggestion," he said. "What if your father is dangerous?"

"If you're scared, just say so," she snapped.

"Did I say I was scared? I'm just worried about you. If you feel the need to carry a gun to look for him, then maybe . . ."

"My father isn't who I'm worried about," she said. "There are some people who would rather not see my father and I meet." Freddie left out the part about the bounty hunters. Though she'd never used her gun before, if she had to, she would.

"Why's that?"

She shrugged. "That's part of the whole mystery. Why would anyone want to keep a father away from his daughter?"

For the rest of the trip, Cleveland and Freddie rode in silence. Though he wouldn't admit it to her, he couldn't help but wonder if he was in over his head.

Chapter 10

Pass Christian looked like a ghost town. A lot of the storm debris was still piled on the streets. White FEMA trailers stood in the place of the destroyed shorefront houses that couldn't withstand Katrina's fury.

Growing up in New Orleans, Freddie always though Pass Christian was a playground for the elite, a place where they docked their yachts and lived in fancy mansions on the beach. They must have thought their money protected them from nature. What Camille didn't teach them, Katrina did, Freddie thought as she looked around the rubble. It was the kids that she felt for the most. Some had lost their parents, some had lost their homes, and all of them lost their schools and libraries. She stopped the car in front of what looked like a diner.

"So, what's the plan?" Cleveland asked as they stepped out of the car.

"I don't know, let's just play it by ear. People around here don't like it when you ask a lot of questions."

Cleveland nodded. "But you know what, asking questions is just what we need to do. We can say we're looking for someone that fits your father's description if you don't want to mention him by name. You'll get the privilege of pretending to be my wife."

"Don't flatter yourself," she said as she closed the car door. As much as she hated to admit it, Cleveland's plan had merit. She reached out and took his hand as they walked into the restaurant.

The chatter stopped instantly when Cleveland and Freddie walked inside. Most of the people there knew each other, they were either residents or long term volunteers.

"Morning," Cleveland said to a patch of people who kept staring at him.

They mumbled a greeting before returning to drinking their coffee. "Tough group," Cleveland whispered to Freddie.

"I guess we stand out more than I thought we would," she said as she tugged gently on one of Cleveland's locs.

"Then why don't we just ask a few questions?" he said as they took a seat in a booth near the rear of the restaurant.

She shrugged. "I guess you're right," she said. Still, she was afraid that they may ask the wrong person the right question. "The last thing I want to do is put him in danger or be the reason that he's caught," Freddie admitted. "He's been running for a long time and I'm sure some people would do anything to send him back to prison—not that he doesn't belong there. But he is my father."

Cleveland focused his intense stare on Freddie. "Why do you think your father is here?" he asked.

"Before Lillian's wedding, I heard my mother say something about Jacques being around and all his presence was going to do is cause problems for us. When I asked her about it, she said if I wanted to find out why he'd returned, that I'd have to do it without her help. Pass Christian has always been one of his favorite places."

Cleveland furrowed his brows in confusion. "Has your mother said why she doesn't want your father in your life?"

"She's never given me a concrete reason. It's beyond frustrating," she said.

He shook his head. "I don't mean to sound judgmental, but your mother shouldn't stand in the way of you and your father getting to know each other. Obviously, she thought enough of him to have you."

"People change, I guess," she said. "There is no justification for what my mother or my father have done. The least either of them can do is just explain everything to me."

Cleveland nodded in agreement. "Wow. Even though you're dealing with all of this, you're holding up pretty well."

"One thing I can say my mother taught me is how to hide my emotions," she said as she crossed her legs.

Before Cleveland could reply, a red-haired waitress wearing a tight uniform walked over to their table and asked them if they would like to order.

Cleveland ordered coffee, grits and toast. Freddie, who didn't have much of an appetite, ordered just a cup of coffee and raisin toast.

"Excuse me," Cleveland said, before the waitress walked away. "We're looking for someone, a man that may be volunteering with some of the people working on the reconstruction. Do you know where they meet in the mornings?"

"Usually at the town hall," she said. "Who are you looking for?"

"A family friend," Freddie interjected. "He was so

moved by what was going on here, that he took off and didn't tell a soul where he was going."

The woman nodded as if she didn't believe the story Freddie was weaving, but she didn't say a word.

"You're not going to make many friends here," Cleveland said once the waitress was out of ear shot.

"Who said I was trying to make friends? I just want to find my father and get out of here."

"What happens when you find him?"

Freddie shrugged. "I just want to talk to him and get the answers that I need."

"And then what?"

"You agreed to help me find my father, but that doesn't mean that I have to tell you everything that I need from him," she said.

"That's true, but—"

"You volunteered to help me, I didn't ask for your help. I knew this was a mistake," Freddie railed.

"Calm down," Cleveland said. "You're right, I did volunteer, but I didn't know that we were going to be playing cloak and dagger. You have a gun and you haven't been forthcoming with any information."

"Because it doesn't matter," Freddie said. "Once we find my father and get back to New Orleans, we're going to go our separate ways."

"You really think it's going to go down like that? We're not finished, not by a long shot," he said.

"So, you're not helping me from the kindness of your heart?" Freddie folded her arms across her chest and rolled her eyes.

"There's something going on between us and as much as you'd like to ignore it, I'm not going to let you."

"This isn't the time or the place for this discussion," Freddie said through clenched teeth. "And for the record, there is nothing between us but two incidents that shouldn't have happened."

"Incidents? So that's what we're calling it now?"

She rolled her eyes and tugged at her ponytail. "Cleveland, don't do this, okay?"

"Do what?" he asked innocently.

"Can we just go now?" she said with a hint of an attitude in her voice.

Cleveland rose to his feet, took enough money out of his wallet to cover their breakfasts and stepped aside so that Freddie could exit the booth.

She stalked out of the restaurant in silence, because the last thing she wanted to do was think about what she and Cleveland had done between the sheets. Everytime she thought about the feel of his lips against hers or the way he felt inside her, she got weak. Weakness was something she couldn't show. Not now, not ever.

Still it felt as if his gray eyes cut through her soul every time he looked at her. Maybe that's why she couldn't eat or look him directly in his eyes at the restaurant. The sooner she found her father, the sooner Cleveland could get back to Atlanta and they would never have to see each other again.

Could she handle that? *Of course I can,* she thought as she slipped into the car. *Cleveland will forget about me as soon as his feet hit the Georgia red clay.* She glanced at him as she drove. If things were different, then maybe she and Cleveland would've had something more than a few rolls in the hay. But he had to understand that she didn't want a relationship with him or anyone else. Not until she knew why her father was running and why he'd abandoned her.

"Are you all right?" Cleveland asked after Freddie started the car.

"I'm fine."

"Listen, I know this is hard for you. But after you find your father, you're going to have to ask yourself, how am I going to live without Cleveland."

She rolled her eyes and shook her head as she threw the car in reverse. "What you should ask yourself is, 'Why am I so stupid that I'd piss off the woman driving, who will leave me in the middle of nowhere.'"

"You'd be back," he quipped.

"Please shut up," Freddie snapped. "Do you take anything seriously?"

"I do, but you need to loosen up. You're wound way too tight and you're too young to have a heart attack."

Freddie pressed the gas pedal down and took off, causing Cleveland to hold on to his seatbelt extra tight.

"I won't say another word as long as you slow down," he said, shooting a sharp glance at Freddie.

"That was me loosening up," she said as she slowed the car.

"Uh-huh," he said. "Judging from that crowd, I think that's the town hall up ahead."

As they approached the town hall, Freddie scanned the crowd looking for her father. Did he look the same as he did when she'd last seen him? Her father had a distinct look, long black wavy hair pulled back in a ponytail, a caramel complexion and a beard like a pirate.

Scanning the crowd, she didn't see him. Freddie felt like a ten-year-old all over again, sitting on the front steps waiting for her dad to show up.

"Why don't you park the car so that we can look around," Cleveland suggested.

"That's what I was going to do, but you've noticed that they don't take too kindly to strangers around here," she said.

"Then I guess we need to make friends," he said once she stopped the car and parked.

Cleveland hopped out the passenger side and headed to the throng of volunteers standing near the entrance of the town hall. Everyone turned and looked at him, immediately sensing that he wasn't one of them.

"Hey," he said to the crowd. "Who do I need to talk to about volunteering?"

One man stepped up and gave him the once over. "You're not from around here are you?" he asked.

"No. I'm from Atlanta, but my wife and I saw what was still going on here and we want to help," Cleveland said smoothly.

A red-haired woman, dressed in a pair of denim overalls and a pink baseball cap, pushed the man aside. "Don't pay attention to Earl. We're glad to have you. Come over here so we can sign you and your wife up."

Cleveland turned around and saw Freddie standing behind him with a fake smile plastered on her face.

"I'm Estelle," the woman said as she led them to the booth where the volunteers were to sign in.

"Cleveland and this my wife . . ."

"Winfred Babineaux," Freddie said.

Estelle stopped in her tracks. "Babineaux? Are you from New Orleans?"

Freddie nodded.

"Oh dear, I have to ask you this, you're not related to Jacques Babineaux are you?"

"Has he been here?"

"Not that I know of, thank God. But everyone in the Gulf knows what he did. We don't need your help or that kind of trouble around here."

"Ma'am," Cleveland said. "We're not here to start any trouble and we just want to help."

"What did Babineaux do to make him the pariah of the Gulf Coast?" Freddie asked, her voice desperate.

Estelle motioned for Freddie and Cleveland to step to the side with her. "All my life, I've always heard that the only good Babineaux is a dead Babineaux. Jacques Babineaux is a cursed man for what he did. If I were you, I'd go back to where you came from and I wouldn't tell anyone else that you're a Babineaux."

"Look, lady," Freddie said. "If you know something other than conjecture and legend about my father, then tell me."

"Father?" Estelle said, her eyes widened in disbelief. "Jacques is your father?"

"Yes, and I think he's here."

"Mon dieu," Estelle said, pushing her hat back from her forehead. "Wait here."

Freddie and Cleveland exchanged confused looks. "Let's just go," Freddie said. "This is just another dead end. I'm sick of this."

"Wait, maybe Estelle knows more than she's letting on. Why did you tell her that you were his daughter?" Cleveland asked.

"Because I don't do subtle and I'm tired of this bullshit. I want to find this man and get the hell away from here." *And you,* she added silently. "If my father is here, he's probably . . ."

"Right behind you, darling," a man said. Freddie and Cleveland turned around. The man that they thought was Earl stood in front of them. "Can't believe you got married, I always hoped I'd be able to give you away."

Freddie folded her arms across her chest. "I have a hard time believing that."

Babineaux nodded. "I guess you would. How's your mother?"

"I didn't come all this way for small talk."

"I imagine not, but this isn't the time or the place." He nodded toward Cleveland. "Can he be trusted?"

She nodded. "Why don't we go somewhere private," Freddie suggested as she tossed the car keys to Cleveland. "Will you wait for me?"

Though Cleveland figured Freddie and her father needed privacy to hash out whatever they had to talk about, he didn't want to leave her alone with a purported murderer, father or not.

"Don't have much of a choice, do I?" he asked as he headed for the car.

Freddie looked at her father; he was truly a master of disguise. He was completely bald, had lost the earring and started wearing a pair of tortoiseshell eyeglasses.

"You look different," Freddie said.

"That's the plan. After all, people are looking for me," he said.

"Tell me about it."

Jacques smiled and opened his arms to her, but Freddie didn't move. "So, you can't give your old man a hug?"

"When I needed to hug you, you were nowhere to be found," Freddie snapped.

Folding his arms across his chest, Jacques rocked on his heels and sighed. "There was a reason for all of that and . . . Is that man really your husband? How do you know he isn't like the other guy and is trying to catch me for the money?"

Freddie shook her head. "Don't you dare try and change the subject," she said. "Don't worry about who he is. You owe me some answers."

"We can't talk out here," he said. "Someone might hear us."

"But that lady knows who you are," Freddie whispered. "How do you know that you can trust her?"

"She's family," Jacques replied as he pulled a scrap of paper and a pen from the pocket of his overalls. "This is where I'm staying. We usually get back there around six. Come alone. I don't trust that guy. He looks shifty."

"I can't help that I'm attracted to shifty men, look at who my father is."

Jacques leaned in and kissed Freddie on the cheek. "Let me walk you to your car, unless you are really here to work. I mean, we need all the help that we can get."

"No, I have my own rebuilding to worry about. I'll drop Cleveland off at the hotel and then come back. Will you still be there around seven?"

"I'll wait for you," he said. "That's the least that I can do. And I promise I'm going to answer all of your questions." When they got to the car, a slow smile spread across Jacques' face. "I see you kept her in good condition." He ran his hand across the fender.

"It's the only thing of yours that Mom didn't get rid of," she said as she slipped inside the car. Cleveland was already behind the wheel.

"And you let him drive?" Jacques said through clenched teeth. "This is a Babineaux baby."

"Then I guess that explains why you abandoned it," she snapped, her voice filled with attitude.

"If you feel this way about me, then why did you go through all this trouble to find me?"

She shrugged her shoulders. "Because I want to know why you . . . Let's just talk about this later."

"Fine," he said as he leaned in to kiss Freddie on the cheek. She turned her head quickly.

"Let's go," Freddie said to Cleveland as she closed the door.

"Is everything all right?" he asked.

"Yes. Thank you for coming here with me, I appreciate it."

Cleveland glanced at her as he pulled out of the parking lot. "Well, I'm glad that I could help, but you and your father didn't look as if you all had resolved anything."

"Look, your concern is touching, but misplaced," she said as she leaned back in the seat.

"So, I'm supposed to act like I don't care after coming all this way with you?"

Freddie closed her eyes and didn't answer. The sooner that they got back to New Orleans, the sooner she could get rid of Cleveland and get back down to Pass Christian and talk to Jacques.

"Freddie," he pressed.

"What?"

"Are you going to tell me what happened with you and your father?" he asked, cutting his eye at her.

"There's nothing that you need to worry about," she said. "We're going to talk later, especially since I know where he is."

"He didn't seem too happy to see me behind the wheel."

Freddie sighed, "That's because he doesn't really trust a lot of people. Especially after what happened with the last person who tried to help me find him."

"Oh, I hope I didn't make things worse," he said, his voice filled with concern.

"No, you didn't, but I really wish that you'd just drive and be quiet," she said. "I'm sorry, you've done nothing but help me and I'm being rude."

Cleveland chuckled, "I wasn't going to say anything, but you are."

Freddie ran her hand over her hair. "Let me make it up to you, I'll buy you lunch when we get back to town. I know a great restaurant off the beaten path where we can get some gumbo and crawfish."

"Well this I can't believe, Winfred Barker eating humble pie," Cleveland said as he turned on to the Interstate.

Chapter 11

Once they made it back to New Orleans, Freddie directed Cleveland to a restaurant near the lower Ninth Ward. It was one of the few businesses that came back after the hurricane. Smiling as they pulled into the parking lot, Freddie remembered coming here with her mother and father when she was about four years old. It was one of the only fond memories that she had of her family.

Once upon a time, they had been happy. Though it was a long time ago and much of it was a hazy memory. Just like the day her father disappeared. It was just like the clichéd tale of a dad going out for a pack of cigarettes and never coming back. Freddie had heard the rumblings about her father as she was growing up. Things had gotten so bad that by the time she was going to elementary school, she had a new last name.

The only thing her mother would say about her father was that he was in prison where he belonged.

"You're quiet again," Cleveland said as he parked the car in the gravel lot.

She smiled, "I guess I'm tired. It's been a long day."

"And seeing your father was a shock, huh?"

"Yeah, you could say that. Can we not talk about him, though?" Freddie said as she stepped out of the car.

Cleveland nodded as he looked around at their surroundings. "Wow," he whispered, "I guess Mardi Gras didn't make it down here?" There were still piles of storm debris on the side of the road. A few buildings were gutted and in need of repair. The marks were still on the walls detailing if bodies were found in the houses. It was a different look from the revelry going on in the French Quarter.

"It's a shock, isn't it," she said.

"You'd think this place would be rebuilt by now."

"It would be if the people that lived here weren't black and poor," Freddie said bitterly. Glancing down at her watch, Freddie noticed that she and Cleveland weren't going to be able to have a leisurely meal because she had to get back to see her father. "We'd better get inside. I have to get back to the hotel and check on everything that's going on."

He nodded and headed toward the door. "You were right about this place, it is off the beaten path." Cleveland opened the door and held it for Freddie.

"And they have the best food," she said as they walked into the greasy spoon. In a way, it reminded Cleveland of some of the restaurants in Five Points or Sweet Auburn.

There was no hostess to seat them and no pretentious crowd of buppies.

The couple took a seat near the window. Cleveland looked out over the neighborhood and saw no signs of life, no signs of renewal or rebuilding.

"Wow," he mumbled.

"What?" Freddie asked.

"It's just the fact that there's nothing going on out there. No bulldozers moving, no signs of life. It's just bleak; this can't be America."

Freddie stared out the window. "You know, since the storm, I hate cloudy and rainy days." They both looked up at the sky simultaneously. The sun shined brightly, but from the look in Freddie's eyes, Cleveland knew a different kind of storm was brewing.

"Is everything all right?" he asked.

"Yes," Freddie said quickly. "I'm just hungry and tired. It's been a long day already."

"You can relax when you get back to the hotel, right?" he asked, his voice filled with concern.

She sighed. "Not really, I'm sure there's some crisis there. That's just how things work during Mardi Gras." Nervously, she toyed with her ponytail.

"Don't you think you've done enough today?"

She shook her head and dropped her hands on the table. "Cleveland, I appreciate your concern, but you're wasting it. I've been taking care of myself for a long time and I don't need you to look after me."

Cleveland placed his hand on top of Freddie's. "I don't doubt that. But does it hurt to have someone watch over you?"

Slowly, she slipped her hand from underneath his. "Let's order so that I can get back to the hotel."

Leaning back in his seat, Cleveland studied Freddie as she glanced over the greasy menu. A smarter man would cut his losses. He'd gotten a chance to taste her, feel her wetness, and she made it clear that the only thing she wanted from him was sex. He should've been fine with that, because that's how he normally dealt with women. Nothing serious, no entanglements that would last longer than he wanted. But Freddie was different. She was the gazelle and he was the lion.

"Why are you staring at me?" she asked as she peered over the menu.

Before he could answer, an older woman walked over to the table to take their orders. They both settled on the crawfish special and iced tea. When the waitress left, Cleveland folded his arms across his broad chest and looked at Freddie. She met his smoldering gaze.

"What is it?" she asked.

"You tell me," he said. "I get the feeling that you want to get rid of me because you've gotten all that you want from me."

"I don't want or need anything from you. See, this is why I didn't want you to help me. Do you think I owe you something now?"

He shook his head. "Not at all, Freddie."

She rolled her eyes and watched the waitress walk over to the table with a basket of hot water cornbread. "Why don't we eat and then go our separate ways? Your visit is almost over and you haven't had a chance to experience New Orleans. I sucked you into my drama and . . ."

"And we had a great time in your suite and you know that we have something between us. A fire. It's been building since Lillian's wedding. I'm game to see where it leads, but you . . ."

"Don't want anything from you and there isn't anything between us. You really flatter yourself too much. The sex was good, but it wasn't earth-shattering," she spat.

Shaking his head, Cleveland grinned. "You keep saying things like that, but you know that if we weren't in this restaurant, you'd be all over me."

"But since we are in this restaurant, I'm not going to tell you what you're full of and where you can go."

"What are you afraid of?"

"Nothing," she snapped. "And why are you pretending that we have some deep connection when all we've shared are a few orgasms? Just because you rode to Mississippi with me doesn't mean that we're going to be a couple or you're going to have some huge role in my life. You live in Atlanta."

"I know where I live," he said.

"Good. Remember that. When this week is over, you're going back to Atlanta and I'll be a distant memory."

I'm never going to forget you, Cleveland thought as he watched Freddie go through the motions of convincing herself that they meant nothing to each other. Cleveland knew they had a connection and he felt that she knew it too. Passion like what they shared couldn't be faked. "If you say so," he finally said.

The waitress brought their entrees out and the duo ate in an awkward silence. After they finished eating, Cleveland stood up and smiled. "Are you ready to get back to your work now?" he asked.

"Yes, and thank you for taking this trip with me today," Freddie said as she stood up and headed for the door. Cleveland took one more look at the bleak neighborhood around the restaurant. Something about New Orleans was calling him. Or maybe that something was just Freddie.

I'm truly losing my mind, he thought as they got into the car. *My home is in Atlanta and she doesn't want me here. So when this week is over, I'm going home and back to my life.*

Cleveland sat in the car, silently mulling over what he should say to Freddie, if anything.

She glanced over at him and smiled tersely. "Is everything all right?" she asked.

"Yeah, guess I'm tired too," Cleveland said.

"Ruining your vacation, huh?"

Shrugging his shoulders, he didn't reply. Cleveland was tired of this dance with her. Tired of Freddie running hot and cold and the mystery surrounding her.

"I wouldn't say that," he said.

"Then what's the problem? Because you did offer to . . ."

"I'm tired of watching you fight," he said.

"Fight what? What are you talking about?"

"I'm talking about you fighting what you really want."

"And just what do you think I want?" Freddie asked.

"Me."

"You? Are you kidding me? I don't want . . . we're not going there again."

Cleveland tugged at his locs and smiled. "Going where? Back to your bed? We both know that's the one place where you don't have a problem saying what you want. Then when you've reached your release you go back to denial."

"What happened between us was a mistake and it won't happen again."

"Denial."

"I'm not denying anything. You live in Atlanta, your life is there and . . ."

"But the heat is here, burning between you and me like an inferno," Cleveland said in a low voice, causing a throbbing between Freddie's legs.

"Whatever," she snapped, hating the way her body responded to him. "It's Louisiana, there's always heat here."

Cleveland ran his index finger across Freddie's thigh. She shivered inadvertently then swatted his hand away. "You're disgusting," she said in a quiet tone.

"If you say so. But I'll make a deal with you," Cleveland said. "If you will admit that you want me, then I'll give you everything you desire."

"All I want from you is to be left alone," Freddie said as she pulled into the parking lot of the hotel. "Get out of my car."

"So, I'll see you later?" Cleveland joked as he got out of the car.

* * *

When Freddie walked into her office, she fell into her chair and closed her eyes tightly. She'd hoped that finding her father would answer her questions, but it left her with more unknowns. Picking up the phone, she called her mother in Houston.

"Hello?" said Loraine.

"Mom, how are you?" she said flatly.

"Where have you been, Winfred? It's Mardi Gras and your staff said you haven't been in all day. Is that how you're running my hotel?"

"Your hotel? When's the last time you did a day's work at your hotel? If you must know, I spent the day looking for my father and I found him."

After a moment of total silence, Loraine said, "Are you determined to ruin your life? You are going to ruin everything that I spent my life building. Do you think there's a million-dollar bounty on Jacques' head because he's a nice guy?"

"Why don't you just tell me the truth? If you would've answered my questions a long time ago, I wouldn't be running around the Gulf Coast chasing a convict," Freddie snapped.

Loraine released a heavy sigh. "There are some things that you're better off not knowing."

"Damn it, Mother, I'm twenty-seven years old, stop treating me like I'm a damned baby."

"I have to go."

"You're not doing this to me, not this time," Freddie said, feeling like the twelve-year-old who'd been asking when's Daddy coming home.

"Doing what? Protecting you from that man as I've done all of your life? The Babineaux name isn't held in high regard around here, in case you haven't noticed. I shielded you from that, made people forget that he was your father and he was a part of this hotel that you seem to be running into the ground. Stop worrying about that man when he doesn't give a damn about anything but himself."

"Then I guess that's something the two of you have in common," Freddie snapped. "You don't give a damn about me either."

"How can you say that?" Loraine demanded. "You don't know what it was like. When your father . . . you know what, I'm not explaining anything to you and if you think that finding your father is some sort of prize, you will soon see that you are wrong." Loraine slammed the phone down.

Freddie placed her phone in the cradle and closed her eyes tightly. What was her mother hiding? Was her father going to be any more forthcoming with answers and—The shrill ring of the telephone interrupted her thoughts. "What is it?" she snapped when she picked up the phone.

"Is that how you speak to your guests?" Cleveland asked.

"What do you want? I'm busy."

"I was concerned about you," he said. "Since you have so much work to do, I was wondering if you're going to have time for dinner."

"No, I'm going to be working through the night and I thought we agreed to stay away from each other?"

"I'm not good at following directions, and I'm not going to spend the rest of my vacation ignoring you."

"Please, I don't need this," she said. "I have to go."

"I'll see you at eight with a couple of Po-Boys."

Before Freddie could protest, Cleveland hung up the phone. She wasn't worried about Cleveland because she was going back to Mississippi to talk to her father. Still, it bothered her that the sound of his voice heated her blood. Bothered her that the entire time she was alone with him, all she thought about were the things they did in her bed. He made her pleasure his priority and when he touched her, it was electric. Freddie crossed her legs as her sexual core throbbed at the thought of Cleveland burying his face between her thighs, lashing her heated button with his tongue. Opening her eyes, she nearly expected him to be there.

She glanced at the clock on the wall. It was time to go. Freddie prayed that she could sneak out of the hotel without running into Cleveland, because she had an idea where their meeting would lead. Though she'd be satisfied in one respect, having sex with Cleveland wouldn't give her the answers that she needed about her father.

Chapter 12

Lying in his bed, Cleveland looked up at the ceiling, thinking of Freddie. Why had he let this woman get under his skin? If Freddie was a woman in Atlanta would she have gotten to him this way? What if Louis was right? Maybe the only reason he wanted Freddie so badly was because she was unattainable. Perhaps that was true when they first met, but these few days with her had shown him a different side of her, a different type of woman. A woman that he would never be able to get out of his mind.

Even if he wanted to, Cleveland couldn't erase the memory of Freddie's taste from his psyche. She was like an addictive drug that he couldn't get enough of and right now he wanted more.

But Freddie was fighting him and what they were feeling. He could tell that she wanted him every bit as much as he wanted her. Still, at every turn, Freddie fought it.

Sitting up, Cleveland swung his legs over the side of the bed. In three days, he'd be back in Atlanta and where would that leave them? Freddie made it clear that she thought he was going to forget about her, which made him wonder if that's what she planned to do.

Rising from the bed, Cleveland decided that he was going to leave her with a memory that she wouldn't soon forget. He headed downstairs and prayed that the talkative desk clerk he'd met earlier was on duty.

Questions swirled in Freddie's head like hurricane winds as she drove to Mississippi. What was her father going to reveal to her? Was he even going to show up?

"This is madness," she muttered as she approached her exit. The entire trip, Freddie kept looking behind her to make sure no one had followed her. She couldn't shake the feeling that someone was going to try and collect the million-dollar bounty that was on Jacques' head. The sting of Marcus's betrayal still weighed heavily on her. What if Cleveland had found out . . . Cleveland.

He wouldn't do that to her. Would he? What did she know about him other than the fact that he made her scream out in pleasure every time he touched her, kissed her and pressed his body against hers. Freddie yearned for him, more than she wanted to admit. But what kind of future could they have? He lived in Atlanta and her home was and always would be in New Orleans. Long distance relationships didn't work. Waiting hours and hours to see each other for a couple of days wouldn't allow them to build something real. And Freddie was tried of rebuilding and waiting for something to tear it down.

It was laughable for her to think that what she and Cleveland had shared was anything more than a fling. The smart thing for her to do would be to ignore him, suppress what she was feeling and never fall into bed with him again. She had real issues, real problems that were going to get worse if Cleveland stuck his nose in it.

"I can't even think about him, and I need to stop talking

to myself," she said as she took her exit for Pass Christian. Glancing at the digital clock on the radio console, Freddie noticed that she was late. She'd hoped that she wouldn't have a problem finding the boarding house where her father was staying. She didn't because it was one of the few places in town that was still standing. As Freddie approached the house, she saw two men sitting on the wide porch, smoking cigars and sipping from Mason jars. She pulled her car behind a beat up pick-up truck. Cautiously, she stepped out of the car and headed over to the porch. The chattering men stopped talking as soon as she came into their line of vision. The three of them looked each other up and down. Neither of the men was Jacques.

"Hi," Freddie said. "I'm looking for a gentleman I met earlier today."

The fatter of the two men leered at Freddie, drinking in the way she filled out her jeans and cotton T-shirt. "If he ain't here, I'll be more than happy to be of service to you."

Glaring at him, Freddie bit back a sarcastic comment. "He was bald and was wearing overalls, and . . ."

"You talking 'bout Earl, eh?" the other man said as he expelled a plume of smoke. "He's inside; said he was expecting a visitor."

Freddie approached the steps. "Is it all right if I go in?"

The fat man bounded down the steps. "Let me be your escort," he said then extended his arm to her.

"I don't need you to escort me anywhere," Freddie said as she pushed past the man. She looked up at the door and saw her father standing there with a smile on his face.

"Baby girl," he said. "You're late."

Freddie's right eyebrow shot up. "I've waited a lot longer for you," she snapped.

Jacques looked over his shoulder. "Let's take a walk," he said as he stepped out on the porch. When she and

Jacques headed down the steps, she heard the fat man mumble, "Lucky bastard."

Jacques took Freddie's hand in his. "I have a lot to atone for, don't I?"

She snatched her hand from his grip once they were out of sight from the other men. "Why the hell did you leave us? What are you running from?"

"No small talk with you, huh?" Jacques laughed. "You look just like her, y'know. Got her attitude too."

"Are you referring to my mother?"

Jacques nodded. "How is feisty old Loraine doing these days? I bet she's still cursing my name."

"Why wouldn't she? You left us damn near penniless with that hotel that was mortgaged to the hilt. Do you think she should have warm fuzzy feelings for you?" Freddie stopped walking and faced her father. Despite his adeptness at disguising himself, she still noticed their similarities. They had the same dark eyes and thin noses, revealing the Creole blood that flowed in their veins. His sunburnt skin told her that he spent many hours in the sun without the use of sunblock.

"All right, I know it seems that I left because I wanted to, but things happened and I did what I had to do to protect my family. That's a fact that your mother seems to forget."

Freddie shook her head. "What are you saying?"

"Tell me this, what has your mother told you about us?" Jacques asked. He placed his hand on his daughter's shoulder.

"She told me that I'd be better off if I forgot about you and pretended that I didn't have a father."

Shaking his head, Jacques laughed hollowly. "Guess your last name ain't Babineaux, huh?"

"Hasn't been for as long as I can remember."

"I'm a murderer, according to the law. But I didn't do it.

Someone else did and set me up. When I broke out of prison, I set out to clear my name. Went directly to your mother—you must have been ten years old. Your mother knew the truth, but by the time I'd met up with her after spending five years in prison, she tried to pretend that she forgot what happened. Loraine called the cops on me. I had to get out of there, had to go underground." He shook his head as if he was reliving an unpleasant memory. "Kept me away from you and lied about the murder."

Freddie shook her head. "She wouldn't do that. You're a liar."

Jacques dropped his hand from her shoulder. "Figured you'd react like this."

"So it is true. You are the killer that I've always heard you were. But why? All I want is to know the truth. Who was this person that you killed and why did you do it?" Freddie's voice wavered as she spoke.

"The Reverend Nolan Watson," he said in a voice barely above a whisper.

A Pass Christian police cruiser passed them. Jacques looked over his shoulder as the officer slowed his car and turned around. "There's a curfew here," Jacques said. "We'd better head back and you need to go back to New Orleans."

Freddie shook her head. "You can't drop this on me and expect me to just leave. Who the hell is Nolan Watson? Why did you . . ."

The police officer pulled up to the duo. "You folks aware of the time?" the officer asked from his car.

"Sorry 'bout that, sir," Jacques said in a tone that sounded like a docile slave. "We're heading back to the house."

The officer nodded, "Make sure you do that."

Jacques and Freddie turned toward the boarding house. "You have to go. These cops are enforcing that curfew like fascists. And I'm going to be leaving here soon, too. I can't stay in one place for too long. Besides, your new husband might be like the last one and call the cops."

"First of all, Cleveland isn't my husband. And he doesn't know anything about you," Freddie snapped.

"Oh no? Then he must not be from New Orleans."

Folding her arms across her chest, Freddie said, "He's not."

Jacques enveloped Freddie in his arms. "Go home. I'll find you soon, all right?"

She pushed away from him. "I don't believe you. And I don't want to see you again so that you can tell me more lies. Maybe my mother is right about you. It's best that I pretend you don't exist."

Cleveland smiled at Celeste. Man, could she talk and for the last three hours, she'd been talking about everything New Orleans when all he wanted to know about was Freddie. He wanted to know if she had a man, how long she'd been living in the hotel and what, if anything, impressed her. Celeste hadn't given him a clue about what kind of woman Freddie was or the type of things that she liked. Just as Cleveland was about to tell Celeste good night, a frazzled looking Freddie burst through the entrance. Her eyes were red and puffy. Despite the evil look she shot him, Cleveland crossed over to her. "Are you all right?" he asked.

"Not now," she snapped. "Celeste, what are you still doing here?"

"Avery called in sick," Celeste said nervously. "I tried to reach you, but . . ."

"Why don't you take off and I'll take over down here," Freddie said in a calmer voice.

Celeste turned to Cleveland and smiled. "Thanks for keeping me company tonight," she said before breezing out of the hotel.

Freddie shook her head as she walked behind the front desk. Cleveland watched her intently, wondering what had caused her to cry and what he could do to make everything right?

What am I thinking? She doesn't need me to protect her, but I can't help but want to do just that, he thought.

"What?" Freddie asked, noticing Cleveland's heated gaze.

"Since you stood me up for dinner, you know you owe me one," he said as a slow smile spread across his face.

Freddie pressed her palms against the desk. "You know, I don't have the energy to go back and forth with you. If you haven't noticed, I have work to do."

"Why are you so upset?" he asked. "Does it have anything to do with your father?"

Freddie ignored his question. Instead of answering him, she turned to the computer and started entering guest information.

"Can I at least get you a Po-Boy? Have you eaten dinner?"

She looked up at him, her face filled with a mix of sadness and annoyance. "Just go," she said in a weak voice. "It's been a long night and I . . ." Tears sprang into her eyes and Cleveland knew he wasn't going anywhere. He headed behind the desk and drew Freddie into his arms.

"Will you stop acting like you don't need anybody?" he breathed into her ear. "If you want to talk, I'll listen."

Pressing her hand against his chest, she looked up into his eyes and shook her head. "I don't want to talk."

"What do you want to do?" His lips were inches from hers, she could feel the heat from his breath dancing across her mouth.

Freddie stepped back because being that close to him rendered her unable to think. "My father isn't who I thought he was and I think my mother was right. All of this searching that I did for him just uncovered a monster. What kind of man kills a priest?"

Cleveland hugged her tightly. "So, you drove back to Mississippi? I would've gone with you," he said.

Freddie shook her head. "I needed to go alone. He probably wouldn't have talked to me if you had been there," she said.

"I'm sorry," he said.

"So am I. All of these years, I've been so angry at my mother for keeping my father away from me, but I see now why she did it. He was so matter of fact when he was telling me about what he did. Then he had the nerve to have an attitude because my mother didn't drop her world to help him when he first escaped from prison. What was she supposed to do?"

"What are you going to do now?"

Freddie stepped back from Cleveland and wiped her wet cheeks. "I don't know. I wish I didn't know about him."

Cleveland planted a comforting kiss on Freddie's forehead. "Let's get out of here. Do you have to man this desk?"

She shook her head. Freddie knew that she wasn't going to be of any use to anyone tonight anyway. "Let me lock the front door and put the sign up," she said as she reached for the "Hotel guests use pass key to enter" sign.

After locking up the lobby, Freddie and Cleveland headed out to the party on Bourbon Street. The area was packed wall to wall with people in various stages of drunkenness. The sounds of jazz, blues and R&B became one as the clubs tried to entice revelers to come inside. Cleveland pulled Freddie closer to him so that they wouldn't be separated by the crowd. Looking at her face, he could tell that she wasn't in the mood for a loud club. At the end of the street, he found a run-down-looking bar that didn't have a line or loud music coming from the establishment. "You know anything about this place down here?" he asked.

"Lupe's Joop Joint? It's the oldest club down here and very locally supported." Freddie peered around Cleveland's shoulder. "I'm surprised it's even open."

"Let's go inside," Cleveland said, reaching out and grabbing Freddie's hand. When they entered the dark club, Cleveland and Freddie were happy to see very few patrons inside and the ones who were in the bar were too drunk to notice anything.

They walked to the bar and sat down on the only two wooden stools that were there. The bartender, a burly man with a neck full of colorful plastic beads, grunted as he ambled over to the couple. His gold tooth glimmered in the faint light of a Budweiser sign.

"We serving Hurricanes and that's it. If you want something else, go someplace else," he said.

"That's fine," Cleveland said. "We'll take two."

Freddie nodded, not really looking up at Cleveland or the bartender. Maybe the alcohol would make her forget. Forget her father was a priest-killer and a liar. It wasn't as if she thought Jacques was some hero. After all, her mother spent years telling her that he wasn't worth a damn. Still, hearing he was connected to something so heinous. . . .

"Freddie?" Cleveland said. "You want to leave?"

"What? No, just give me my drink," she said quietly.

He closed his hand around hers as the bartender slammed their drinks down in front of them. "My offer still stands, if you want to talk, I'll listen."

Freddie ripped her hand away from his and grabbed her drink and then downed it in three gulps. "You know what," she said. "These last few months have been a waste of time.

That was confirmed when I talked to my father earlier tonight. Looking for him just proved that my mother was right and I'm never going to hear the end of that."

"He didn't answer your questions?" Cleveland asked, knowing that he was going to have to tread lightly if he didn't want her to shut down on him again.

She ran her hand over her face. "He said enough."

"I'm sorry," he said softly.

"Hey, bartender," Freddie said. "Give me another one."

The man mixed Freddie another drink and slammed it in front of her. "You must be from New Orleans."

She nodded and gave him a weak smile. Freddie looked at her drink and thought about the last time she'd had too much to drink and was alone with Cleveland. She pushed her glass aside. "Maybe we should get out of here," she said. "I don't think alcohol is going to change anything about tonight."

"So, where do you want to go?"

"Back to my suite," she said.

Cleveland smiled but Freddie shook her head. "Just to talk," Freddie explained. "I don't want to sit in here and drown in Hurricanes."

Rising from the stool, Cleveland held his arm out for Freddie. "All right," he said as he reached into his wallet to pay for their drinks.

As Cleveland and Freddie hit the streets, it seemed that most of the other clubs were turning out their guests as well. But no one was going home, the party had just moved to the streets.

"This is madness," Freddie said as the crush of humanity enveloped them. Instinctively, Cleveland pulled her into his arms. With their bodies pressed against each other's, he captured her lips and kissed her with an ardent passion that made her knees quake. His hands roamed her back, slipping down to her ample bottom.

Gasping, she pulled back from him and they exchanged heated looks. "Why—why'd you do that?"

"I couldn't help it, been wanting to do that all day and . . ."

She cut him off with a kiss of her own, which was hotter than before. Hip to hip, they kissed as if no one else were on the street. Cleveland's body sprang to life as he grabbed her buttocks and pressed her against his throbbing manhood. Breathlessly, she broke off the kiss, knowing that if they continued kissing, she'd want to strip his clothes off in the middle of the street.

"Let's get out of here," she said.

The couple dashed down the street, half running and half walking through the crowd. Freddie hoped being with him tonight would erase the day. Erase the revelation that her father was really the monster that people said he was. This, she thought as they arrived at the hotel, was just mindless sex and it didn't mean anything else. Because she was not falling for Cleveland Alexander.

Chapter 13

Once they got to the hotel, Cleveland and Freddie were all over each other. In the stairwell, he pressed her against the wall, not really caring if someone saw them. Kissing her neck, he unbuttoned her blouse and slipped his hand inside, cupping her breast. Freddie moaned as her nipple hardened against his fingers. She lifted her leg and wrapped it around his waist, pulling him closer to her sexual core. Freddie was throbbing between her thighs at the thought of Cleveland ripping her pants off and giving her pleasures that she'd craved since the first time he touched her at Lillian's wedding.

Freddie grabbed his waistband, fumbling with the button and zipper. She needed him, wanted him right now. Cleveland grabbed her hands, lifting them above her head and broke off the kiss. He looked at her, drinking in her image with lust-filled eyes. "We'd better walk up these stairs before we get even more carried away," he groaned.

Freddie nodded, unable to speak because she was so hot, so primed to receive Cleveland. When he scooped her up into his arms, she buried her lips in his neck, kissing and licking him, eliciting throaty moans from him as he took the steps two at a time, rushing to Freddie's suite.

Cleveland put her down once they reached the door to her suite so that she could unlock the door. Freddie fumbled with her purse, looking for her room key. She shook like a leaf as she put the card in the electronic lock.

Once the door was open, Cleveland spun Freddie around. "Do you know how beautiful you are?" he whispered.

She didn't want to hear sweet nothings and didn't want him to make promises of devotion. Men, especially the ones she knew, didn't keep their promises.

"Don't talk," she said as she closed the space between then and wrapped her arms around his neck. "Don't talk."

Cleveland captured her lips and she kissed him with a passionate furor that made him quake. She leapt into his arms, wrapping her legs around his waist. Breaking off the kiss, Freddie pulled at Cleveland's T-shirt, lifting it above his head. Then she ran her hand down his smooth bare chest. His skin felt like silk underneath her fingers. Cleveland looked as if he wanted to say something, but Freddie cut him off with another kiss. She caught him off guard and caused him to stumble onto the bed backwards.

Freddie landed on top of him and continued to strip him, unbuttoning his jeans and sliding them down his narrow hips. As she eased down his body, Freddie let her tongue guide her. Cleveland moaned as he felt the heat of her breath above his crotch. His penis sprang to attention. She ran her tongue across the tip of his manhood and he released a guttural groan that came from his core. As if she was feeding off his reaction, Freddie took his tool into her mouth, licking and sucking him to a near climax. Cleveland's hips rose as he pulled back from Freddie. Now it was his turn to taste her as he flipped her onto her back. He removed her clothes in short order, but left her ruby red thong on as he parted her thighs, raining kisses on them as he explored her wet valley with his finger.

"Ooh," Freddie moaned as his finger found her throbbing bud. "I-I."

"Thought you didn't want talking," he said before replacing his finger with his tongue. Freddie screamed out in delight as Cleveland lapped her flowing juices. She pressed her hips into his kiss, silently begging for more. Gripping the back of his neck, Freddie pressed him deeper between her thighs. Over and over she moaned, "Yes, yes, yes."

With her chest heaving and her breathing staccato, Freddie felt better than she'd felt all day. Her mind was closed from thoughts of her father and his tale of murder. She had a singular focus: pleasure. All she wanted was to have an orgasm and fall asleep in Cleveland's arms while listening to his heartbeat.

No, she thought as the first ripple of climax flowed through her. *This is just about sex. Cleveland isn't any better than my father.*

Her body language changed and Cleveland noticed her stiffness as he kissed her navel. "Are you all right?" he asked.

"I need you inside me," she said, masking the real thoughts in her head. How could she let good sex with this man fool her into thinking that there was something between them? He had a life in Atlanta and when he returned there, would she be forgotten?

"Not just yet," he said as he straddled her body, his throbbing member against her thighs. Cleveland took her hardened nipple between his lips, circling it with his tongue as she writhed underneath his kiss. With his free hand, he stroked her other breast. Freddie's body was on fire and there was only one way to put it out. She locked her legs around Cleveland's waist.

"Please," she moaned. "Need you. Inside."

He looked up at her, still sampling the taste of her

breast. Cleveland smiled and stopped kissing her breasts. "I want to be inside," he whispered as he reached down for his discarded jeans. Cleveland pulled a condom from his wallet and placed it on Freddie's flat stomach. She reached for the sheath, but Cleveland moved it from her reach. "Slow down, I want to take my time with you," he said. "We have all night, there's no need to rush."

"Make me forget," she said in a voice Cleveland didn't hear. Freddie reached down and stroked Cleveland's throbbing member as she kissed his neck. His groans alerted her to how good she was making him feel. With strength that Freddie didn't know she possessed, she flipped Cleveland over.

Straddling his body, she ground against him, exacting a little revenge as she teased his chest with her tongue. Cleveland's hands trembled as he tried to open the condom. Freddie took it from his hands and made short work of putting the sheath on his member.

Grinning, he said, "You like being on top, don't you?"

"You like having me on top. What's with all the talking?" she asked as she guided him to the center of her sexual being. It amazed her how Cleveland fit her, knew just where to go and how to make her come every time they had sex. And that's all it was about: sex. Freddie gripped his shoulders and started to ride him like a prized steed. Her breasts bounced up and down, causing Cleveland's mouth to water as he tried to grab them. When he took hold of them, sucking and squeezing her nipples, Freddie's pace slowed. Her movements became more fluid and Cleveland matched her stroke for stroke, thrust for thrust.

"Oh yeah," he moaned as Freddie arched her back, pulling him in even deeper. "You feel so good."

Freddie closed her eyes and for a moment she felt as if

this was more than sex. This was the union of two souls, this was special. This was a man that she could love, someone who would take care of her.

Stop thinking like this, she thought as she felt herself again beginning to climax.

"Look at me," Cleveland commanded, his own orgasm building in his shaft. "Look at me, baby. Come for me."

Freddie bit her bottom lip, holding back a scream as she stared deep into Cleveland's eyes. Could he tell, she wondered. Did he know what she was feeling and thinking inside?

She collapsed on his chest and buried her face in Cleveland's chest. She allowed him to hold her. And for a moment, she ignored all of the emotions that she was feeling.

It felt right being in his arms. It felt as if he was a man that wouldn't let her down.

That thought startled her, shook her core and she pushed out of his arms.

"What's wrong?" he asked.

"Nothing, I just need to use the bathroom," she lied. Freddie bolted from the bed. Once inside the bathroom, she wet a washcloth and ran it over her face. She didn't like what she was feeling. The episode with her father had confused her enough, adding Cleveland to the mix had been a mistake.

Pull it together, she thought as she looked at her reflection.

"Freddie," Cleveland called out. "You all right?"

"Yes, I'll be out in a minute." Her voice sounded more confident than she actually felt.

Seconds later, she climbed back into bed, still engulfed in a storm of confusing emotions. Inching away from Cleveland she attempted to go to sleep, but it didn't take long for his arms to wrap around her waist and pull her closer to his hot body. His lips rested against her neck.

She shrugged out of his embrace, it was too comforting and easy to believe that this was more than what it was.

"I stink or something?" he asked.

"What? No, I'm just tired. Trying to go to sleep."

"And I'm stopping you from doing that?" he asked, once again pulling her into his arms. Freddie leaned against his chest, despite herself. She didn't close her eyes, instead, she stared at the ceiling.

He glanced over at her. "You know, my offer still stands."

"What offer?"

"You talk, I listen," he whispered.

"I told you I don't have anything to talk about," she replied, snaking out of his arms. "Maybe I could get some sleep if you left."

"That's how we're playing it now?" he said without making an effort to move.

"Didn't you pay full price for the suite across the hall? Don't expect a refund because you're not sleeping there."

Shaking his head, Cleveland laughed. "You're something else," he said.

"Excuse me?"

"I've never met a woman like you. You're hot and cold like a faucet. You let me turn you on, but I never know what's going to come out."

"You know what," she said. "It's easy for you to sit here and pretend that you have some feelings for me, but what happens when you go back to Atlanta? You're going to forget all about me and . . ."

"Wait, wait, what are you saying?" he asked. "Do you really think that I'm the kind of man that would just leave you without a second thought?"

Freddie hopped out of the bed. "Why wouldn't you? Atlanta is a long way from New Orleans and I'm sure you have plenty of women willing and ready to jump into your bed."

"You think this is about sex?" Cleveland said as he sat up in the bed.

"Isn't it?" she snapped. "What else could it be?"

Climbing out of the bed, Cleveland crossed over to her. "If this was just about sex for me, I wouldn't be breaking my neck to get in here." He placed his hand over her chest. "You do something to me that's more than physical. I've never wanted anyone the way that I want you."

Freddie slapped his hand away. "I don't believe you."

"Why's that?"

"Will you just go? It's late, it's been a long day, and I'm tired."

Cleveland shook his head. "I'm not going anywhere and if you were honest with yourself, you'd admit that you don't want me to leave."

She pressed her head against his chest and in a small voice she said, "You're right."

Kissing her on the top of her head, Cleveland smiled. "Let's go back to bed," he said.

Freddie closed her eyes and rested in Cleveland's arms. Part of her wished he'd just get tired of her ranting and leave. Being with him was starting to feel normal. It was a feeling that she was sure wouldn't last. All of her life, her mother force fed her bitterness when it came to men. Freddie hoped she'd find love one day, a man she could depend on and care about. But when she thought she had that in Marcus, she was wrong. Lillian had told her that Cleveland was no good, so was she crazy to think that there was more between them than good sex?

Should she let go and try to see if Cleveland was something more? Freddie knew Cleveland didn't deserve her attitude; he'd been nothing but nice to her, giving up his vacation to help her track her father. But was it smart to get this close to him?

* * *

The next morning, Cleveland woke up and laid in bed staring at Freddie's slumbering frame. All night she'd tossed and turned in his arms, but now she was sleeping like an angel.

He wished she would talk to him and let him inside. Did she think he couldn't handle it? Maybe Freddie thought he was the shallow person Lillian painted him to be. She had to know that if he was just after her body, he'd be gone already. Since the wedding, he hadn't thought of anything but Freddie. He wanted to know what made her tick, what kept her up at night, and how he could make her life less hectic.

It wasn't going to be easy because he did live in Atlanta and his time in New Orleans was winding down. Still, he was willing to work and willing to have something real for the first time in his life. As he was about to lean in and kiss her, his cell phone rang.

Damn it, he thought as he scrambled out of bed and grabbed the phone. In his effort not to wake Freddie, that's just what he did.

"What?" he snapped.

"You're an uncle," Darren said excitedly. "Jill gave birth to a perfect baby girl. She has your eyes, can you believe that?"

"I can't believe you're a father, that's great news. What's her name?"

"Kayla Marie."

"That's beautiful. I can't wait to see her."

"When are you coming back? You know we're still short-handed and you're letting the good times roll in New Orleans."

"Get it right, it's *laissez bon temps roule.* And I am

having a great time," he said as he looked over his shoulder at Freddie, who was stretching in the bed.

"Louis wants to know if you found somebody named Freddie and I'm not even going to ask why you'd be looking for some dude," Darren said.

"Trust me," he said as he winked at Freddie. "Freddie is all woman. Is Louis at the hospital?"

"Yeah. Jill's resting and we're out here chewing on cigars. I can't believe I'm a father."

"I can't believe it's a girl. I see we're going to have to hit the shooting range," Cleveland said with a laugh.

Freddie inched closer to him and whispered to him, "What a double standard. Now what if someone came after you with a shotgun?"

He whispered to her, *They'd better be a good shot, because that's just what it's going to take to get me away from you.*

She smiled, then sauntered out of the bed in all of her naked glory. Cleveland drooled as if he were Homer Simpson as he looked at her naked bottom.

"Clee," Darren shouted in his ear, reminding him that he was still on the phone.

"Yeah, what?"

"Two days, I really need you back here, all right?" Darren said.

"I understand, I know you need to spend some time with the new family," he said. Freddie looked at Cleveland and shot him a look.

"But, bro," Cleveland said, "right now, I got to go." He snapped his phone shut and crossed over to Freddie.

"You have to go home, huh?" she said.

"Wanna go with me? Mardi Gras is almost over, people are leaving and I'm sure you could use a vacation of your own."

She shook her head. "Why don't we just spend these last two days together and make pretty memories? Then you can go back to your life and I'll continue with mine."

Pulling her even closer to him, Cleveland shook his head. "You're not getting off that easy, Winfred Barker."

Freddie licked her lips, her mouth suddenly dry. "Why are you making this harder than it has to be?"

He smiled sinfully and took her hand in his, then guided it to his manhood. "You want to talk hard?"

Despite herself, she laughed. Cleveland made her laugh and made her feel things that she didn't want to feel. But he'd be gone in two days. Back to his family and . . . *Why shouldn't I go to Atlanta for a few days. Maybe some time away from the Big Easy is just what I need.*

"Cleveland," Freddie said. "You're right. I do need a vacation."

"All right, pack your things and let's hit the road," he said excitedly.

Standing on her tip toes, she planted a wet kiss on his lips. "Not just yet," she said, stroking his manhood back and forth. "There's something we have to take care of first."

Cleveland lifted her off her feet and headed back to the bed.

Chapter 14

As Mardi Gras came to an end, Freddie began to regret all of the time that she'd spent with Cleveland, and more than anything, she was dreading the trip to Atlanta. It wasn't that she didn't enjoy spending time with him. She did and that was the problem. Cleveland and Freddie had started the last few mornings with breakfast in bed, then had some hot sex followed by a shower.

Then Freddie would show Cleveland things in New Orleans that only a native would know. But as the trip to Atlanta loomed, Freddie couldn't help but wonder if she was making a mistake going with him.

How did she get here, being so connected to a man that she knew she could never be with. She wasn't moving to Atlanta and she was sure that Cleveland had no plans to make New Orleans his home.

Things should've never gotten this far. After the trip to Atlanta, we're done and I'm getting back to my life, she thought as she stuffed some clothes into her traveling case. *I'll have Cleveland Alexander out of my system.*

But would he ever be out of her system? After tasting the nectar of his passion, would she be able to go back to her bland life? Freddie could almost hear Loraine saying, "That man is no better than your father. He's going to leave you when you need him most."

Jacques hadn't crossed her mind since their meeting a few days earlier. He said he would contact her, but he hadn't. That wasn't a big surprise, he'd never been a man of his word, from what her mother always said anyway. It made sense that he'd lie about what he did. There were many times when Loraine would comment on how irresponsible Jacques Babineaux had always been.

Shaking her head, Freddie decided that the week she was going to spend in Atlanta was going to be about pleasure and fun—not worrying about her lying and deceitful father.

My mother could've ended all of this had she been honest with me when I started asking her about my father, she thought as she zipped her travel bag.

When Cleveland knocked on her suite door, she'd put her mind at ease. Opening the door, she smiled at him brightly.

"Hi," she said.

"You're scaring me," he said as he wrapped his arms around her. "You're never this happy to see me."

She smacked him on the arm. "I've decided to make this trip about pleasure. I haven't had fun in Hotlanta in a long time."

"I wouldn't go there," he said as he squeezed her bottom and pulled her closer to him. "I recall a night after a wedding where you had a great time."

She arched her perfectly manicured eyebrow. "Says you," she quipped. "And technically, we were in Covington."

Smirking, he said, "I can repeat what you said. 'Oh Cleveland, yeah give it to me, Daddy.'"

Again, Freddie smacked him on the arm. "Whatever, Negro. I wasn't that drunk."

Kissing her on the neck, Cleveland said, "Yes, you were. Then again, you've said the same thing sober."

"Unhand me!" she joked. "Because you need to take my bags to the car."

"Car? I thought we were taking the train."

"No, I refuse to let an eight-hour trip turn into a thirteen-hour journey," Freddie said. "Besides, I'm not going to be stuck in Atlanta without a car. Public transportation is not my friend."

Cleveland didn't say anything, but he was sure there was more to Freddie's urge to drive, and it didn't have anything to do with her dislike of buses and trains.

"All right, let me call Amtrak and cancel the reservation." Cleveland leaned in and kissed Freddie's cheek. "I was kind of looking forward to taking the midnight train to Georgia with you."

Freddie shook her head, "Took you all day to come up with that, huh?"

Cleveland grabbed her bag and started singing an off-key version of "Midnight Train to Georgia."

Sticking her fingers in her ears, Freddie called out, "It's not even midnight."

After Freddie's Mustang was packed, the couple hit the highway. Freddie decided to allow Cleveland to drive and she stretched out in the passenger seat. Cleveland glanced at her, taking note of how relaxed she looked.

"That's a good look for you," he said.

"What's that?"

"You looking relaxed and calm, it works for you."

"I guess I have been pretty intense lately," she said.

"Since the day I met you," Cleveland said. "Maybe that's what I like about you."

"Elaborate," she said as she turned in her seat so that she could face him.

Cleveland laughed. "The way you stepped up to me at Lillian and Louis's wedding, it was intense. I was hoping that you were walking over to say something nice. But you made up your mind that you didn't like me."

"That's not what it was," she said. "I was hungry and Lillian was so worried that you were going to take Louis to some strip club."

"Darren's idea, not mine. See, I knew that was going to be blamed on me." Cleveland drummed his fingers against the steering wheel. "Lillian doesn't like me."

"I noticed. Why not?"

He shrugged. "Because everyone has me twisted. People think I'm some playboy because I haven't caught the wedding bug . . ."

"And because you have a harem of women?" she fished.

"That's not true. Most women bore me, but you—you're exciting and you have something to say."

Freddie folded her arms across her chest. What if he was trying to soften the blow of what she was going to discover in Atlanta. "So, you're saying that Lillian doesn't like you because she doesn't know the real you?"

"That and she's never seen me with the same woman twice," Cleveland said.

"Wow. You say it as if you're proud."

He shook his head. "Listen, some of the women I've met at home aren't worth a first date, let alone a second one. I'm not interested in being some woman's personal ATM. I'm not trying to be with a woman who wants to get married only for appearances. Men have standards too."

"I thought those standards included cup, waist, and ass sizes," she said sarcastically.

Cleveland frowned. "Whatever," he said as he shot her

a sidelong glance. "But if that were the case, then you would definitely meet those standards."

"See, that's another reason why I talked to you the way I did at the wedding. You can be so cocky."

"That was too easy," he said. "I'm not even going to comment on how you know all about my *cockiness*."

Freddie rolled her eyes. "Whatever."

"Seriously, people often mistake my confidence for conceit and that's not what it is. I'm a humble little fireman. I love my momma and I like you."

"What?"

"Maybe you're the one I've been looking for," he said.

"Cleveland, let's not go there. You and I are going in separate directions in our lives. I have to rebuild my life in New Orleans and you live in Atlanta." Freddie's smile faded.

"All right, we'll save this conversation for later," he said then placed his hand on her thigh. "Because this is a pleasure trip."

"Yes, a pleasure trip." *And when it ends, it all ends,* she added silently.

With Cleveland driving, the couple made it to Atlanta in less than eight hours. He didn't believe in stopping and as soon as they got into the city, both he and Freddie were famished.

"Do you want to grab something to eat and head to my brother's house? Because trust me, there won't be any food there."

Freddie crinkled her nose. "You mean they don't have a butler? I thought your sister-in-law was 'Oprah rich?' That's all Lillian could talk about was how famous your brother's wife is."

"Jill is very down to earth. She actually tried to hide

her real identity from Darren. She wanted to make sure he was with her for the love and not the money," he said. "It caused a lot of problems, but they worked it out in the end. Jill was the founder of DVA, a multimillion dollar computer firm. Before she met Darren, she had been involved with a guy who wanted to take over her company and he's the one who wrote that nasty story about her, revealing the truth about her identity. At the time, I didn't understand why she didn't tell my brother the truth. But she showed up on my doorstep one night begging me to help her get Darren back."

"And you helped her?" Freddie asked.

Cleveland shrugged. "She had to do some serious convincing. But Darren was miserable without her. They rekindled their love over a game of basketball."

"A fairy tale marriage?"

Cleveland shook his head. "I wouldn't go that far. But they're happy and I guess when you get down to it, that's all that matters."

Freddie had a wistful look in her eyes as she listened to Cleveland. Could it be that he wanted what his brother had? Was Cleveland the kind of man that would be happy with one woman?

Stop it, she thought. *You can't turn this man into what you want him to be. Besides, men don't want stability, they want variety.*

Turning away from him, she tried to make herself believe that she didn't hear the twang of desire in Cleveland's voice. "Does your brother know you're bringing company?"

"No, but Darren knows to always expect the unexpected with me."

When they pulled up to the Lennox Road house, Cleveland punched a code in the gate and drove right in without picking up the phone to call Darren. From the looks of the driveway, though, Freddie thought they'd arrived at a party.

"Don't tell me all of those cars are your sister-in-law's?" Freddie said.

"No, I guess everybody came to see the baby tonight. Look," he said pointing to Louis's black BMW. "Louis and Lillian must be here."

"Oh great," Freddie said. "I can imagine what she's going to say when she sees us together."

"Hey, pleasure trip, remember," he said, pointing his index finger in her face.

Freddie kissed his finger tip. "Got it."

The couple got out of the car and walked up the winding driveway. "Nice house," Freddie said as she looked around the spacious green lawn. Cleveland thought of the place as a McMansion. It looked like every new house that was built in Buckhead: mass-produced, ultra modern, with white paint and high windows.

"Just like every other house on the block. But I think they wanted to start a new life with a new house," he said.

"So, there were demons?"

Cleveland shrugged. "I don't think so. Jill lived in a penthouse, my brother had a small house in the suburbs. All married couples should have a new house, though. That way they can build together."

"Cleveland Alexander, don't tell me you're a romantic," Freddie said with a sarcastic smile on her face as they stepped up on the front porch.

"You think you know me, don't you?" he said as he rang the door bell.

"Maybe I don't," she said, then watched him thoughtfully as the door opened and he hugged his brother.

"Look what the cat dragged in," Darren said when he released Cleveland. "How was the Big Easy?"

"Good, good. Where's my niece?" he asked.

"In the sitting room, entertaining already." Darren looked at Freddie and smiled. "I'm sorry, we're being rude. I'm Darren, this dude is allegedly my brother."

"Winfred Barker," she said, extending her hand.

"Your name sounds familiar," Darren said, when he shook her hand.

"She was Lillian's maid of honor," Cleveland said as he took Freddie's other hand. "Since you have all these people over here, I hope y'all ordered take out."

Darren frowned at his brother. "I cooked, fool."

"You cook," Freddie asked. "Wow."

Darren nodded to her. "Please don't judge me by this guy." He motioned for Freddie to come closer to him. "He was adopted."

"Hey, I can hear you," Cleveland said as he wrapped his arm around Freddie's waist. He brushed his lips against Freddie's neck.

Darren's eyebrow shot up as he noticed the tender moment between the two. "Chicken and rice," he said. "And your mother is going to be so happy to see you."

"Mom's here?"

Darren nodded. "Hasn't left since the baby came home; she's driving my wife crazy."

Freddie and Cleveland headed into the sitting room where everyone was. When Lillian looked up and saw the couple, she gasped.

"Hey everybody," Cleveland said as he walked over to his mother, who was holding the baby and kissed her on the cheek.

"How was New Orleans?" Margaret asked.

"Good," he said. "Can I hold my niece?"

"Who is she?" his mother asked, nodding toward Freddie.

Cleveland smiled. "This is my friend, Freddie."

"Hi," she said, nervously, feeling Lillian's eyes boring into her back.

"Ma," Cleveland said. "Let me hold the baby."

Margaret frowned. "She just ate, I have to burp her."

Louis walked over to Cleveland. "You're not going to hold her, your mother isn't letting anyone touch her granddaughter."

"Louis, you almost dropped her," Margaret said. "You know you need to get practice holding babies because I see children in your future."

"Oh, Mrs. Alexander, we're not ready for that yet," Lillian said. Then she turned to her friend. "Winfred, I'm surprised to see you here."

"Well, it was a long Mardi Gras and I needed a break," she said through a plastic smile.

"Oh," Margaret said, "you two met in New Orleans."

Cleveland cast his eyes toward the ceiling. "No, we met at Lillian's wedding. Where's Jill?"

"Right here," she called out from the top of the stairs. Cleveland couldn't believe this was the same woman his brother had married. He'd never seen Jill without makeup or her hair styled perfectly. But tonight, she was dressed in a sweat suit with her hair pulled back in a ponytail. She almost looked sixteen.

Cleveland dashed over to the staircase and kissed his sister-in-law on the cheek. "How are you, little mama?"

She smiled and he could tell she was blissfully happy. "I could use a little more sleep, but other than that I'm fine."

"She's beautiful and thank God she looks like you and not your ugly husband," Cleveland said, then looked over his shoulder for his brother. Jill slapped him on the shoulder.

"Kayla looks just like her father and she's gorgeous." Jill walked over to her mother-in-law and lifted her daughter from her arms. The baby cooed and gurgled as her mother cradled her in her arms.

"I never thought I'd see the day," Cleveland said. "Jill Alexander holding something in her arms other than a laptop."

Everyone erupted in laughter as Jill sat down. Darren walked into the sitting room. "All right," he said. "Leave my wife alone."

"Where's the food?" Cleveland asked.

"In the kitchen."

Lillian grabbed Freddie's arm. "We'll get it," she said as she ushered her friend into the kitchen.

Cleveland saw the pained look in Freddie's eyes as Lillian dragged her away. He and Louis exchanged knowing looks.

"The kitchen is about to get hot," Louis muttered to Cleveland.

When Freddie and Lillian were alone in the kitchen, food was the last thing that they talked about.

"What the hell, Fred?" Lillian said.

"You know, I'd rather you call me Winnie than Fred."

"How about I call you Winfred or are you a clone? What are you doing with him?"

"Enjoying myself."

Lillian sighed. "You know, Cleveland isn't the kind of man that . . ."

"I'm not trying to marry him, Lillian. I'm single and he's fun."

"Fun? You don't do fun. I know you and how you try to make a man fit your idea of . . ."

"I know what I'm doing and I'd appreciate it if you'd just let me do it without your judgments."

"Don't come crying to me when he breaks your heart."

"My heart has nothing to do with what Cleveland and I are doing," she said, but the words were hollow. She knew she cared about him more than she wanted to admit and it scared her more than anything.

"Famous last words. You always fall for the wrong man and I'm tired of watching you get your heart broken."

Freddie rolled her eyes. "Last time I checked, I was a grown woman and capable of making my own decisions."

"Fine, but don't come crying to me when he tires of you and trades you in for another woman."

"Where's the food?" Freddie said, pushing past Lillian.

"On the stove," she said, leaning against the island and watching her friend in disbelief. "Do you remember what you told me at my wedding?"

Freddie spooned chicken and rice on a paper plate. "No, but I'm sure you're going to tell me."

"Stupid women. That's what you called every woman in the bridal party that threw herself at Cleveland and now look at you. I guess the rumor is true, you did sleep with him after the reception."

Before Freddie could answer, Cleveland walked into the kitchen. "I just came to see if you needed some help with the plates."

Lillian rolled her eyes at him and headed back into the sitting room. He crossed over to Freddie and kissed her on the cheek. "That didn't look like much fun," he said.

"It wasn't," Freddie said as she handed Cleveland the plate she'd fixed.

"Pleasure trip," he said.

"I know. But I'm going to have to find something to do while you're at work."

Setting his plate on the island, he pulled Freddie into his

arms and brushed his lips against hers. "Let's think about that later. We can eat and run, y'know."

She smacked him on the shoulder. "You're so bad."

Winking at her, he said, "I'll show you bad as soon as we get back to my place."

Chapter 15

After they ate dinner and spent a few more moments with the baby, Freddie and Cleveland headed to his town house in Lithonia, a suburb of Atlanta.

"Nice neighborhood," she said as they pulled into the driveway. "It kind of reminds me of the way things used to be at home."

Cleveland nodded. "I can't imagine what you're going through," he said as they exited the car.

"I'm lucky, I had some place to go without leaving the city. But I have to tell you, I miss my house."

"Have you started rebuilding?"

She shook her head. "Still fighting it out with the insurance companies. But this is a pleasure trip, so let's change the subject."

"All right," he said. "I have an idea. Since we had to deal with the only dish my brother can cook, why don't we have dessert?"

"What do you have in mind?" she asked as Cleveland unlocked the front door.

"Go upstairs and make yourself comfortable, I'll be right back."

Before Freddie could ask him what was going on, he had dashed out the door. Looking around his place, she was pleasantly surprised that he didn't live in a stereotypical bachelor pad. The place was spotless, decorated in deep browns and earth tones. He was a collector of fine art with two oil paintings by Celina Hart and Synthia SAINT JAMES hanging on the walls of his living room. Freddie smiled, wondering if those paintings were gifts or if Cleveland picked the sensual artwork himself. She knew he was a sensual man. It still amazed her how they'd connected in bed. Cleveland had awakened a sexual side of her that she hadn't known existed. But this was a feeling she knew couldn't last. She was rebuilding a life in New Orleans that she wasn't sure she wanted. She was trying to process the tall tale of her father and then there was the hotel.

Freddie didn't like running that place, her mother even called it the family curse. The hotel was profitable, but it reminded her of the day her father left. The police had burst into the hotel and tore the place apart looking for Jacques. Freddie, who had been ten years old at the time, was scared to death. That's one of the reasons why she remodeled the place when her mother finally turned over the reins.

It was a decision that didn't sit well with Loraine until Freddie showed her how billing themselves as a boutique hotel would make them stand out among the other hotels in the French Quarter. Had it not been for Hurricane Katrina, the hotel would've turned a profit and Freddie would've felt better about leaving New Orleans and starting over some place where she didn't have a past. Some place where the shadow of her father didn't linger over her.

She still couldn't believe that he tried to blame her mother for whatever happened. Freddie still had no idea what the true story of Jacques Babineaux was.

Pleasure trip, this is a pleasure trip. Standing here and going over and over this stuff in my head isn't going to help me at all, she thought as she headed upstairs to search for Cleveland's bedroom. If he was planning to surprise her, she was going to make sure she had one waiting for him. When she opened the door to his bedroom, Freddie quickly disrobed and stretched out in the middle of the bed.

Cleveland had never been in such a hurry to check out at the supermarket. But as he stood in line at Kroger's, he realized that old women with coupon books needed their own separate line. The woman standing in front of him had to have a coupon for every item in her basket and then some. Part of him just wanted to pay for her groceries and push her out of the way.

He had a can of whipped cream, giant strawberries, chocolate sauce, and the desire to lick Freddie from head to toe. Grandma needed to buy her rations and go. When the woman finally went through her coupons and paid for her items, Cleveland wanted to dance a jig.

As the cashier rang him up, he smiled and hummed an old Stevie Wonder tune.

"Somebody's happy tonight," the clerk said as she placed his items in a plastic bag.

"I guess that's one way to describe it," he said as he handed her the cash. "You have a good night." Cleveland practically skipped out of the store. When he reached his car, his cell phone rang.

"Yeah," he sang.

"Cleveland Alexander, I know you didn't think you were going to slip out of my house without telling me everything about that Cajun beauty?" Darren asked.

"That's Freddie."

"I guess you were right. She's fine."

"This coming from a married man."

Darren laughed. "I'm married, not blind. What I can't believe is that you're with someone for more than five minutes. The way you were looking at her, I know there's something between you two."

"Freddie and I are just enjoying each other," Cleveland said. "While I was in New Orleans, she was dealing with some heavy stuff, so I suggested she come up for a week to relax."

"What hotel is she staying in?" Darren asked as Cleveland started his car.

"My house."

"I'm sorry, can you repeat that? Because I know you didn't just say she was staying at Casa De Cleveland."

"Don't start," he said.

"I'm not starting anything, but little brother, I know that look."

"What in the blue hell are you talking about?"

"The way you looked at her, it wasn't about ripping her clothes off and having your way with her. You're falling in love. Been there, done that, and now I have the daughter to prove it," Darren said.

"There you go again trying to marry off the single population," Cleveland said. "Freddie isn't like any other woman that I've known. She's not like some of these sisters in Atlanta. She doesn't want my bank records and Beacon score. Believe it or not, she reminds me a lot of Jill."

"She must be a hell of a woman, then," Darren said.

"Well, that hell of a woman is at my house waiting for me, so let's talk about this later."

"Don't mess around and fall in love," Darren jokingly said, then hung up the phone.

By the time Cleveland made it home, he couldn't help but think about the bug his brother had dropped in his ear. Could he be falling in love with Freddie? Did he look at her with a longing in his eyes that everyone could see? *This is so crazy,* he thought as he pulled into the driveway. *Freddie and I are just enjoying each other's company and there's nothing serious happening here.*

Cleveland walked into the house, half expecting to see Freddie waiting for him downstairs. "Freddie?" he called out.

"Upstairs," she cooed.

"I'll be up in a second," he said as he dashed into the kitchen. Cleveland washed the strawberries and sliced them. Then he placed the fruit on a plate. Next he grabbed the whipped cream and chocolate sauce and headed upstairs. Walking into the bedroom, Cleveland almost dropped his treats when he saw Freddie lying provocatively on his king-sized bed.

"Damn," he mumbled as she sat up and smiled at him.

"Pleasure trip, remember? Come over here and pleasure me."

Cleveland walked over to the bed, set the strawberries, whipped cream and chocolate sauce on his oak night stand, then dove onto the bed and between Freddie's thighs. She reached over and grabbed a berry while Cleveland licked her inner thigh, making his way to her heated core of sexuality.

When his tongue touched her throbbing bud, it felt as if electricity flowed through her body. She pressed her hips into his kiss, wanting and needing more. Cleveland read her body language like a book and deepened his kiss. Freddie gripped the cotton sheets and called his name out like a mantra as he brought her close to an orgasm. As Cleveland inched up her body, kissing her flat belly, breasts and collarbone, Freddie popped the strawberry in her mouth, offering it to him as he kissed her lips.

She wrapped her legs around his waist and gyrated against his swollen member. The heat from their bodies could've caused an explosion and Cleveland had to pull back from her. Though he wanted to bury himself inside her wetness, he had other plans.

"Remember, we're supposed to be having dessert," he said in a voice that was nearly a growl. Cleveland reached for the whipped cream and circled her nipples with the cool cream. Before Freddie could say anything about the coolness, Cleveland's hot mouth covered her nipple. Closing her eyes, Freddie stroked his neck as he licked each nipple until the mounds of cream were gone.

"Tastes good," he said when he looked into her eyes. Freddie smiled and reached for the chocolate sauce.

"Now I want to taste you," she said. Cleveland nodded and rolled over on his back. Freddie climbed on top of him, rubbing her hands down his chest. Next, she opened the chocolate and drew a line down the center of his chest. Freddie dipped her finger in the syrup and sucked it off seductively. Watching her made Cleveland even harder than he'd been before. Dipping down, Freddie glided down his body, navigating his muscular frame with her tongue, licking away the chocolate. Then she took his manhood into her hand, stroking his hardness. When her lips covered the tip of his hardness, Cleveland nearly lost it. Her mouth was hot and moist and she captured all of him.

"Oh," he cried as she bobbed her head up and down. Cleveland buried his hands in her hair, relishing in the sensual sensations Freddie was causing. His blood was hot as lava as Freddie pulled back from him and poured chocolate over his rigid penis and licked it off. It took every ounce of self control in him to keep from climaxing.

"Sweet," she said as he reached for a condom and handed it to her. Freddie opened the package and rolled it into place. Then she mounted him and slowly ground herself against his body. Cleveland matched her stroke for stroke, pressing his pelvis into hers. Freddie's breasts jutted upward as they increased the pace of their lovemaking. The movements were fluid and sensual. Sweat covered their bodies as they rocked on, riding the waves of ecstasy until they collapsed in each other's arms.

Cleveland held Freddie tightly, burying his face in her hair. "You feel so good," he whispered.

"So do you," she replied, tightening her grip on him. "I could almost get used to this."

"Why almost?"

"This is only temporary, let's not kid ourselves."

"It doesn't have to be," he said.

Freddie rolled off him and got out of the bed. "Please, Cleveland. Not again."

Cleveland rose from the bed and crossed over to her. "We could make this work. We're only eight hours apart and . . ."

"You're insane if you think a long distance relationship will work. You're a hot-blooded man with needs and if you think that something real is developing here, I'll go home right now."

Stepping back from her, Cleveland nodded. "Wow," he said. "You really don't trust yourself to be happy do you? Always looking in the shadows for something bad to happen. That has to make your life boring as hell. What do you really want, Freddie?"

She picked up her clothes from the chair next to the bed and started to get dressed. Cleveland started to stop her, but didn't. Instead, he folded his arms and shook his head. "Do your feet get tired? All this running that you do."

Freddie whirled around and looked at him. "What?"

"Everytime we get out of bed, you dash off like a sprinter in a hundred-yard dash. You just don't want to be happy, do you?"

"Here we go with your dime store analysis. You don't know anything about me, you don't know what these last few years have been like for me. Jumping into a relationship with a man like you isn't on my agenda."

Cleveland shrugged his shoulders and masked his disappointment by saying, "Your loss, sweetheart."

"You ass! It's all about you, isn't it? Why did I think you were different? Why did I think you actually had a soul? You're just like every other man, just like my father." Freddie snatched the rest of her clothes and jetted down the stairs.

It took him about two seconds to follow after her. She was at the front door when he reached her.

"Don't leave," he said. "Look, I won't bring it up ever again. We can't be together because you said so. I'll accept that, but this trip was supposed to be about having fun and . . ."

"You know what?" she said in a low voice, her hand on the door knob. "In a perfect world, you and I would be together. We'd have a lot of fun and a relationship would work. But the world isn't perfect. My father is a notorious criminal. I have to keep a hotel afloat that I wish Katrina would have destroyed, and I can't get my house rebuilt. So, I'm sorry if you think I'm a runner, but I call it surviving."

He placed his hand on the small of her back. "Come here," he said.

She dropped her hand from the door knob and turned to

him. He opened his arms to her and hugged her tightly. "Things are going to get better, but you have to stop living in the past."

Freddie looked up at Cleveland. Was she living in the past? Trying to recreate the childhood that she'd missed out on? Did she think she and her father could build the relationship that she never had with him as a child and somehow her life would be better?

"Cleveland, I'm sorry," she said contritely. "I'm tired and I shouldn't be so rude to you."

"No, you shouldn't. I know you're stressed out, but I need you to recognize that I'm on your side."

She looked into his gray eyes and her heart skipped a beat. Having a man on her side was something that she wasn't used to. Maybe she should stop fighting it and allow Cleveland to help her in everyway. First, she was going to have to stop getting in her own way.

"Are you all right?" he asked, taking note of her silence.

"Somewhat," she said.

"There's a bed waiting for you right upstairs, and if you want me to, I'll sleep downstairs."

"No," she said. "It's your bed and I'm not going to ask you not to sleep in it."

Cleveland scooped Freddie into his arms. "Good, because I was lying anyway."

The next morning, Freddie woke up before Cleveland and dipped down to the second floor of his three-story town house where the kitchen was. She figured she could cook him breakfast. Besides, it had been awhile since she cooked in a real kitchen. Once again she was surprised to see Cleveland didn't live like a bachelor. His refrigerator was fully stocked with eggs, turkey bacon, cheese and

other breakfast staples. Most guys, she figured, would be
doing well to have a carton of expired milk and a box of
baking soda in their refrigerators.

Freddie found the pans she needed to make cheese
omelets and bacon, then she spotted a box of pancake mix
on the top of the refrigerator. She was elbow deep in mixing
pancake batter when Cleveland came downstairs, clad only
in a pair of cotton boxer briefs that hugged his sexy body
like a second skin.

Freddie nearly forgot what she was supposed to be
doing when she saw Cleveland standing at the end of the
staircase nearly naked.

"I must be dreaming," he said. "You're the last person I
would've expected to cook."

She returned to her mixing. "Why do you say that?"

"Most beautiful women I know don't cook," he said.

"I'm a New Orleans chick, cooking is just like breathing to me," she said.

Cleveland crossed over to the island in the middle of the
kitchen between the stove and the dining area. He hopped
up on a stool and propped himself up on his elbows. Smiling, he watched Freddie pour the pancake batter on the
griddle pan.

"Need any help?"

"Um, why don't you make the coffee," she said.

"How do you like it?" He hopped off the stool and headed
for the coffee machine on the corner of the counter.

"Like you, strong, black, and sweet."

Cleveland cast a sidelong glance at her. "Sweet? Me?"

"When you're not being an insufferable jerk, you can
be quite sweet," she said. "And I'm sorry I've been such
a bitch."

Cleveland frowned as he measured the correct amount

of French vanilla gourmet coffee grinds to put in the brew basket. "You cook and apologize? I must be dreaming."

Freddie, who was cracking eggs, burst out laughing. "Yes, you are dreaming. I have a question. Why does Lillian dislike you so much?"

Cleveland shrugged as he poured just enough water into the coffeemaker's tank to make a pot of strong coffee. "I gave her a hard time when she and Louis started dating. I guess she's never forgiven me for that."

"What do you mean by hard time?" Freddie asked as she flipped the pancakes.

"I just wasn't very nice to her. Called her stuck up a few times because she was always complaining when she came to the firehouse. I had no idea she was so sensitive."

"Well, according to Lil, you're the devil."

He shrugged again. "Misunderstood is more accurate. Everybody thinks they know me and the kind of man that I am."

"But they don't?"

He shook his head. "You ever want something but didn't know exactly what it was?"

Freddie shook her head, not quite sure where he was going with this.

"Most men, whether they admit it or not, have been hurt by a woman. Once a man has been hurt, he'll spend his life trying to inflict pain on every other woman he runs across. That hasn't happened to me because I don't let anyone get too close. When I fall in love, it's going to be for real and last forever. If my dad were still alive, he and my mother would be celebrating their fiftieth wedding anniversary. Some of the women I've dated wouldn't even last fifty days."

She raised her eyebrows. "Okay."

"What I'm saying is, I want something that's forever

and I'm very selective. Some people, mainly Lillian, think I'm a womanizer. That isn't true, it's just that I don't waste my time or someone else's when I know it isn't right."

"So, how do you know when it's right?" she asked.

He shrugged again. "One day, I'll know." What he didn't say, in order to avoid another argument with her, was this: he felt as if what they were sharing was right.

Chapter 16

After breakfast, Cleveland had to go into the fire station for his first shift since his vacation. Freddie decided that she was going to spend the day with Lillian, since Cleveland was going to be gone for the next twelve hours. She knew that her friend was going to have a lot of questions about her being with Cleveland. Questions that Freddie wasn't sure she had the answers to.

Listening to him this morning really made her wonder if she had pegged him all wrong. Was he different? Was he the kind of man that she could actually fall in love with?

"No," she said to her reflection as she stepped out of the shower. "He could've been saying what he thought I wanted to hear."

She dressed quickly and headed downstairs. Cleveland had left his house key so that Freddie wouldn't be stuck in the house all day. As she locked up, Freddie was amazed at how comfortable she was in Cleveland's house. And a small part of her, a part that she desperately wanted to ignore, felt as if this could be the start of something good and fresh. That tiny part of her said she was falling in love with Cleveland Alexander.

Shaking her head and hoping to push those notions of love away, she got into her car and headed to Lillian's. Maybe she needed to hear her friend's voice of reason to get her back on track. This thing with Cleveland was just about sex and just about pleasure. There was no substance, no future, and no way she was going to give in to that tiny voice.

As she drove, Freddie called Lillian. "What's up girl?" she said when Lillian answered the phone.

"I should be asking you the same question, Flavor."

"Flavor?"

"That's what you are, Cleveland's flavor of the month."

"Oh will you stop it?"

"Not until you tell me when you lost your mind," Lillian said. "I mean really, even if this wasn't Cleveland 'Playa, Playa' Alexander, you guys don't even live in the same city or state for that matter."

"Stop yakking my ear off, I'm in your driveway." She hung up the phone and looked up as Lillian opened the front door to her Stone Mountain home. Freddie had to admit it, Lillian had come a long way from the Ninth Ward of New Orleans. Sometimes she wondered how her life would've been different if Loraine had followed the Thomas family to Georgia.

Can't change the past, can't control the present, she thought as she stepped out of the car. "Lillian, aren't you at least happy to see me?" Freddie said as she bounded up the steps.

"I saw you last night, remember. Anyway, Cleveland is not the man for you."

Freddie shook her head. "Did I say I wanted to marry the man? And just for argument's sake, how do you know he isn't what I need?"

Lillian threw her hands up like an African dancer. "You've really lost your damned mind. The only difference between Cleveland and Marcus is that Cleveland doesn't know that finding your daddy would make him a millionaire. He's that same kind of arrogant jerk that's going to do nothing but break your heart."

"It's not like that and you know what? You don't know Cleveland."

"I'm sure I don't know him like you do, but every time I see him he has a new woman on his arm. A new flavor of the month, like I said before. You're better than that and I don't want to see him use you and toss you aside."

Freddie sat down on the sofa in the living room and looked up at her friend with a cat-that-ate-the-canary grin on her face. "Who says that I'm not using him?"

Sitting down beside her friend, Lillian shook her head. "You don't do casual relationships any more than I do. The moment Louis and I met at Gladys Knight's Chicken & Waffles, I knew I was going to marry him."

Freddie cocked her head to the side. "Rewriting history, aren't we?"

"What do you mean?" Lillian asked.

"You didn't even like him when you first met him, according to what you told me. It wasn't until our senior year at Xavier that you gave him the time of day because you were lining up your MRS degree."

"Whatever," Lillian said. "I wouldn't have gotten closer to him if I hadn't known that he was the man for me. Our wedding was no accident. It had been planned since we met in Atlanta our freshman year. Sure Louis isn't the man of my dreams, but he loves me and respects me. I've never seen Cleveland show a woman—other than his mama—respect."

"Have you ever sat down and had a conversation with the man?"

"Why would I?" she said. "Do you want something to

drink or eat? All of this stuff about Cleveland is giving me a headache and it's very unpleasant. Do you remember when my mother moved to Georgia? I really didn't want to come. But I think being in Georgia allowed me to grow as a person, to really get a grip on the kind of woman I want to be."

"Why are you telling me all of this?" Freddie asked, looking at her friend with questions dancing in her eyes.

"Maybe you need a change of scenery, a chance to rewrite some of the history of your life and meet the right man. North Carolina is close to Atlanta, but far enough away from Louisiana . . ."

"What if I want to start over in Atlanta, with Cleveland?" Freddie said then laughed. "Let's eat something, I'm starved."

"You're playing with fire," Lillian said as they headed into the kitchen.

"Good, Cleveland can put it out," she said and playfully swatted Lillian on the bottom.

Cleveland sat on the ratty sofa next to the widescreen TV in the fire station. He was so sick of Louis and Roland questioning him about Freddie. Roland ate barbequed chicken, which was dripping sauce on his thigh and asked Cleveland, "How the hell did you swing that?"

"For the last time, I'm not talking about Freddie."

Louis nodded in agreement. "I'm sick of hearing about you and Freddie. Lillian acts like she's that woman's mother and you're the big bad wolf. Ever since you two walked into Darren and Jill's place it's been, 'I can't believe Freddie is with him.'"

"Your wife," Roland said in between bites of chicken, "is evil."

Louis smacked the chicken bone out of Roland's hand. "I've warned you not to talk shit about my wife. She just doesn't think Mr. Playa over here is good enough for her friend."

Darren walked into the break room. "You guys haven't gotten it out of him either, huh?"

Cleveland stood up. "First of all, there's nothing to get out of me. I have nothing to say."

"Aw, whatever man!" the three men exclaimed in unison.

Roland picked up his chicken bone and walked over to Cleveland. "Your dating stories got us through a lot of long shifts. Now you're with this bona fide babe that has got to be a freak-and-a-half and you're not sharing stories."

"Roland, get a life," Cleveland said. "Freddie is different."

Darren raised his eyebrow and looked at his brother, who had a goofy smile on his face. "Different? Say it ain't so? My baby brother has fallen in love."

Cleveland tugged at his locs and looked at his brother. "Did I say I was in love? The woman is different, not like a lot of these other woman that I've run across, but I didn't say I was in love."

"Where is she now?" Louis asked.

"At my house."

"Alone?" Roland asked. "You left a woman alone in the bat cave? You know she is going through all of your stuff."

"Freddie's not like that," Cleveland said. "Besides, I don't have anything to hide. We know where we stand."

"You need to stop lying to yourself," Darren said. "I've known you all your life and you don't like to leave Ma alone in your house, but this chick is at your place alone? Who are you and what did you do with my brother?"

"Man, I'm tired of all of you," Cleveland said. "I'm going to wash the truck or something."

As he left the break room, Cleveland thought about

some of the things that the guys said. Everything that he was doing right now when it came to Freddie was out of character for him. What if Freddie was in his house looking for proof that he was the womanizer that Lillian said he was? It didn't matter to him what the guys thought. Freddie, the woman who cooked him breakfast and made his toes curl, wasn't the kind of woman who would ramble through his house.

How did they figure that leaving her alone in his house meant that he loved her?

Why am I lying to myself? Cleveland thought as he filled a bucket with water. *I'm falling hard and fast for a woman that has made it clear that she doesn't want anything more than this physical relationship we share. She's going to go back to New Orleans and I'm going to spend the rest of my life searching for someone that measures up to her.*

"Cleveland," Darren said, walking up behind his brother. "Hey, sorry about giving you a hard time. But I saw this coming."

"Man, I don't feel like talking about this. Freddie and I are two adults, having fun. She's going though a lot right now. Her house was blown away by Katrina, she has these family issues, and she needed to unwind after Mardi Gras," he said. "She's made it clear that she doesn't want a serious relationship."

"Your line, huh? I can see in your eyes that you want more than just a bedroom buddy with this woman. If she's all that, enough to make you bring her to Atlanta and . . ."

"So what if I want more? She doesn't," Cleveland said in a low voice. "All I can do is go with it."

Darren shook his head. "Not if you feel about her the way I think you do. You've never been in love or even in deep like this. You never let a woman get close, but this one is in there." Darren pointed to Cleveland's chest. "Are you sure you can handle it?"

"This might be a little more than I can handle. Freddie is an amazing woman, but she has this wall that she just doesn't want to let me cross."

"What kind of family issues does she have?"

"I have to go and check something out," Cleveland said. "Why don't you finish up washing this baby?"

Darren shook his head at his brother. "And I thought I was in charge here."

Cleveland dashed inside and headed for the computer. He needed to know exactly what Freddie was dealing with when it came to her father. He typed Jacques Barker into the Google search bar, but came up empty.

This man is a mystery, he thought as he typed in Jacques Barker and New Orleans. Still there was nothing.

Cleveland hoped that Freddie would tell him about her father, and he could tell her that he was falling in love with her and would do whatever he needed to do to help her work out her past issues.

"What are you doing?" Louis asked as walked up to Cleveland and looked over his shoulder at the screen.

"How much do you know about Freddie's family?"

He whistled. "Sore subject. Her pop is a big time felon. She doesn't even have his last name anymore."

"What's his last name?"

"Babineaux," he said as he headed down the hall.

Cleveland typed the name Jacques Babineaux into the Goggle search bar. Ten pages of information popped up. An article from Crime.com caught his eye.

Its headline read, *Evil has a name and it is Babineaux. Wow,* he thought as he started reading.

In 1986, New Orleans pastor Nolan Watson was found dead behind a French Quarter hotel. His body had been mutilated, his genitals nearly severed off. Watson, a proud member of the New Orleans community, was known for helping any and everyone who needed help. His church in the upper Ninth Ward was a stop for presidential candidates and anyone seeking office in the city of New Orleans. That's why his murder was so shocking.

Who would kill this man of God?

"This crime shook New Orleans because people don't kill preachers. That's real evil when you do something like that," said Bishop Thomas Brodreaux. "Reverend Watson was a beacon of light in the community when there was a lot of negativity. When he was killed, a feeling of evil just settled over the city."

A few weeks later, New Orleans saw the face of evil when Jacques Babineaux, the owner of The French Garden Inn, the hotel where the Reverend was found, turned himself in for the crime. He offered no explanation and avoided trial with a guilty plea.

But he wouldn't stay in prison long. Though Babineaux was sentenced to life in prison, he escaped after serving only five years of his sentence. Though many people thought he'd return to New Orleans, he was never spotted in the city. The FBI and the New Orleans Police collected over $1 million in reward money hoping the public would flush him out.

Police and federal authorities questioned his ex-wife, Loraine, who dropped her husband's last name after the trial. For three years, she and her daughter were under police protection. Police thought that Babineaux would return, kidnap his family and go underground.

He didn't. Loraine Barker, his ex-wife, declined several requests for interviews. Police don't suspect that Barker helped her ex-husband escape because she has never shown public support for her husband.

Cleveland printed the story and shook his head. No wonder Freddie wanted answers from her father. How could a man do something like that? He was beginning to think that there was more behind the story than what was on the Web site. But how was he going to get Freddie to open up about it? Did he really want to know? Taking the story from the printer, he folded it and placed it in his jacket pocket. When the time was right he and Freddie could talk about her father and why she'd even want to find him. But not while she was in Atlanta. This was a pleasure trip that he was determined to make her enjoy.

Chapter 17

Stuffed from a lunch of fried chicken breast sandwiches with cheese and onions, fried potatoes covered with hot mustard and vinegar, and thick slices of chocolate cake, Freddie and Lillian lay on the floor listening to John Coltrane. Freddie closed her eyes, feeling as if every calorie of their sinful lunch had settled on her stomach.

"We overdid it," she moaned.

"Who are you telling? I haven't eaten like that in years. The last thing I want is to get fat before Louis gets me pregnant."

"I should've known that was next on the agenda for you. The perfect little family," Freddie said with a laugh.

"What's wrong with that?"

"Nothing, I just wonder if you realize that things don't always work out the way you plan them. I never planned to fall . . ."

Lillian propped up on her elbows. "I knew it," she shrieked. "I knew it! You're falling for Cleveland Alexander. Damn, Winfred, you're going to get your heart broken."

"My heart will be fine. When this week is over, Cleveland and I will go back to our lives and that will be the end of whatever this is," she said.

"What is this that you and Cleveland have going on?" Lillian asked. "And don't say it's nothing. You're starting to care for him."

Freddie shrugged. She wasn't ready to admit the obvious and she didn't want to hear Lillian go on and on about what a bad guy Cleveland was. Lillian didn't have a clue as to what kind of man Cleveland Alexander was.

"I can't explain what's going on with me and Cleveland, but I'm tired of trying to defend it to you, though." Freddie sat up on the floor. "So, I'm going to go back to his place and wait for him to come home so I can burn off some of the calories we just ate."

"Please, spare me the details."

Slowly Freddie rose from the floor. "But," she said. "Before I go back to his place, you know there is something we need to do. You know that boutique near Lenox Mall? I want to go there."

A slow grin spread across Lillian's face. "I can't believe you. You're going to buy some lingerie. And I'm going to help you. This is crazy."

"If you pick up something for yourself, you and Louis might be making that baby sooner rather than later," Freddie quipped as she and Lillian prepared to leave.

Three hours later, Lillian and Freddie had purchased enough lingerie to put on their own version of the Victoria's Secret Fashion Show.

"I think I went a little overboard," Lillian said as she picked up a black, lace see-through teddy that was going to leave little to the imagination when she put it on. "Louis is going to think I lost my mind."

Freddie smiled, thinking of the reaction she'd get from Cleveland tonight when she greeted him at the door in the sexy red satin bustier and matching thong she'd purchased. "Well, I'd better go. I want to beat Cleveland home."

Lillian grunted. "I still say this is the biggest mistake of your life."

"Whatever, Lil. I'm not trying to marry the man, all right. Unlike you, my goal in life has never been to be a wife."

"That's a lie. Exhibit one, you are the same person who has a wedding book. You picked out that ugly dress with the bell sleeves because you wanted an October wedding."

"How old were we when we made those books?" Freddie said. "Just because you kept yours it doesn't mean I have mine. Besides, Katrina washed that book away."

Lillian covered her mouth with her hand. "I keep forgetting how much you've lost. Thank God you had that hotel, huh?"

Freddie groaned as she pulled on her collar. "I don't want to think or talk about that place. Sometimes I think that I'm being punished for what my father did. Loraine doesn't want anything to do with the hotel, except to spend the profits. For years, she ignored that place until I turned it around."

"Maybe she thought having a Barker run the place would make people forget that it was a Babineaux property. Of course she couldn't be the face. Everyone knows she used to be married to your dad."

Freddie sighed. "I saw him, Lillian. Cleveland and I found him in Pass Christian."

"What? What did he have to say for himself? I've never understood why you've chased after that man. He's a criminal, and he left you and your mother destitute and with your reputation tattered. What possible reason would you have to want to find or talk to him?"

"You can't understand. Your father died, but you got a chance to know he loved you and his name isn't cursed by everyone in New Orleans. Maybe I was thinking that if I had a conversation with the man, I could understand why he left and why he did what he did."

"What happens if Cleveland finds out that . . ."

Freddie threw her hand up. "He isn't Marcus. Cleveland doesn't even know about the bounty and he's not going to find out."

"What if he does?" Lillian asked as she pulled out more of her lingerie. "Can you be sure that he won't sell your father out for a million dollars? I know for a fact that Atlanta firemen don't make a lot of money."

Chewing on her lip out of nervous habit, Freddie shook her head, but a little voice inside her told her that she didn't know for sure that Cleveland wouldn't sell her out. "Let me go," she said. "I hear Atlanta traffic is murder."

"Definitely makes you want to commit one," she said as she walked Freddie to the door. "Be careful. That's the last thing I'm going to say on the subject."

Freddie and Lillian hugged then Freddie dashed down the stairs and hoped she would make it home before Cleveland did. *Why do I consider his place home? I shouldn't be that comfortable with him and in his place,* she thought as she drove. *I'm not falling in love with this man. It will never work. It's just physical. Just physical.*

When Freddie arrived at Cleveland's house, she had just enough time to shower, change, and cook him a light meal. Rushing up to the bathroom, she took a shower. Standing underneath the five-speed showerhead, Freddie lost track of time and before she knew it, Cleveland was slipping into the shower behind her. He took her breasts into his big hands.

"Hey there, beautiful," he breathed against her neck.

She moaned in response. "What are you doing here?"

Cleveland spun her around and slipped one hand

between her thighs. "Making you very happy," he said as he parted her wet folds of skin. With his finger, he sought out her tender bud. Freddie melted against him as his fingers found her sexual center. Cleveland moved his finger in a come-hither motion and her knees buckled. "This isn't how things were supposed to happen," she whispered. "I was supposed to surprise you."

"Surprise," he said, then slipped on a condom and pulled her onto his erection. Then he captured her lips and kissed her until she felt heady with desire. She parted her legs and Cleveland molded her body around his. She burned and yearned to feel him inside her and to make her need known as she ground against him. She was so wet that Cleveland was drawn in. The heat from the shower and their bodies made them feel as if they were going to explode. He pressed her against the wall of the shower, slowly pumping in and out and palmed her breasts, tweaking her hard nipples and pushing her over the edge. Her body shook as he hit her spot time and time again. Freddie bit down on his neck, muffling her screams of passion. As the warm water beat down on them, they both reached their climax, exploding from the inside out.

Cleveland reached back and shut the shower off, then he smiled at Freddie. "I've never had a shower like that before."

She gave him a quick peck on the lips, "You ruined my surprise."

"I couldn't resist. I heard the shower going as I came upstairs." Cleveland scooped her up in his arms and stepped out of the shower. Freddie wrapped her arms around his neck and looked into his eyes. Could she be falling for this man? She took one of his damp locs between her fingers. How did this happen? How did she let herself fall for this man?

"Hey," Cleveland said. "Why don't we go out to dinner? Houston's?"

"Okay, but let's have dessert in," she said then smiled seductively.

"You don't have to tell me twice. But I have to warn you, I'm on call this evening and I may have to go back to the station," he said as he sat her down on the bed.

"Okay," she said, feeling a little disappointed that she was possibly going to have to share him with the City of Atlanta. "I forgot that you're a superhero."

"That's right," he said, winking at her. "Up, up and away."

Freddie laughed as Cleveland made swooshing sounds as if he were flying.

After they dried each other's bodies and dressed, they headed to the restaurant. Instead of going downtown, they headed for the location that had just opened up on Covington Highway.

"Atlanta's constantly growing," Freddie commented as they passed construction sites. "Does this make your job harder, all the new communities and what not?"

"Only when you can't find a new street on the GPS system. Our system is one of the fastest and growing."

Freddie nodded. "So, why did you become a firefighter?"

Cleveland smiled wistfully. "It's the family business, though my mother was hoping that I'd be the one to pick another career path."

"Why? It seems like such a noble thing to do."

Cleveland exhaled. "It's noble and dangerous. We lost my father to a fire. He was a fireman. And he was the closest thing to a hero that I've ever knew. For Darren and me this was the best way to honor him. Then last year, I got hurt in an explosion and my mother wanted Darren and me to quit. But we've been doing this for so long, we don't know how to do anything else."

"Wow," Freddie said. "Your mother must go out of her mind every time there is a fire."

Cleveland nodded. "Especially after that big fire at that warehouse in Charleston. It's a risk, but anything that's worth having or doing is worth taking a risk over."

Freddie didn't say anything. She wondered if she should take a risk on Cleveland? He was worth having, but she didn't know if she could be happy in Atlanta. Would he move to New Orleans and help her rebuild her tattered life?

Do I really want to rebuild in New Orleans? she thought as he pulled into the restaurant's parking lot. As they got out of the car and Cleveland wrapped his arm around her waist, Freddie seriously considered taking the risk to love him and leave everything that had been destroyed behind.

I could be happy with Cleveland. I really think I could, she thought as she stared into his gray eyes.

Chapter 18

After dinner, Cleveland and Freddie headed back to his place, but before they could have dessert, Cleveland was called to the station to take over for a fireman that had gotten sick. It was a quiet night, but Darren didn't want to take any chances by being short-handed.

As he headed out the door, Freddie told him that she understood. She was, however, disappointed that he wouldn't see her naughty fashion show, which she knew would knock him off his feet. Seeing Cleveland in his element and so dedicated to his job, she had to wonder why Lillian didn't see this side of him. He was a fun-loving and sexy man, but he had a tender side. That's what scared Freddie, because she couldn't write him off or lump him in the same group as her father. It was hard for her to admit that Cleveland was a good man. Admitting that would almost be like giving herself permission to fall in love with him.

This isn't good, she thought as she paced back and forth in the living room. *I can't fall in love.*

Freddie's cell phone rang as she headed upstairs to Cleveland's bedroom. She dashed back down the stairs and grabbed the phone. The caller ID said that the caller was unknown. She knew who it was when she pressed the talk button.

"Hello?"

"Chere, it's your father."

"What do you want?" she asked as she sat at the base of the stairwell.

"Well, I told you that I was going to get back with you and try to see you."

Freddie rolled her eyes. "And that was last week. What, do you have more lies to tell me about my mother?"

"Listen, I'm in New Orleans because I'm tired of running and I wanted to let you know that I'm going to tell the authorities the truth."

"The truth? Do you even have a clue what the truth is? It's unbelievable to me that my mother is a murderer."

"Believe what you want to believe, chere, but the truth is, I thought I was making your life and your mother's life better by taking the blame for what she did. I had no idea who that dead man was at first."

"That doesn't make a difference. You're still a part of this murder. You and mom."

"I was trying to protect you all," he said.

"That's what you say, but how do I know that's the truth?"

"I need to see you before I turn myself in."

"That's going to be hard. I'm in Atlanta."

"With that Rasta boy I saw you with?" His voice was filled with fatherly concern. Freddie had to laugh.

"Don't you think it's a little too late to play 'daddy'? I don't need you to approve who I date. When I needed that kind of stuff, you were on the run."

"And what would you rather have happened? Me spend the rest of my life in prison and you grow up thinking that I was a murderer?"

"Wouldn't have made a difference. At least if you were in

prison I would've known where you were." Freddie was tempted to snap her phone shut and close her father out of her life, but she had to know what he had to say for himself.

"How do you know he isn't like the other one?" Jacques asked.

"Because he isn't. You do know what your lies are going to do to Mother, don't you?"

"What about what your mother's lies have cost me? I've been running for a long time. Do you think it's been easy for me? All of this has been hell and the worst part of it is that I missed seeing you grow up and become the woman that you are."

"Don't give me that bullshit," Freddie exclaimed. "You made your choices."

"I'm telling you for the last time, I'm not guilty."

Unable to listen to any more of her father's lies, she slammed the phone shut and threw it against the wall. Tears of frustration poured down her cheeks. Part of her wanted to call her mother and ask her if any of Babineaux's claims were true. Then again, her mother had never been forthcoming with information about her father.

Sitting on the base of the stairwell, Freddie allowed tears of frustration to spill down her cheeks. She was no closer to finding out the truth about her family.

Wiping her eyes with the backs of her hands, Freddie decided to busy herself by picking up Cleveland's discarded clothes, hoping that it would give her something else to think about.

As she picked up his jacket, a folded piece of paper fell out. Curiosity got the best of her and she unfolded it. Reading the words jabbed her in the heart. She was wrong, she'd misjudged who Cleveland was. It was like finding out about Marcus all over again.

Son of a bitch, she thought as she took the Crime.com

story and ran upstairs. Freddie stuffed her bags with her clothes and the lingerie that she'd purchased. Anger coursed though her veins and heated her blood. She had to get out of there before Cleveland returned or she would be tempted to reach into her glove compartment, get her gun and use it for the first time ever. Why did she think Cleveland wouldn't find out about her father? But to hide this from her, did it mean that he was going for the money? *Bastard!*

Freddie, once she was packed, dashed out of the house, not bothering to lock the front door, and headed for Lillian's. Though she didn't want to hear "I told you so," she needed her friend. She just hoped that Louis wasn't at home.

Cleveland and Roland rolled up the fire hose after putting out a bushfire near Peachtree Industrial. It was nearly two A.M. and this had been their first call of the night. Nights like this were a firefighter's dream. No death, no serious property loss and limited danger.

"That woman still in your house?" Roland asked as they hopped onto the truck.

"Yep."

He shook his head. "The death of a playa. Can't believe you got that chick in your house and you're not there. What if one of your freaks from way back call?"

"I don't do booty calls, so that's not an issue or a problem."

"Whatever. Cleveland, what's so special about this woman?"

The driver started the loud engine and over the rumbling, Cleveland said, "I don't know. She's the one."

"What?" Roland called out.

Cleveland shook his head. He wasn't going to try and explain his relationship with Freddie to Roland. Cleveland knew he wouldn't understand it, because he barely had a grasp of what was going on between them himself. Although they'd been trying to pretend that they only had a physical relationship, Cleveland knew it was deeper than that. Talking to her was so easy, it felt as if she was listening and not just waiting to put her two cents in the conversation.

Freddie was smart, witty, and he loved her sarcasm. So many women he met didn't have a clue how to hold a real conversation. But Freddie kept him on his toes and he loved that. At times he felt as if she was just a little more than he could handle. But these last few days with her, Cleveland knew that she was just right for him. He couldn't wait to end his shift and get home to her.

One day, this is going to be a permanent arrangement, he thought with a smile on his lips.

Freddie pulled up to Lillian's house and sat in the driveway. She pressed her forehead against the steering wheel. Did she really want to go in there and listen to Lillian's tirade about Cleveland and a laundry list of I-told-you-sos?

How could she have made such a gross misjudgment of Cleveland Alexander? Was it always going to be like this? Was every man going to see her as a lottery ticket? How long had Cleveland known about the bounty on her father? Was he trying to use her to get information about her father so that he could collect the reward?

Damn it, lightning is not supposed to strike twice, she thought as she called Lillian from her cell phone.

"Hello?" Lillian said, her voice thick with sleep.

"Lil, it's me," Freddie said. "I'm sorry to call you so late, but I need some place to stay tonight."

"Okay, sure, come over. What happened with you and Cleveland?" she asked.

Freddie stepped out of the car and walked up the steps. "Open the door, I'm on the front porch."

A few moments later, she head Lillian fumbling with the door locks. "That was fast."

"I was calling from your driveway," she said as she walked in.

"What if I would've been making a baby tonight?"

Freddie shrugged, she was in no mood to joke with Lillian. "Just show me where I'm crashing and I'll be out of your hair in the morning."

Lillian touched Freddie's elbow. "What happened? One of his other women showed up at the front door? Don't say I didn't tell you that . . ."

"Lil, please," Freddie exclaimed. "I don't need this shit right now."

"Well, I-I . . . Let me get you a blanket and a pillow," she said then headed upstairs.

"I'm sorry," Freddie called after her. "It happened again."

Lillian bounced down the stairs. "What happened?"

"Cleveland must have done some investigating and found out about my father. Tonight, after he went back to work, I was picking up his clothes and found this." She reached into her pocket and pulled out the story from Crime.com.

"That rotten bastard," Lillian said as she read over the story. "So, it's Marcus all over again."

Tears sprang into Freddie's eyes, but she refused to cry. "I can't believe how wrong I was about him. It's just that he made me feel so . . . It doesn't matter, I'm going back to New Orleans in the morning and Cleveland Alexander will become a distant memory." She started to tell her friend that Jacques was back in the Crescent City and wanted to see her. Instead, she didn't say another word and Lillian went upstairs to get her a blanket and pillow.

As Freddie settled on her friend's sofa, she buried her face in the pillow and cried silently. How could she have been so close to falling in love with a man who was only out to betray her?

Cleveland didn't usually leave the fire station in the middle of the night, but he wanted and needed to see Freddie. They still had dessert to eat. The thought of her lying in his bed, sound asleep in something sexy, turned him on as he drove. He couldn't wait to see the look on her face when he kissed her lips and woke her up. As he pulled into his driveway, Cleveland noticed that his front door was ajar. He brought the car to an abrupt stop and slowly exited. His heart raced as thoughts of a robber or rapist being in the house with Freddie danced in his mind. *Dear God, please let her be all right,* he thought as he quietly pushed the door open. He grabbed an umbrella, which was at the door, and called out for Freddie.

Silence greeted him. Looking around the house, he saw that nothing looked as if it had been disturbed. Cleveland turned all of the lights on in every room he passed as he headed up the stairs.

"If anybody is in here, I have a gun," he said in a gruff voice. Cleveland walked into the bedroom. "Freddie!" He turned the light on. Looking around the room, he noticed that the only thing missing, other than Freddie, was her luggage.

"What in the hell is going on?" he muttered as he grabbed his phone from the night stand next to his bed. Cleveland was about to dial 9-1-1, then he reversed his decision and called Lillian. It was becoming clearer to him that Freddie hadn't been kidnapped, but had more than likely left on her own accord.

"What do you want?" Lillian snapped.

"Have you seen Freddie?" he asked, not bothering to say hello.

"So what if I have?" she said.

"I walked into my house and the door was open and Freddie isn't here."

"There's no need for you to worry about her or seeing her again, you ass."

Cleveland furrowed his brows. "What's with the attitude?"

The next thing Cleveland heard was the dial tone. Slamming the phone into the base, Cleveland swore loudly. "What in the hell is going on?" he exclaimed. Without giving a second thought to Lillian's attitude, Cleveland rushed downstairs and out to his car. Freddie was going to tell him what was going on and why she left.

Chapter 19

Lillian hung up the phone and turned to her friend. "You know he's going to be on his way over here," she said as she ran her hand over her face. "I shouldn't have answered the phone."

"What did he say?" Freddie asked, despite herself.

Lillian huffed and plopped down on the sofa. "All of this drama. I told you Cleveland Alexander was bad news, I just had no idea he was slimy like Marcus. Hell, he doesn't need money, he can borrow whatever he needs from Jill and Darren. I just can't . . ."

Freddie crossed over to Lillian and grabbed her shoulders. "Lil! What did he say?"

"Something about the door being open, worried about you, blah, blah," she said. "If he was so worried, he wouldn't have been snooping about your dad behind your back."

Freddie nodded. "I've got to leave, I don't want to see Cleveland."

Lillian pushed her friend's hands away and shook her head. "You're not running out of here in the middle of the night to avoid this fool. He's the one who's wrong. Besides, you need to rest before you drive back to New Orleans and I don't want to read about you crashing your car on the highway because you fell asleep." Folding her arms across her chest, Lillian continued. "Besides, I can handle Cleveland."

Freddie shook her head. "This isn't something I need you to handle. If he shows up here, then I'll take care of him."

Lillian rolled her eyes. "Don't get soft on me. Cleveland is going to come in here and try to sweet talk you back into his bed and his house so he can turn your father in. Remember what Marcus did, right?"

Nodding, Freddie didn't need to be reminded that she'd played the fool twice. "I can handle this, all right?"

"One day, you're going to meet the right man and you two are going to have a wonderful life," Lillian said as she gave her friend a tight hug. "I'm going upstairs, but if you need it, I've got a bat in the closet."

Freddie smiled weakly. "If I scream, bring the bat down."

Plopping down on the sofa, she waited. Though she didn't want to admit it, she wanted Cleveland to come, to hear why he'd done what he'd done. Was he really in it for the money?

Pleasure trip, she thought bitterly. Freddie felt as if her heart had been slammed against a brick wall and shattered like a glass vase. How could a man be so cold and fake the feelings that she thought were developing between them? Did he think she wouldn't know where the money came from? She was so close to believing that she had found Mr. Right, a man that loved her for the woman whom she was. A man who could grow with her and provide her with the safety and security that she never had growing up in New Orleans.

Freddie refused to cry. Her tears would be a reminder of how foolish she'd been. How could she have allowed him so deep in her heart when she'd barely known him? Cleveland, she surmised, was the worst kind of man. He not only said he was different but he had an act that fooled her jaded heart.

When the tears finally came, Freddie was helpless to fight them. Wiping her eyes with the back of hand, she made up the sofa so that she could bunker down and get a few hours of sleep before she headed to New Orleans. She laid down on the sofa and closed her eyes but before she drifted off to sleep, there was a loud knock at the door.

Freddie laid there for a moment; she knew who was on the other side of the door and didn't hurry to get there. Lillian appeared at the top of the stairs with the Louisville Slugger in her hands.

"Is that him?" she asked.

"Go back to bed," Freddie said as she rose from the sofa. She took a deep breath as she walked to the door. Pulling the curtain back, she saw Cleveland standing there with a worried look on his face.

"What do you want?" Freddie said through the door.

"Is everything all right? I mean did something happen that spooked you tonight?" he asked, concern peppering his tone. "Will you let me in?"

"Hell no!" she spat. "I'm not letting you in and you can get off Lillian's doorstep."

Cleveland furrowed his brows in confusion and placed his hand on the doorknob. "Freddie, open the door so we can talk."

"Now you want to talk? I trusted you, Cleveland, and you're a snake."

"What are you talking about?"

"Crime.com," she hissed.

"Huh?" He pulled on the door. "Open the door, because I'm not going to stand out here screaming through this glass."

"Then leave. There is nothing I have to say to you."

"Freddie, tell me what you think I did." Cleveland was nearly pleading with her, but she was unmoved.

"What I think you did? You think the sex is that good that I should turn a blind eye to what you were planning to do?" Her voice rose as her rage grew.

"Do you want me to break this window? Open the door, now!"

"You're in no position to make demands on me," Freddie snapped, though she did open the door once she saw a few porch lights come on. Cleveland walked in, his face still a mask of confusion.

"Tell me what's going on," he said.

Lillian bounded down the stairs. "Oh, you ain't slick, brother," she said as she pointed the bat at him. "I can't believe you're such a sleazy, lying bastard."

Cleveland grabbed the end of the bat and took it from Lillian's hands. "What in the hell is going on?" His voice boomed like thunder. Both Lillian and Freddie jumped a little. "Since I walked into my house, my mind was racing, I thought something bad had happened to you and now I come in here and I"—he said holding the bat above his head—"Lillian wants to play 'Crazy Joe.' One or both of you is going to tell me what the hell is going on."

"Put the bat down," Freddie said, her voice forceful and angry. She was tempted to take it and hit him with it. "And get out."

Cleveland dropped the bat, but he didn't make an effort to move. "If I did something wrong, at least tell me what it was," he said. His eyes pleaded with her to talk to him. Freddie stared into those gray eyes and remembered how she thought those eyes held love and comfort in them. Now it just looked as if he were a liar, a liar with a silver tongue. Tears sprang into her eyes again, but she blinked rapidly to keep them from falling.

"How could you?" Lillian exclaimed.

"How could I what?" Cleveland said. "Freddie, talk to me." He reached out to touch her but she recoiled at his touch.

"Don't touch me, don't ever touch me again."

Cleveland threw his hands up in frustration and groaned loudly. "This is bullshit, if you don't tell me what's going on, how am I supposed to know what's wrong?"

"You want to talk bullshit," Freddie said, stepping closer to him, her voice gruff and angry. "Bullshit is you pretending to care about me so much and then going behind my back to collect the reward."

"Reward? What are you talking about?" he exclaimed as he tugged at his locs.

"Don't give me that," she said, pushing him in his chest. "I saw the story you printed. How long have you known?"

"Known what?" he asked, confusion replacing the anger on his face.

"About her father, you jerk!" Lillian cried. Cleveland turned to her and frowned.

"Please tell me what this has to do with you?" he huffed. "This is between me and Freddie."

Lillian placed her hands on her slender hips. "First of all this is my damn house and I told you not to mess with my friend. Freddie is . . ."

"Lillian," Freddie said, "I told you that I can handle this. Give us a minute."

She shot her friend a look that said, 'Are you sure,' then snatched the bat from the floor. "Sixty seconds and I'm coming back with the bat."

Cleveland shook his head and waited for Lillian to disappear upstairs before he said anything. "Tell me what this is all about," he said, attempting to touch her shoulders, but she swatted his hands away.

"It's about you being a lying, conniving bastard," she said. "How long have you known?"

"What am I supposed to know?" he said, growing tired of the back and forth with her.

"About my father and the million-dollar bounty that's on his head? You just couldn't wait to get me to Atlanta so that you could call the authorities and collect the money."

Shaking his head, he said, "That's not what's going on. I had no idea that . . ."

"I saw the story. You went on the Internet and did a search on my history. What did you expect to find? The number for the FBI?"

"I looked up that information because I wanted to know more about you and what you didn't want to talk about. I wanted to know why it was so important for you to find your father and why you felt as if . . ."

"You could've asked me! Talked to me instead of going behind my back!" she exclaimed. "I don't believe a word you're saying anyway. You've never had a problem speaking your mind or asking me uncomfortable questions. What made this time so different?"

"Because I didn't want this trip to be about. . ."

"Save it, Cleveland. I'm not going down this road again."

"Again? So, you're holding me up for what someone else did? I don't need the money from your father's bounty, and why would I do something to hurt you?"

She shrugged. "Why not? You'd gotten what you'd wanted. We had sex in every way you could imagine. What was left?"

"How about the way I feel for you? How about what's in my heart?"

She rolled her eyes, willing herself not to believe what

he was saying. Marcus claimed to love her and had no qualms about turning her father in. What made her think that Cleveland was any different?

"Go to hell."

"That's where I'll be if you walk out of here believing the worst about me."

Folding her arms across her chest, Freddie glared at him. "You can stand there and say all of this crap, but the truth is, you lied to me."

"I've never lied to you. I just needed some clarity and you didn't want to talk about it."

"I don't want to hear that," she said, pushing against his chest. "I was ready to give you everything. I wanted to love you and now I find out that you were nothing but a lying sack of shit."

"I already love you," Cleveland said, his voice low and deep. He took two steps toward her and pulled her into his arms. Freddie pounded her fists against his chest as tears welled up in her eyes.

"Don't say that. Don't say you love me when you and I both know that isn't true."

Cleveland dropped his arms and shook his head. "What do you want me to say? Is now the time to lie to you? Do you want to be right and find out that I was trying to find out information about your father so I could break your heart? After all we've shared, do you really believe I'm a cold bastard who would do this to you?"

Though her heart screamed *No*, Freddie didn't say a word. Part of her knew that every word Cleveland said was true, but still the Internet story made it difficult to believe that he hadn't changed his mind after learning how much money he'd get from turning her father in.

"I'm going back to New Orleans in the morning and

I never want to see your face again," Freddie said. "Leave, now."

"But, Freddie, I love . . ."

"Get out," she screamed. "It's over, Cleveland. Don't make it harder."

Backing away from her, he shook his head. "This isn't over. Not by a long shot, and if you think you're walking out of my life, you're wrong." Cleveland opened the door and walked out. When he was gone, Freddie collapsed on the sofa and sobbed like a hungry newborn baby. As Lillian crept down the stairs, Freddie didn't hear her. She was torn in several different directions over Cleveland. Was he telling the truth? Did he really love her? Could she trust him?

"Freddie, are you all right?" Lillian asked in a quiet voice.

"Do I look all right?" Freddie replied through her tears. "How could he do this? How could he do this and then say that he loves me."

"Pish, he would say whatever to get you to . . ." The front door opened and Louis walked in yawning. He looked down at the bat in the middle of the floor.

"What in the world is going on in here?" he asked as he took a sidelong look at Freddie and Lillian.

"Nothing," Lillian said. "No, I take that back. Your no-good friend was here. Didn't I tell you he was no good? Look at her."

Louis shrugged his shoulders. "Why is it our business? Freddie and Cleveland are adults, but every time I turn around, I'm getting cussed out because of something you said he did. Lillian, I'm tired of it and maybe you ought to start minding your own damned business."

She shot a bone piercing look at her husband. "You're going to defend him?" Her voice rose with every word she spoke. "I guess it doesn't matter that he was trying to . . ."

"Lillian," Freddie said. "Louis is right. This has nothing to do with either of you and I'm going to leave and stay at a hotel tonight. There's been enough drama here tonight."

Louis shook his head. "Freddie, you're family, you don't have to go anywhere. I don't know what's going on with you and Cleveland, but he can't be as bad as you two think. Since the day he got back from New Orleans, all he's been talking about is you."

Placing her hands to her ears, Freddie rocked back and forth on the sofa and Lillian rolled her eyes at her husband.

"I thought we were supposed to be minding our own business," Lillian said sarcastically.

Louis threw his hands up. "I'm going to bed," he said. "It's late and I don't have the energy."

Once Louis had disappeared upstairs, Freddie looked at her friend. "Don't make my problems yours," she said.

"I'm not, but I told Louis that I didn't think you and Cleveland were a good idea. He was the one who said Cleveland was a good guy. Whatever."

"But Louis is a good guy and your husband. This has nothing to do with you guys, all right? I'll be gone in the morning," she said.

Freddie and Lillian hugged tightly. "Girl, it's going to be fine," Lillian said.

She nodded and smiled weakly. "I know," she said. "I'm going to go home and forget all about Cleveland Alexander." But Freddie knew those words were lies as soon as they left her mouth. She would never be able to forget Cleveland.

Chapter 20

Cleveland didn't close his eyes to sleep, so when the sun crept over the horizon he hopped out of bed, still dressed from the night before in his jeans and AFD T-shirt, and dashed downstairs.

Heading for his car, Cleveland could think of nothing but going to New Orleans and telling Freddie that he meant every word he'd said and that he loved her too much to let her go. *Damn it,* he thought, *this isn't how this week was supposed to turn out.*

He started the car and headed for Louis and Lillian's house. He didn't see Freddie's car parked in the driveway and he was not going to knock on the door and take more abuse from Lillian. If she weren't Louis's wife, he would've given her a piece of his mind last night, but out of respect for his friend, he held his tongue.

Turning his car around, he headed for the station and prayed that Darren was in. Knowing that it was going to be a long shot for him to take more time off, all he could hope for was his brother's belief in the power of love.

Pulling up at the station, Cleveland slammed his car door shut, ran inside and called out for Darren. As he ran down the hall, he saw Roland peak his head out of the sleeping quarters. "What's all this damned racket?" he demanded.

Cleveland ignored him and walked into Darren's office, where he found his brother leaned back in his leather desk chair sound asleep.

"Darren," Cleveland said, slamming his hands against the desk.

Darren nearly fell out of the chair as his eyes fluttered open. "What—Cleveland, what's wrong?"

"I've got to go to New Orleans, I need at least two days to get her back."

Darren blinked several times in succession as if he was trying to get his bearing straight. "Okay, you're in here at the crack of dawn because you and your girlfriend had a fight? And you're asking for more time off, even though you've just gotten back from a week's vacation? I've got to be dreaming, because you have lost your mind." Darren wiped his eyes and yawned.

"I don't ask for much," Cleveland said, "and I'm not one to ask for favors, but D, I love Freddie and she thinks that I've betrayed her when I didn't."

Darren sat straight up in his chair, fully awake now as if he'd just drank a pot of coffee. "Did you say that you love her?"

Cleveland nodded. "I've never felt this way about a woman and if she doesn't love me back, then at least I need to clear my name."

Darren motioned for his brother to sit down. "What happened?"

Cleveland told his brother the story, how he'd done some research on her father on the Internet, printed the story and Freddie found it. "I don't want the money that comes from turning her father in. Why would I do that? Why would I break her heart for money?"

Darren nodded. "I understand that. But do you think that she's going to listen to you if you run down there?"

Cleveland shrugged. "I can't go on wondering what if. Maybe Freddie is that woman who I've been waiting for. I've never had these kinds of feelings for any other woman. When you and Louis were talking about love and all that mess, I knew I'd never feel it. Then she walked into my life. A woman who speaks her mind and isn't afraid to think outside the box. Freddie is the kind of woman who will keep me on my toes. She's not . . ."

Darren threw his hand up and said, "She's your soul mate."

"Yes."

"I saw the look in your eyes when you were talking about her a few days ago and I recognized it."

"What look?" Cleveland asked.

Darren smiled, "The same look that I have in my eyes when I look at Jill. Now, I'm glad that you're in love, but we're still short-staffed here. I can only let you go for two days. So whatever the two of you have going on between you better be cleared up in forty-eight hours."

Cleveland nodded and hugged his brother. "Forty-eight hours, huh?" Cleveland said.

"If you love her as much as you say you do, it's not going to take that long," he said. "Hell, if it wasn't for you, Jill and I wouldn't be together now. But please take a shower before you go to that woman."

Cleveland laughed for the first time since his fight with Freddie and took off for the showers.

Freddie had driven for about four hours before she stopped to gas up her car. She wanted to put as much distance between herself and Atlanta as she could. What was she thinking anyway? Even if Cleveland wasn't a liar, the relationship was doomed from the start. They lived too far away from one another and she couldn't trust that he wouldn't break her heart.

Oh, he's already done that. I hope he didn't think telling me that he loved me was going to turn me into a glob of Jell-O and I was going to believe everything he said. I know he was after the money. For once in his life, my father was right, she thought as she filled her car with gas. She walked into the store, paid for gas, and purchased a cup of coffee and a bran muffin. Looking at her watch, she saw that it was nearly ten A.M. She had to wonder if her father had turned himself in yet. She didn't want to deal with him either. *Why is it that every man in my life is nothing but a huge disappointment?* she thought as she climbed into the car and started it up. The engine sputtered a bit, but soon roared to life. As she got back on the highway, Freddie decided that she was going to get rid of her father's Mustang. Just like Jacques, it was more trouble than it was worth. Loraine had been right all along and admitting that to her was going to be the hardest thing she was going to have to do.

Was that her destiny? To end up alone and bitter just like her mother? Maybe she was listening more than she cared to admit when Loraine told her that men couldn't be trusted and would always disappoint you when you needed them most. Cleveland had certainly let her down. But she was partly to blame for that, because she'd been the one to bring him into her world and her problems. Cleveland hadn't asked her to take him to Pass Christian. She allowed him to find a place inside her heart and she fell in love with him all on her own.

How was she going to pretend that she hadn't fallen in love with Cleveland?

Love? She thought. *I don't love him, I can't.*

A few hours later, Freddie was back at the hotel. Just as she was getting out of the car, someone grabbed her from behind, and a hand covered her mouth, stopping her from screaming. Freddie struggled against the body as the man dragged her into a corner.

"Shh, chere, it's just me," Jacques Babineaux said when he released her. "I've been waiting for you and hiding from your mother."

"Are you trying to give me a heart attack? Or better yet, get arrested? There are cameras everywhere these days," Freddie said once her heart stopped racing.

"I told you that I'm turning myself in today. My lawyer and I are meeting in an hour. Where's your mother?"

"In Houston, I guess. Why?"

"Because this is her last chance to come clean," he said. Freddie shook her head and turned her back to her father.

"Why don't you just keep running? You're going to open a can of worms that no one wants to deal with. I read a story about what you did and . . ."

"I didn't do anything but protect your mother and in turn you. But I've spent too much of my life paying for it. It's time for me to stop running and time for your mother to admit the truth."

She turned around and faced him, her eyes shining with tears. "What about me and what this is going to do to me? Do you think I want both of you in prison?"

He shrugged his shoulders. "I'm getting too old to run. You don't need my protection anymore and your mother didn't hold up her end of the deal. She didn't tell the truth, she just left me holding the bag for all of these years. If she would've told the truth, she would've been able to tell the authorities what really happened that night."

Pushing her hair behind her ears, Freddie asked, "What did happen that night?"

"Your mother is going to have to answer that question," he said with a far away look in his eyes.

"No, I'm asking you," she said. "Tell me what happened or I swear to God, I will call the police right now."

Jacques shook his head. "You're not going to do that and you know that I'd be gone before the NOPD showed up."

"Fine, let's find out," Freddie said as she reached into her pocket to pull out her cell phone. Jacques touched her wrist gently.

"All right," he said. "I'll tell you."

She closed her eyes and braced herself for the story she'd been waiting her entire life to hear. Jacques cleared his throat and began.

"That night, your mother and I were in the hotel, we'd just wrapped up a Baptist convention that the good Reverend was hosting. I was tired and left Loraine down at the front desk to run the night audit. I always told her to lock the door at eleven and she never did. It must have been around midnight when I heard her scream. See, at that time, we'd been living in the hotel to make ends meet. The hotel hasn't always been this nice, either. Anyway, I rushed downstairs and saw Nolan Watson sprawled on the floor with a steaming gunshot wound to his chest. Your mother's shirt was ripped, she had scratches on her chest and face and in her hands was the .38 special we kept underneath the counter.

"She was incoherent when I asked her what happened. We had two guests in the hotel and they must have been too drunk to hear anything. I told your mother we should call the police. She shook her head and screamed 'no.'

"'The cops are going to take his side. He's so well-known in the community and no one is going to believe that he tried to rape me.' Then she started sobbing and crying like a wounded animal. We couldn't leave the body in the middle of the lobby and I said we had do something."

"Your mother wanted to dump him in Lake Pontchartrain. But that was too risky. New Orleans was in the middle of a big crime wave and I told her that we should take the body and dump it somewhere in the Lower Ninth. Police would think that he'd been shot in a robbery gone wrong or something like that. Of course, when the time came to move the body, she was too distraught to do it. So I wrapped him up in some old carpet and took him out back in the alley. Someone was coming and I had to leave him there. Inside, your mother had cleaned up all the blood and herself. When the cops found his body, I was the first and only suspect."

Fingering her throat, Freddie asked, "Why?"

"Watson and I had a public feud that went back years. It was my hotel where he was found and . . ."

"What was the feud about?" she asked.

"Watson was a damned fraud, the public thought that he was a good man and a holy man, but he was nothing but a charlatan. Chasing women, drinking like a fish and defrauding people with his insurance policies. When my mother died, her life insurance policy didn't pay a damned thing. I went to him and he basically laughed me out of his office. Claimed that my mother hadn't paid her premiums. But I knew she had. I hated that man and he knew it. He'd always had a thing for Loraine and it burned him up that I'd married her."

"If that's really what happened, then why didn't you and Mom go to the police?" Freddie asked.

"When the police questioned your mother, she turned everything around on me," he spat bitterly. "It's like she wanted me in prison. That other stuff that happened to him, I know she did it."

Shaking her head, Freddie didn't know what to say, whether she should believe her father's story. "So, why now? Why turn yourself in now?" she asked.

"I told you, I'm tired. And it's time for someone else to pay the price for that night."

"I have to go," Freddie said as she attempted to push past her father.

"Chere, I know this is a lot to take in, but it's the truth," he said. "Make sure you watch the news tonight and you might want to tell your mother to watch as well."

Freddie watched as her father took off down the alley. It was only a few minutes after one, New Orleans time, and she was exhausted.

Cleveland pulled into the parking lot of The French Garden Inn's parking lot and looked up at the building. She was in there and he was going to find her come hell or high water. He sighed as he got out of the car and slowly walked to the front door. Upon entering the lobby, he looked for Freddie and hoped she'd be behind the front desk. But he was greeted by a perky, but older woman who had eyes like Freddie.

"Welcome to The French Garden Inn, do you have a reservation?" she asked with a plastic smile on her face.

"I'm looking for the owner," Cleveland said, his voice clear and strong, not showing an ounce of the desperation that he felt.

"That would be me, I'm Loraine Barker," she said as she extended her perfectly manicured hand. Cleveland shook her delicate hand, pleased to meet Freddie's mother, but wondering why she was here and not her daughter. "What can I help you with?"

A door slammed behind them and Freddie walked in.

She locked eyes with Cleveland and glared at him. "Why are you here?" she demanded.

Loraine looked from Freddie to Cleveland. "Is there a problem? Do I need to call security?"

"No, Mother," Freddie spat. "Because from what I hear calling the police isn't your strong suit."

Loraine clutched the pearl choker around her neck. "Winfred, what has gotten into you?"

"Freddie," Cleveland said. "Can we talk?"

Looking from her mother to Cleveland, she shook her head. Casting a heated glance at her mother, she said, "I'll deal with you later." Then she shot the same hot look at Cleveland. "You and I have nothing to say to each other. Everything was said in Atlanta."

Crossing behind the counter, he pulled her into his arms. "You had your say on my turf, now it's my turn to say what I have to say to you on yours."

Loraine smacked Cleveland hard on the shoulder. "Get your hands off my daughter. She just said she didn't want to talk to . . ."

"Mother! I can handle this," Freddie said, then she motioned for Cleveland to follow her outside. He rubbed his shoulder as he followed her out the door.

"Your mother packs a hell of a punch. That hurt," he said.

Freddie stared coldly at him. "Did you come to collect your reward? You're too late because my father is turning himself in today."

"How many times and how many ways do I have to tell you that I don't give a damn about a reward, what your father did or any of that? Do you think I drove eight hours to get here with barely three hours of sleep because of him? I came for you, I love you."

"No, you don't. You love who you think I am. You love

the fact that I don't chase you and you love the fact that you don't have to see me every day. You . . ."

Cleveland took her face into his hands and kissed her with a fiery passion that started her knees shivering. Pulling back, Cleveland peered into her eyes.

"Tell me you didn't feel that, tell me you don't know what that kiss was all about. You think I'd be here if you weren't the most important woman in the world to me. What's it going to take for you to open your eyes and see that this man, standing right here in front of you, loves you?"

"Please," she said, her voice low and hoarse. "Don't do this."

"Do what?"

"Make me love you when we know that it won't last," Freddie said. Tears sprang into her eyes. "I can't deal with this today, please just go away."

"No," he said. "I'm not leaving until you admit that you feel the same way about me that I feel about you."

"Cleveland, you don't understand, you don't want to get involved with me and this family and everything that's about to happen."

"What are you talking about?" he asked, his face lined with confusion.

"Take this chance and leave."

He grabbed her by the shoulders and pulled her against him as if she were Scarlett and he was Rhett Butler. "I'm not going anywhere and I don't care what kind of drama you think is . . ."

"My father's back, he's turning himself in and he's going to accuse my mother of murder. Still something you want to attach yourself to?"

"You're who I'm attaching myself to," he said. "I'm standing here beside you to support you."

She wrapped her arms around him and squeezed him tightly. "I shouldn't have doubted you," she said.

Cleveland kissed her on the top of her head. "No, you shouldn't have, but I know you've never had anyone in your corner before, but you do now."

Freddie stepped back from him. "I have to take care of something. Will you meet me at Jackson Square in an hour?"

He eyed her suspiciously. "You're not trying to get rid of me, are you?"

"No, I'll be there in an hour, I promise," she said. "I have to deal with my mother right now."

Cleveland pulled her close and gave her one last kiss. "I'll be waiting," he said when they parted.

Chapter 21

Freddie burst into the hotel, looking for a fight and looking directly at her mother.

"You know what," Loraine said when she saw her daughter at the entrance, "I don't appreciate you disappearing for nearly a week and then coming back here giving me . . ."

"Save it," Freddie snapped. "You've been absent from my life a lot longer than I've been gone from *my hotel*. Am I supposed to be impressed because you put in a few days' work?"

Loraine folded her arms underneath her breasts and glared at her daughter. "How dare you come in here filled with your self-righteous indignation because you've been chasing some man? Did you get your fill of sex? That's every woman's downfall, a man with bedroom skills. Did he curl your toes and make you forget everything that I've ever taught you?"

"What you taught me? All you taught me was bitterness and I thought I was doomed to be like you, Loraine. But why don't you come clean, *Mother*. Tell me how you're the reason my father was never around because you killed Nolan Watson! Tell me how you told me so many lies over the years that I've lost count. Tell me that!"

Loraine crossed over to Freddie and slapped her as hard as she could. The force of the blow made Freddie jump back. "You don't know what you're talking about. He-he's been filling your head with these lies."

"If you mean my father, then yes, he told me everything," Freddie said. "Now, you tell me the truth."

"I was tired of being a pawn in everybody's game," Loraine said, covering her ears with her hands.

"What are you talking about?" Freddie's eyebrows furrowed in confusion.

"Your father, that charming son of bitch, hated Nolan Watson and I was dating him."

"Dating who?"

Loraine cocked her head to the side. "Nolan. He was in seminary school, and your grandmother loved him. But Jacques Babineaux was different. So worldly and handsome. When he started paying attention to me, it was exciting and turned me on. What I didn't know was your father courting me was just a part of his vendetta against Nolan."

"I don't believe you. If that's the case, why would you and Dad have gotten married?"

Loraine looked pointedly at Freddie. "Things haven't always been as loose as they are now. When I got pregnant, there was no way my parents were going to let me be a single mother. Since Nolan and I weren't having sex, there was only one man who could've done the deed. At first I thought he was going to try and deny it, but he wanted a huge wedding in Jackson Square with all the stops." Loraine shook her head as if the memory was too much to bear. She walked over to the window and looked out over the French Quarter. "So, on my wedding day, I heard your father telling Nolan that he finally beat him. That he finally had something he wanted and could never have." A single tear rolled down her cheek and she wiped it away quickly.

Freddie crossed over to her mother and placed her hand on her shoulder. "Are you telling me that you planned the shooting, set Jacques up and everything because of what he said on your wedding day?"

Loraine whirled around and glared at her daughter. "No, I did it because I deserved better. Your father was never a good husband. Do you know how many chambermaids I had to fire because Jacques was sleeping with them? And Nolan. He'd come around with his trophy wife on his arm, telling me that he'd dump her in a minute if I left Jacques. These men didn't love me, I was a bone of contention for them and I was tired and angry. So yes, I shot Nolan that night and let your father take the blame for all of these years. And I'm not sorry."

Shaking her head and backing away, Freddie felt as if she didn't know who this woman was. "Did you think about how this would affect me?"

"Tell me, what do you really remember about your father? When you needed something or someone, I was there for you, not him. Our lives were better without him."

Freddie threw her hands up. "I'm done with this," she said. "Both of you are sick."

"What are you done with?" Loraine asked. "You're going to turn your back on me?"

"Yes, I'm leaving. You wanted this hotel, take it."

Loraine stood between Freddie and the door. "No, no," she said. "This is your legacy, your future so that you never have to depend on a man for a damned thing. Winfred, you turn your back on this and you're going to suffer for it."

Freddie pushed past her mother and headed out the door, then turned around and said, "By the way, you might want to tune in to the newscast at six."

"What?"

"Jacques Babineaux is turning himself in," Freddie said before walking out the door and heading for Jackson Square.

Cleveland walked around Jackson Square wondering if he'd been a chump. Was Freddie going to show up or had he driven all the way to New Orleans to be made a fool of?

She's going to be here, I know she is, he thought as he headed for a vendor who was selling roses, carnations and daisies. As cliché as it was, Cleveland bought a bouquet of roses for Freddie. Smiling as he paid the vendor, he couldn't remember when he'd gotten so corny. He was never the flowers-and-candy kind of man, but if it would make Freddie happy, then he could occasionally be corny. He glanced down at his watch, it had been an hour and still there was no sign of Freddie. He walked over to the statue of Jackson and wondered what it would cost to have a wedding out here. *That's just crazy,* he thought. *Freddie and I aren't ready for marriage, yet.*

A hand touched his shoulder and Cleveland turned around hoping to see a smiling Freddie, but she looked troubled. "What's wrong?" he asked.

"Can we go? Just take me away from here, please."

The flowers in his hand were nearly forgotten when he asked, "Where do you want to go? Back to the hotel?"

"No, absolutely not," she said, shaking her head.

"What happened?" he asked.

Freddie sighed, "Just get me away from here. We can talk later." She looked down at the flowers in his hand. "This isn't how this was supposed to go, was it?"

He handed her the roses with a lopsided grin on his face. "This went totally differently in my mind."

"I told you that you had a chance to leave and you decided

to stick around," she said, smiling through her sadness. "Welcome to the madness."

"Is it really that bad?"

Freddie brought the roses to her nose and looked at Cleveland. "Worse. My family is about to be a part of a huge scandal, again. This time, it's not just my Dad, it's my mother too." Her eyes glossed over with tears. "That's why I want to get away. Before the media comes looking for me."

"Whatever you want," he said as he wrapped his arm around her waist. "Where do you want to go?"

"Back to Atlanta, if you don't mind. I'm going to have to get away from here to figure out my next step and I promise, no more running to Lillian," she said.

"Good, because your friend has it in for me," Cleveland said.

Freddie smiled weakly. "My bags are still in the car at the hotel. Hopefully we can get in and out without anyone, particularly my mother, seeing us."

Cleveland nodded, noting that Freddie wasn't in the mood to joke. They walked back over to the hotel and grabbed her bags from the Mustang. "You're not taking the car?" Cleveland asked.

She glanced at it, thought about how long she'd worked to get it on the road and how she'd thought that having this car was like having a piece of her father. Now, she didn't want it. She didn't want to be reminded that both of her parents were vindictive and ruthless people.

"I don't want to take it," she said. "I'll look into getting something else later."

Cleveland looked at her, not knowing what to say. He had thought that her car meant a lot to her. "All right," he said, "then let's go."

"I'm sorry that I'm bringing you into all of this drama; it's like a bad episode of Jerry Springer or something."

He held her against his chest. "You'll come out stronger when this blows over. And I'm going to be right by your side."

She nodded as they headed for Cleveland's car. Once they were inside the car, Freddie sat silently as he drove down the Interstate. Sensing that Freddie needed her quiet time, Cleveland didn't say a word either, he just stole glances at her every couple of miles.

Freddie reached down and turned the radio on in time to catch a news brief about her father.

"In a shocking turn of events today, one of New Orleans' most wanted criminals turned himself in," the radio reporter said. "Jacques Babineaux, subject of a nationwide manhunt, is in custody at the Jefferson Parrish jail until the FBI takes custody of him. Babineaux was convicted for the murder of the Reverend Nolan Watson but escaped from prison and has been on the run for years. In a statement through his lawyer, Babineaux proclaimed his innocence and said that his former wife, Loraine Barker, is the killer."

Freddie shut the radio off.

"Wow," Cleveland murmured.

"See what I'm saying," she said. "That's why I have to get away from here."

He nodded, "I see. That's crazy. Did your mother open up to you?"

Freddie smiled sardonically. "Let's just say the truth is even stranger than fiction. I think I liked it better when I was in the dark," she said. "For years, I tried to ignore the media reports and whispers, but now I can't drown this out."

"When we get to Atlanta, you won't have to think or talk about it if you don't want to," Cleveland said. "But if you do want to talk, I'll listen."

She sighed, her heart swelling as Cleveland spoke.

Maybe he did love her and maybe he wasn't trying to hurt her. But would she be able to allow herself to love?

Turning to Cleveland, Freddie asked, "When you were on the Internet doing that search about my father, what were you trying to accomplish?"

"Honestly, I just wanted to know what the big secret was. Why you were looking so hard for your father and how he could possibly not want to be a part of your life. Every time I talked to you about it, you shut down on me. I wasn't trying to invade your privacy or anything like that."

She touched his knee gently. "I didn't want to tell you about my father because the last time I confided in some-one about him, it turned out that he was trying to profit from my father's capture. He was using me to get to the million-dollar bounty. So, I didn't trust you with the whole story about my father."

"I can respect that, but there's something you should know about me. I'm not the kind of man who uses people and I don't put my heart on the line often, so when I say I love you, that's no bull, no games, and no hidden agenda."

Freddie wished that she could tell him that she loved him too—that she was ready to open up and tell Cleveland that she loved him too—but she was too wounded and too hurt to say those words. Instead she just smiled and held his hand. Cleveland didn't press Freddie to say anything and they fell into a comfortable silence as he drove. It was so comfortable that Freddie drifted off to sleep.

Cleveland stole glances at Freddie as he drove, smiling at the peaceful look on her face as she slumbered. She deserved the rest. She'd been running since he met her and now it was time for her to rest and receive what she deserved, a man in her corner who loved her.

He had a lot to prove and he knew that. Freddie didn't seem as if she was going to be too quick to open up and he could understand it, but he was still ready to prove to her that he wasn't like any man who'd hurt her in the past, including her father. Now that he had her, he was going to have to do everything in his power to keep her. Cleveland had to do more than tell her that he loved her, he was going to have to show Freddie in every possible way that he loved her.

After they had been driving for awhile, Cleveland stopped and woke Freddie up.

"Hungry?" he asked as he pulled into the parking lot of a diner.

Freddie stretched her arms above her head and yawned. "Starved," she said. "Where are we?"

"Montgomery, Alabama. I figured we'd put enough distance between us and New Orleans before we stopped."

"Thank you."

They exited the car and headed inside the small restaurant. Since it wasn't dinner time, but way past lunch, the place was nearly empty. A waitress pointed to the empty tables and said, "Seat yourselves."

Cleveland nodded and chose a table in the corner near a wide window. Freddie plopped down and gazed out the window.

"Are you all right?" he asked her, noticing her melancholy disposition.

"I have to start all over," she said. "Find a job, a place to live and everything. It's like a second hurricane has blown through my life."

"Well, you can stay with me until you find a place of your own. And maybe Jill can offer you a job with . . ."

"No, I'm not going to let you recreate my life for me. This is something I have to do on my own."

Placing his hand on top of hers, Cleveland said, "I know

you're not used to having someone looking out for you, but that's changed."

"Cleveland," she began.

"Good evening," the waitress said. "Here are some menus. Our special is fried chicken and mashed potatoes with sweet tea."

The couple took the menus and asked the waitress for a few minutes to go over them. As soon as she left, Cleveland turned his full attention to Freddie. "I'm not going to let you talk me out of helping you."

"Cleveland."

"I don't want to hear it. This is how things work, I love you and you're about to go through . . ."

"Will you shut up for two seconds?" she said. "I want to say thank you."

"Oh," he said, heat rushing to his cheeks. "I just thought you were doing that 'being difficult' thing that you do."

"Whatever," Freddie said with a slight smile on her lips. "I'm not difficult."

"And the sun doesn't shine," Cleveland quipped. "If I can take you back to the night of Lillian's rehearsal dinner?"

"Please, you were being an ass. All you did was complain about missing a pep rally."

"You don't understand how much I love football," he said. "And it's not often that the Falcons are playoff bound. Besides, with all of those bridesmaids looking at me like I was going to be their ticket to a trip down the aisle it was just too much. Besides, my plan was to attend the wedding, not the rehearsal dinner."

"Uh-huh. You loved every minute of it. Never have I seen a man strut around the way you did that night."

Cleveland leaned back in the booth with his arms folded across his chest. "Do you really want to go back to that night? Go on and admit that you were fighting how bad you wanted all of this."

"Wanted to deck you."

Chuckling, he reached across the table and stroked her arm. "We both know you wanted more than that. When you walked over to me that night, it took my breath away and then you started talking. So beautiful, yet so bitter."

Freddie balled up a napkin and tossed it at Cleveland. "Whatever. Lillian really had it in for you. She really thought you had a night of debauchery planned for her man."

"All I wanted was a night of debauchery with you. Especially when you tried to pretend that you didn't want me."

"I wasn't pretending, I didn't want you then," she said with a smile on her lips. "But now is a totally different story."

"Is that so?" he asked with a wide grin on his face.

Raising her right eyebrow, Freddie returned his smile. "It is."

He waved for the waitress and then said, "I suggest that we order the special and get the hell out of here."

Chapter 22

After eating their meal, Cleveland and Freddie couldn't get back to Atlanta fast enough. He drove at a neck-breaking rate making the two-and-a-half-hour trip in about an hour and forty-five minutes. As they pulled into his driveway and exited the car, Freddie remarked, "You're lucky we didn't get stopped by the police."

"Well, had the officer taken one look at you, he would've understood."

She playfully swatted his shoulder. "And just what would you have said to the officer?"

Cleveland pulled her against his body. "It's a man thing, you wouldn't understand if I told you." Gently, he brushed his lips against her neck. "Let me get your bags."

Freddie slipped her hands in the front pockets of his jeans. "My bags aren't going to grow legs and walk out of your car. Besides, there's something else you need to do first."

His body responded to her hot words and gentle touch. "What would that be?" he asked, his lips close to her ear. She wrapped her legs around his waist and Cleveland cupped her ample bottom.

"I could tell you or you could carry me inside and I can show you," she said before leaning in to kiss his lips.

Cleveland couldn't get Freddie in the house fast enough. With one hand, he secured Freddie around his waist and unlocked the front door with the other one. Crossing the threshold, Cleveland kicked the door closed and then captured Freddie's lips, kissing her with an urgent hunger. She returned his kiss, thrusting her tongue into his mouth and probing the depth of it. A soft moan escaped his throat as his groin tightened in anticipation. Backing against the wall, Cleveland ripped her shirt open and Freddie grabbed at the waistband of his jeans. She dropped one leg from around his waist and planted her foot on the ground as he kissed her neck. Soft moans escaped her throat as his lips traveled down to her collarbone and across the tops of her breasts. With nimble fingers, she unbuttoned and unzipped his pants. Cleveland's hardness spilled out of his boxers and Freddie stroked him as he continued to kiss her breasts.

"Umm, I need you," she moaned. "Need you inside."

Cleveland ripped his mouth away from her breasts. He didn't have to tell her that he needed to bury himself inside her and forget that they'd ever been apart. Scooping her up in his arms, Cleveland headed upstairs to his bedroom, taking two steps at a time. Once he got into the room, he laid Freddie on the bed and looked at her for a moment. She was a thing of beauty with her hair fanned out on the pillow and her eyes filled with a combination of love and lust. When she sucked her bottom lip in, Cleveland grew harder and hotter. He stripped her clothes from her body, kissing each inch of skin that he exposed.

Freddie writhed underneath his touch, his kisses heated her body up like an inferno. She reached for his pants, but Cleveland grabbed her hand. "I want to take my time with you," he said. He kissed her flat stomach, using his tongue to slide down to her heated core. Gently, Cleveland spread her thighs apart and buried his face between them and lapped her womanly juices. She seized the back of his neck, pressing him to go deeper, to taste more of her. He obliged her, deepening his kiss and wrapping his tongue around her throbbing bud. Intense waves of pleasure rippled through her body causing her legs to tremble. Freddie arched her back, pressing her hips into his mouth as her breasts heaved and her nipples hardened like diamonds. Cleveland alternated his finger and his tongue inside her, nearly bringing her to climax. Freddie hadn't noticed that Cleveland had disrobed until she felt his thick hardness against her thighs. Covering her body with his, he kissed her, allowing her to taste the saltiness of herself. Freddie drew his tongue deeper into her mouth, silently telling him how urgently she needed him. Cleveland slipped his hand between her thighs as they kissed and stroked her core until she cried out.

"Need. You. Inside," she said, her breathing labored.

"Wait," he whispered against her ear. "I have to protect you."

Cleveland reached in his nightstand drawer and pulled out a condom. Freddie watched him as he slid the sheath in place. Would it be horrible if they had a child together? She knew that she'd be a better parent than her mother or her father had been to her. *What am I thinking? He probably doesn't even want to have children and why would anyone want to get involved with my crazy family?*

"Are you all right?" Cleveland asked when he noticed how quiet she was and the frown on her face.

"Yeah," she said, her voice far off. "I'm fine."

He eased into the bed beside her and wrapped his arms around her. "Talk to me," he whispered as he stroked her forearm.

"This feels so easy, so right, but it can't always be like this."

He rolled Freddie on top of him and brushed his lips against hers. "Why not? This thing between us is only as difficult as you make it," he said.

She rolled her hips against his and Cleveland groaned. "There you go with the 'd' word again," she said as she guided his hardness to her wetness. He gripped her hips as she tightened herself around him. They rocked back and forth, their conversation saved for another time. Freddie threw her head back in ecstasy as Cleveland matched her stroke for stroke.

"You feel so-so good," she cried as she gripped the sheets while they ground their bodies against each other. Cleveland wanted to speak, wanted to describe how good it felt inside her hot valley, but he was rendered speechless when she gyrated her hips like a trained belly dancer and brought him nearer to his climax.

Freddie handled his body like no other woman ever could, she knew where to kiss him, how to ride him and what drove him wild. Grabbing her back, he flipped her over and dove deeper into her wetness, causing her to cry out his name. They fell into an intense rhythm, pushing and pulling each other to dizzying heights of pleasure. Cleveland slowed his pace as he felt the eruption of an orgasm building in his belly. But Freddie wouldn't slow down. She tightened her grip around his waist with her legs and ground against him with wanton desire. Sweat covered their bodies as their dance continued. Freddie closed her eyes, reveling in the powerful sensations attacking her nervous system.

Grunting, Cleveland was no longer able to hold off his climax and he exploded inside her. Shivering, Freddie collapsed on his chest, smiling and satisfied. Cleveland wrapped his arms around her and kissed her forehead. There was no need for words because their hearts were beating in sync. Freddie closed her eyes and silently admitted to herself that Cleveland Alexander was her soul mate.

The shrill ringing of Cleveland's cell phone woke him and Freddie around three A.M.

Cleveland tumbled out of bed and grabbed the phone. "Yeah?"

"Where are you?" Darren asked.

"Was in bed. On the floor now. What's wrong?"

"I hope you're back in Atlanta, because we had a man go down tonight," Darren said solemnly.

"Who was it?" Cleveland asked, now fully awake.

"Roland. He's in intensive care. About three hours ago, we were working a fire in a warehouse and the roof collapsed. He was inside and we couldn't get him out before the collapse. He's in bad shape. As much as we teased him, Roland's a good man."

Cleveland cursed and rubbed the bridge of his nose. "Where is he?"

"Grady. He had burns on eighty percent of his body, inhaled a lot of smoke," Darren said with a heavy sigh. "I'm going to need you to come to the station in the morning. Sorry if you didn't get to win your woman back yet, but . . ."

"I'll be there. I'm back in town," Cleveland said.

"Thanks."

"It's times like this when we have to come together. Were you there?"

"Yeah," Darren said. "This is the first time that I've been at a fire and was scared. I have to think about my little girl, I don't want her growing up without me. I got an offer to be moved up to the arson investigations unit. After tonight, I'm seriously considering it."

Cleveland didn't know what to say, though he understood what his brother was feeling. Still, he couldn't imagine working without Darren. "Do you think this is a decision to make while you're so emotional?" he asked.

"Jill's been pushing me to do it," Darren said. "And you know who's been backing her up on it."

"Well, if you take this job the next thing Mom is going to do . . ." Cleveland said.

"Push me to hire you. She's been trying to get us out of the fire service since the day we went to the academy," Darren said with a low chuckle. "I guess it's times like this when I can understand where she's coming from."

Cleveland shot a glance at Freddie and wondered if she would understand the life of a firefighter and the dangers that went along with it. She'd lost so much in her life, was it fair to bring her into his life when he faced death and danger on every call? "Yeah," he finally said. "I know what you mean."

"So, did you find her and plead your case?"

"Yeah, I sure did." A slow smile spread across his lips as Freddie shifted in the bed and the sheet dropped from her chest and exposed her breasts. As her chest rose and fell, Cleveland felt a warm feeling spread across his body and he wanted to wrap his arms around her and never let her go.

"Is she there now?" Darren asked.

"Yeah, she is."

"Well, I'll be damned. How did you swing that?"

"I can't even get into that right now," Cleveland said as he crawled back into bed. "What time do you want me to come in?"

"I'd love to say six, but I'll deal with eight," Darren

said. "I'm going to head back to the hospital for awhile then I'm going home to kiss my baby."

"See you in a couple of hours," Cleveland said then snapped his phone shut. As he wrapped his arms around Freddie, her eyes fluttered open. "Did I wake you?"

Freddie snuggled closer to him. "Yeah," she said. "Is everything all right?"

"One of the men from our station was injured in a fire. Times like this always make us think of our father. Darren is even thinking about going into the Fire Marshal's office for arson investigations because he doesn't want his daughter growing up without him."

"I can understand that. It's really admirable that he wants to be there with his child. Too bad I can't say that either one of my parents did the same thing." A lone tear slid down her cheek. "I'm not going to think about that." Cleveland wiped her cheek with his thumb.

"Whenever you want to talk about it, I'm willing to listen," he said, kissing the track of her tear.

"Thanks. I guess you'd better go to sleep since you have to work, right?"

Cleveland nodded. "Yeah, I'm going to have to go into the station and pick up the slack. It's a good thing I didn't have to do much talking to get you to come back with me."

"Whatever," she said. "You provided an escape plan."

"Are you saying it could've been anyone that you would've left with? Yeah, right," Cleveland said then tickled her underneath the covers. "You know you wanted to come with me."

"And I did, several times," she quipped.

Cleveland pulled her on top of him. "I can make it happen again," he said.

Spreading her legs apart, Freddie smiled and said, "Don't talk about it, be about it."

Chapter 23

The next morning, Cleveland struggled to pull himself out of Freddie's arms and head to work. But she pushed him out of bed.

"Don't let me be the cause of you losing your job," she said. "You get in the shower and I'll start some coffee."

Cleveland groaned as he glanced at the clock. It was ten minutes after five. "All right," he said as he rolled out of bed. As he walked into the bathroom, Freddie grabbed Cleveland's T-shirt, put it on and headed downstairs to brew him some coffee and scramble a few eggs. While she cooked, Freddie thought about her situation. She didn't have a job, she wasn't going back to New Orleans and she couldn't live off Cleveland. Maybe Lillian would help her find a job somewhere in Atlanta.

Lillian isn't going to be happy about Cleveland and me being together, but she's going to have to get over it, she thought as she heard Cleveland walking down the stairs. *I think I love this man.*

"Breakfast and coffee? Don't get me used to this, I may never let you leave," he said as he walked up behind her and wrapped his arms around her waist.

"Don't get used to it," she said as she turned around and kissed him on the tip of his nose. "I'm not a morning person and hopefully I'll be employed soon."

"So, you're going to make Atlanta home?"

"For a while, I guess," she said. "I don't want to go back to New Orleans right now, especially with all of that stuff going on with my family."

"When do you want to move your stuff in?"

Freddie crinkled her nose. "Move my stuff in? Cleveland, I don't want to be dependant on anyone, including you. I've got to make my own way."

He sighed as he dropped his hands from around her waist. "Dare I say it?"

"Say what?"

"That you're being difficult again?"

Freddie threw her head back and groaned. "Cleveland, eat these eggs before you end up wearing them."

"You're just not used to someone helping you out, are you? You don't have to live here forever. Do you even know how much a decent place in Atlanta is going to run you?"

"So, I haven't thought this whole thing out," she said as she walked over to the stove and moved the pan with the eggs in it from the burner. "But, you have to let me do this my way. I'll stay here for a few weeks, but I am going to get my own place, all right?"

Cleveland raised his hand in mock salute. "Yes, ma'am."

"Good, now get some plates so that we can eat and you can make it to work."

He glanced down at his watch. "Um, I'm just going to have time for coffee on the run. I want to head to the hospital before I go into the station."

She poured him a mug of java and kissed him on the cheek. "Have a good day," she said. "And be careful."

Cleveland winked at her and headed out the door with

his coffee in his hand. Before he left, he told Freddie that she could use his truck if she needed to go somewhere and that the keys were in the utility drawer in the kitchen.

When he was gone, Freddie leaned against the kitchen counter questioning what her next move should be. Maybe she could live with Cleveland until she found something more permanent. But Freddie was scared, afraid that loving him would lead to heartbreak. Even though he'd offered safety, love and support, there was still a part of her that was waiting for the other shoe to drop. There was no way she could be happy, especially when her past showed her that it's always the ones who love you the most that lie to you and break your heart.

Freddie cleaned the kitchen after eating some of the eggs and toast she'd cooked, then headed upstairs to take a long hot bath. As she luxuriated in the oversized tub in the master bathroom, Freddie closed her eyes and wished that she was still on her pleasure trip with Cleveland and they were upstairs in the bed making love this morning. Just as she was about to drift off to sleep, the loud chiming of her cell phone jarred her awake. Freddie sprang from the tub, wrapped herself in a towel and dashed into the bedroom where her phone was. She grabbed it without looking at the caller identification. "Hello?"

"Chere, I'm a free man," Jacques said happily. "Well, save for the electronic bracelet on my leg. But now that I don't have to go back to prison until a new trial is ordered, I can finally clear my name."

"Am I supposed to rejoice because one parent is free and another one is on her way to prison?" Freddie asked sarcastically.

"Your mother may not even go to prison. Can you really blame me for wanting to clear my name?" he asked. "I'm innocent. Sure, I made some bad decisions, but I gave up my life for your mother. The least she could do is be honest about her role in the whole thing."

"Maybe you're innocent of murder, but from what I understand, you set all of this in motion, didn't you Dad?"

Jacques chuckled. "Then your mother got to you first, huh? I really did love your mother, she was the one who thought I had an ulterior motive for marrying her."

"So, this war with you and Nolan Watson had nothing to do with you getting Mom pregnant?"

"At first, I wanted to be with her because he loved her and I wanted him to crumble. You don't understand how hard it was for us after my mother died and he wouldn't pay out the insurance policy that she'd been paying for all of those years."

"That doesn't make it right. I don't really want to hear your spin on this," she said. "I guess between your story and Mom's the truth is in there somewhere."

"The truth is, your mother and I made mistakes and . . ."

"And I paid for it," Freddie said. "That's the one thing that you and Mom don't seem to understand. I needed both of you."

"Chere . . ."

"Don't give me that 'chere' bullshit! While you and Loraine played games, I was suffering. I needed a father and a mother who could protect me. I grew up in a city where I couldn't tell anyone who my father was because everyone hated him. My mother would never tell me about you and I walked around my entire life feeling as if part of me was missing."

"What do you want me to do? I can't change the past. We're going to have to find a way to get past it or . . ."

"Or maybe I should pretend that I don't have parents. I have to go," Freddie said then clicked her phone off. She tossed the phone against the pillow and exhaled loudly.

She couldn't accept one version of what happened without wondering if she was being lied to by one of her parents. Since she couldn't unravel the mystery herself, she was going to have to put it behind her and move on.

Once she calmed down from her father's phone call, she dressed and headed for Lillian's. She knew that this was going to be another argument, but she felt as if this was the time to get it over with.

Cleveland sat back on the leather sofa in the lounge area of the fire station and closed his eyes. He'd been at work for three hours after stopping by the hospital to visit Roland. Seeing his buddy in that hospital bed with all those tubes and machines hooked up to him, affected Cleveland in a way that he hadn't expected. Much like Darren, he was beginning to question if he wanted to continue to be on the front lines of firefighting. He'd already faced death and won. But would he be that lucky again if he was in Roland's shoes?

"Hey man, you're not falling asleep already are you?" Louis asked when he walked into the lounge area.

"Nah, I'm just thinking," he said.

"About?"

"Life, Freddie, Roland."

"Freddie? Aw, shit," Louis said as he took a seat on the end of the sofa. "What's up with you and that chick? And think before you answer that, because whatever is going on with you two has an effect on my marriage."

"What?"

"Lillian doesn't want you two together."

"It really doesn't matter what Lillian wants. Freddie and I are adults."

"Uh-huh, I wish someone would tell my wife that," he

said. "She seems to think that she's Freddie protector and I've never understood that."

"I can," Cleveland said. "Freddie's been through a lot, but Lillian needs to mind her own business."

Louis nodded in agreement. "Well, at least Freddie's tucked away in New Orleans and I don't have to worry about . . ."

"Well, that's not exactly true," Cleveland said. "Freddie came back to Atlanta with me yesterday."

"What? Are you kidding me? All right, Cle, tell me the truth, are you in love with her?"

"I love her more than I thought I would ever love a woman. She's different. She's more than I ever thought I wanted. You know how you just feel that something is right and your life isn't going to be complete until you make sure that you have that person with you?"

Louis's right eyebrow shot up and he peered at his friend. "Who are you and what have you done with Cleveland Alexander?"

"This is me, man. Isn't this what you and Darren have been trying to get me to see? How many times have you all talked about how great love and marriage is? Now that I've found someone I want to spend my life with, you want to have my head examined?"

Louis rolled his eyes. "Whatever," he said. "Just make sure that this is what you want and you're really ready to commit."

Cleveland sat there silently for a moment. He'd never thought about committing to one woman, never thought about spending the rest of his life with one woman and never making love to anyone else. That is until he met Freddie. He was ready, he was ready to commit to her, but was he ready to be a husband?

"Cleveland?" Louis asked. "Are you ready?"

He exhaled loudly. "Yeah, I'm ready. I've never felt this way before. Man, I drove all the way to New Orleans to get my woman. Do you think I would've done that if I wanted a playmate? There are enough of those in Atlanta and trust me, it was fun but I want more."

"More what?" Darren asked as he entered the lounge with a dozen Krispy Kreme doughnuts and three cups of coffee.

"More Freddie," Louis said. "Is this breakfast?"

"Yeah, it's a tribute to Roland," Darren said as he set the items on the coffee table. "I was at headquarters meeting with the chief. He said that we're going to get a few more men in here."

"Great," Cleveland said as he picked up a cup of coffee. "When is this going to happen?"

Darren sighed. "Right after you guys get a new battalion chief. I was offered a position with the Fire Marshal's office for arson investigations."

"What?" Cleveland and Louis said simultaneously.

"It's not official, so I'd appreciate it if you two keep this under wraps for a while," Darren said. "But, I have a family I have to think about these days. I won't be any good to you all if I'm worried about going in to back you guys up because I don't want to get hurt."

Cleveland stood up and walked over to his brother, clasped his hand on his shoulder and nodded. "I understand, but I can't say that I'm happy about it."

"You will be."

"Why?"

"Because you may be promoted," Darren said.

"What? Why me?" Cleveland asked.

Louis laughed. "Duh. Your last name is Alexander. You guys are AFD royalty. Your life is just changing at every turn, huh?"

"Life changing? Ah," Darren said as he opened the box of doughnuts and pulled out a chocolate-covered one. "This is about Freddie."

Cleveland smiled and sipped his coffee. "This is about Freddie and how much I love her."

Darren nearly choked on his doughnut, and Louis patted him on the back. "Love?" Darren said. "Did I just hear you?"

"Since you married Jill, you've been trying to shove love down my throat. Now I tell you that I'm in love, and you're choking."

"It's just that you and love don't exactly go together," Darren said then chuckled. "What did that woman do to you?"

"Must be voodoo," Louis quipped.

"Oh, so that's how Lillian got you?" Cleveland asked.

"Ha, ha," Louis said as he reached for a doughnut. "I love my wife and it has nothing to do with voodoo."

Before the men could say anything else, a fire call blared over the PA system. The pastries were forgotten as they ran to get their gear and head to the call.

"Freddie, what are you doing here?" Lillian asked when she opened the front door.

"I'm finally taking your advice," she said as she and her friend embraced.

"What advice is that?"

"I'm starting over in Atlanta."

Lillian stepped back from Freddie and eyed her suspiciously. "Hmmm, I've been trying to get you to move here since you told me that the hurricane destroyed your house. This wouldn't have anything to do with Cleveland, would it?"

Freddie smiled. "Well, he's part of the reason," she said. "But it's more than that."

"More? Are you pregnant?!"

"No, drama queen. Can we sit down and talk?"

Lillian stepped aside and Freddie walked into the living room then took a seat on the sofa. "All right," Lillian said. "What's this 'more'?"

"My parents." Freddie closed her eyes and leaned back on the plush sofa. She told Lillian the sorted story of the murder her mother finally admitted to, the revenge plot that set everything in motion, and the media frenzy that was building around the sordid case.

"Ooh," Lillian said. "I think I would've come here too. But from one sordid case to this sordid man. If you're going to be living in Atlanta, then you need to know that Cleveland Alexander isn't the man you need to be planning to make your life with. You should let me introduce you to some nice men that go to church with Louis and me. There is this one brother that . . ."

"Lillian, stop."

"Stop what?" Lillian said. "I'm just trying to look out for you, I mean, you're my best friend and I love you too much to allow . . ."

"All right, Lillian. Stop. Seriously. I love Cleveland and you're about two seconds away from getting cursed out. No one stopped you from being with the man you love and I'll be damned if I allow you to try and do that to me." Freddie rose to her feet. "You know, you have this nasty habit of trying to make decisions for other people."

"What?"

"Oh, don't 'what' me. If people don't do things your way, you don't think they're living their lives right."

"You think I'm that judgmental?" Lillian asked, her voice filled with shock.

"I love you like a sister, but yes, you are judgmental," Freddie said in a calmer voice.

"I'm only looking out for you. I know what kind of man Cleveland Alexander is, and he's going to hurt you."

Freddie closed her eyes and shook her head. "You don't know what kind of man Cleveland is and that's what is so maddening about your irrational dislike of him. But you know, it doesn't matter how you feel about him because I love him."

"And you loved Marcus, too. How did that work out for you?" Lillian's words stung like a slap to the face.

"Go to hell, Lillian," Freddie snapped. "Just because you snagged Louis, that doesn't make you some love expert. You know what, I'm going to leave before I say something I'll regret later."

"Winfred," Lillian called out as Freddie stormed out the front door. "I'm sorry."

Freddie didn't look back because she wasn't interested in Lillian's apology. In the back of her mind, she always felt as if Lillian and her mother had a superiority complex when it came to her family. She knew that was why their mothers stopped being so close all of those years ago. Though she didn't want the same thing to happen with Lillian and her, she wasn't going to let her friend tell her who she was supposed to love. When her cell phone rang, Freddie had no doubt who it was.

"What?" she snapped.

"Freddie, I'm sorry," Lillian said.

"You should be," she said, not giving her friend a break.

"But you have to understand that I'm just trying to look out for you."

"It certainly feels like a judgment to me. I don't need that from you. I'm starting my life over from scratch, again. If you're not going to be in my corner, then just leave me alone."

"Fine, but when he breaks your heart, who are you going to turn to?"

Freddie clicked her phone off and tossed it on the seat beside her. She wished that she knew how to get to the fire station so that Cleveland could wrap his arms around her and tell her that everything would be all right. If he said it, she would believe it.

Chapter 24

Cleveland and Louis rolled the fire hoses in after successfully knocking down the apartment fire without any injuries. Their minds were on Roland as they hopped into the truck and headed back to the station. Why hadn't the last fire been so simple? Cleveland stared out of the window and heard his mother's voice telling Darren and him that her life would be a lot easier if she didn't have to worry about them dying in a fire every day.

Still, he couldn't leave the fire department. It was in his blood and if his accident didn't cause him to want to give up his job, why was he questioning it now? Still, knowing that his brother wasn't going to have his back and he was going to be the man that everyone depended on at the fire station gave him a queasy feeling. He couldn't have these kinds of doubts and expect to do his job well.

"You're quiet over there," Louis said.

"Just thinking about what Darren said earlier and about Roland."

Louis nodded. "And Freddie?"

Cleveland smiled and looked away from his friend. "I'm always thinking about her lately."

"That voodoo that she do, done got you," Louis sang off key. "What are Freddie's plans? Is she moving here or will she be going back to New Orleans?"

"It looks as if she's going to be staying here, but you know how she is, she wants to do everything her way. Doesn't want to be helped or anything."

"That's the Freddie I know. Maybe Lillian can learn a little bit of her independence. I don't know if I can deal with this happy homemaker routine of hers much longer."

Cleveland slapped him on the shoulder. "You knew she wasn't going to work when you married Ms. High Maintenance."

"You don't like my wife, do you?"

"It's the other way around. She doesn't like me. I guess I shouldn't have given her such a hard time when you two were dating. You know women don't forget things like that."

Louis nodded. "Guess you two are going to have to get along now because you're in love with her best friend."

"Well, tell her that she needs to let go of the past. We can have a dinner party or something and kiss and make up."

Louis laughed. "I don't know if I want you kissing my wife."

"Trust me, Freddie is the only woman I really want to kiss," he quipped.

When they arrived at the fire station, Cleveland called Freddie at his house to see if she was all right.

"Hello?" she said when she answered the phone.

"How are you, beautiful?"

"Fine," she said flatly.

"You don't sound fine," he said. "Did something happen?"

"Lillian and I had a disagreement today," she said. "But it's nothing. How's your day been?"

"Just one fire, so far. Louis and I are going to see Roland later, but I was wondering if you wanted to meet for a latte."

"Um, huh," she said, her voice sounded distracted.

"Are you sure that you're all right?" Cleveland asked.

"I guess. Cleveland, I'm sorry, you asked me if I wanted to go to get something to eat, right."

"Yeah, but if you need to talk, then I'll listen. What happened with Lillian?"

She sighed into the phone and told him about the argument that she and her friend had.

"She'll get over it," Cleveland said.

"I hope so," Freddie said. "I don't understand why she thinks that she can live my life better than I can."

"Babe, I don't know," he said. "But you can't worry about what Lillian thinks. She's going to have her opinions and you don't have to deal with that."

"She should be happy for me, you know. I'm starting my life over and she's been trying to get me here since Hurricane Katrina happened. Now that I'm here, all she can do is complain about me and you."

"That's funny, because Louis and I were just talking about going out to dinner."

"It doesn't seem like that's going to happen any time soon," Freddie said. "I have to find a job."

"Why don't I call Jill and see if she can . . ."

"No," she said. "I don't want you calling in favors for me, I need to make my own way."

"I'm going to start calling you Miss Difficult."

"Cleveland, let's not have the same argument. I've never depended on anyone before and I'm not going to start now. Are we eating or what?"

"Sure. Do you want me to pick you up?"

"How long will it take you to get home? I'll cook something special for you."

"If you keep spoiling me like this, then we're going to have to make this arrangement last a little longer."

"Don't say that. You make me think you want to get married or something," she joked.

"Would that be such a bad thing?" Cleveland asked.

"Don't talk like that unless you mean it."

"Who said I didn't?"

"Bye, Cleveland," she said then hung up the phone.

Once he closed his cell phone and grabbed his radio, he turned to Louis and told him that he was going to dine with Freddie. "I'll be back in a few hours," he said with a wide grin on his face.

"That voodoo that she do," Louis sang at Cleveland's retreating figure.

Freddie was putting the finishing touches on blackened chicken breasts, brown rice and cabbage when Cleveland walked through the door.

"Smells really good in here," he called out.

"I'm in the kitchen," she said. "The food is almost ready."

He walked into the kitchen and encircled Freddie's waist then kissed her on the neck. She wanted to melt against him and forget about the reason why he'd come home in the first place. He kissed her again and pulled her closer to him.

"I've been thinking about this all day," he said, then flicked his tongue across her neck. "Will the food be as tasty?"

Freddie pushed away from him. "Not if you distract me and I burn my rice."

Cleveland took a seat on one of the bar stools and watched her cook. "I guess I can taste the cook later, huh?"

"That's mighty presumptuous of you," she said then winked at him. "Have you gone to see your friend again?"

"Nope. There have been a lot of changes going on at the station. Darren's going to take a job in the fire marshal's office and I'm going to become the new battalion chief."

"Really?" Freddie said. "That's a good thing, isn't it?"

Cleveland shrugged as Freddie began to spoon rice and cabbage on a plate for him. "When I think about why Darren's leaving, it makes me wonder if he has a point."

"Why is he leaving?" she asked as she placed a chicken breast on his plate.

"He doesn't want to end up like our father. He has a family to think about and every call we go out on, we're putting our lives on the line," Cleveland said.

"What about you?"

"What do you mean?"

"Do you want to give it up too?" She turned her back to him and tried not to think about what losing him would do to her. Though she was trying to remain independent, it was too late. She was getting used to the security Cleveland provided. Used to his touch, his kiss and the beat of his heart when she lay against him at night.

"In the past I've wavered on staying or going into the fire marshal's office, but with this promotion coming up, how can I leave?"

She fixed her plate and joined him at the bar. "I guess you can't," she said.

Cleveland eyed her as she cut into her chicken. "Do you think you're going to be able to deal?"

"Deal?"

"With me being in the fire service. Never knowing what each day is going to bring."

Freddie shrugged her shoulders. "That's true with anything. It's not like I grew up in a crystal tower. But I can't say that I'm not going to be worried every time you walk out the door."

Cleveland stroked her cheek. "You're going to make a brother think you got love for him."

She smiled but couldn't quite bring herself to say the words. "Well, it's true," she said.

"What's true? That you love me or you're going to be worried?"

"Why don't you eat before your food gets cold?" she said, desperately wanting to change the subject.

Cleveland smiled as he spooned some rice into his mouth.

Just tell him, she thought as she watched his lips close around the fork. *Tell that man how you feel.*

"How's the food?" she asked.

"Good," he said. "But I believe that the cook tastes a lot better."

Freddie tossed a balled up napkin at him. "You're so wicked," she said, then dropped her fork against her plate. "Want to find out?"

He dropped his fork, turned to Freddie and scooped her up off the stool. Hungrily, he captured her lips, kissing her until she was breathless: Freddie wrapped her arms around his neck and plunged her tongue into his mouth. A soft moan escaped her throat and heat spread throughout her body as Cleveland's hands stroked her back.

He pulled back and smiled at her. "Delicious. But we'd better stop."

"Why?"

"I'm on call and the last thing I want to do is start something that we can't stop," he said then quickly pecked her on the lips.

Freddie groaned. "That's messed up."

"Want to come back to the station with me? There is this room where we can have all the privacy in the world, no matter who's in the station," Cleveland said.

"You talk as if you've used this place before," she teased.

"I plead the fifth," he replied with a wide smile. "Come on, let me show you my world and more."

She smiled at him and kissed him on the cheek.

"Let's do it," she said as she hopped out of his arms.

Freddie followed Cleveland in the truck to the fire station and she didn't know what she was more excited about, seeing where Cleveland worked or being naughty with him in the fire station.

They dashed down I-285 at a breakneck speed. As they got closer to downtown Atlanta, traffic was pretty much at a stand still. Freddie had almost forgotten that every hour in Atlanta was some sort of rush hour.

The moment they arrived at the station, Cleveland hopped out of his car, with his cell phone in his hand. He rushed inside, not saying anything to Freddie, who stood near his truck with a puzzled look on her face. What had the phone call been about, she wondered. Seconds later he was back outside. "That was about Roland," he told her as he ushered her inside. "He's taken a turn for the worse. We're going to the hospital."

"Do you want me to drive you?"

Cleveland nodded. Freddie noticed that he was trembling and his eyes were wet with unshed tears. She stroked his cheek gently, unsure as to what she should say to him. Somehow it didn't seem proper to say, "everything will be all right," when it looked otherwise.

Darren and Louis bolted out of the station house and hopped into the battalion chief car then sped out of the lot. Freddie struggled to keep up with Darren as he weaved in and out of traffic. Cleveland gripped his seat belt as Freddie drove, but he didn't comment on her driving. She glanced at him and saw that he was whispering a prayer.

Once they arrived at the hospital, there were about twelve other firefighters in the lobby with tear-stained cheeks.

"No," Cleveland whispered.

A man with a white shirt walked over to him and Darren. "I'm sorry," he said.

"Chief," Darren said, his voice choked up with emotion.

"He passed away about fifteen minutes ago," the fire chief said.

Tears flowed freely from Darren, Louis, and Cleveland. Freddie reached up and caressed Cleveland's arm, but he didn't seem to feel her touch.

Louis shook his head. "This is unbelievable. He's gone, but Roland . . ."

The three men fell silent as the other firefighters offered their condolences. Freddie backed away from the group and watched the moments between the men. Closing her eyes, she thought about being on the other side of those handshakes. She didn't know how she would be able to handle this. But on the other hand, she never knew how connected the firefighters were. It really was a brotherhood and a family. Something that she'd never had.

"Louis!" Lillian cried out as she burst into the waiting room. She flung herself into her husband's arms. "Baby, are you all right? I couldn't believe it when you called from the car."

"No, I can't believe Roland's gone," he said in a hoarse voice.

She held his face in her hands. "I know." Lillian turned to Cleveland and Darren. "Are you guys all right?"

They stared at her with blank expressions. Freddie walked over to Cleveland and tapped him on the shoulder. "I'm going to get you a cup of coffee."

Lillian nodded. "That's a good idea. I'll come with you."

"That's all right," Freddie snapped.

Lillian grabbed Freddie's arm and whispered in her ear, "Even if you're pissed with me, this isn't the time for us to fight."

"I'm not fighting with you," Freddie said. "But I'm not going to pretend that we're best friends either."

"This right here isn't about us."

"So, why are you trying to make it that way?" Freddie asked. "I'm here for my man because he just lost a friend."

"Not just a friend, but a brother and my husband is hurting too," Lillian said.

"I know that, Lillian," Freddie said calmly. "I'm going to get coffee, if you're coming let's go because the last thing that any of us need is for you to start with your dramatics."

Lillian shook her head and followed Freddie to the elevator. "Okay, I was wrong," she relented when they stepped on the elevator.

"Did I hear you correctly?" Freddie said sarcastically. "You're admitting that you're wrong?"

"Yes. Who am I to tell you that you can't love Cleveland? I don't have to like him, but it's your life."

Freddie smiled at her friend. "I'm glad you came to your senses because I really thought I was going to have to kick your butt."

Lillian hugged her friend. "How long have you been my sister? You really think I was going to let that dude come between us?"

"I'd hope not," Freddie said as she squeezed her friend back.

Lillian sighed. "They're going to need us, now. They ribbed on Roland a lot, but they loved him."

"How do you deal? Every day that Louis walks out that door, you don't know if he's coming back," Freddie said as they stepped off the elevator and headed for the hospital cafeteria.

"It's a struggle. But I knew what I was getting into when I fell in love with a firefighter."

I didn't know it was going to be like this, Freddie thought as she and Lillian ordered enough coffee for all of the men in the lobby. *I don't want to lose Cleveland.*

After getting the coffee and some cream and sugar, the women headed back to the waiting room. Cleveland, Darren and Louis were joined by more firefighters and Jill. Freddie passed the coffee cups to the men who wanted them. Then she took a seat beside Cleveland, who looked as if he was deep in thought.

"I got you some coffee," Freddie said quietly.

Cleveland took the cup from her hands and set it on a table beside the chair where he was sitting and then he drew her into his arms. He didn't say a word, but after a while, Freddie felt warm tears seep through her blouse. She rocked back and forth, kissing Cleveland's forehead.

"I-I can't even remember the last thing I said to him," he said. "He was doing me a favor, you know. Covering my shift for me because . . ." Cleveland's voice trailed off.

"Because you were in New Orleans looking for me," she said quietly.

He cast his eyes upward at her but didn't reply to her statement. Freddie exhaled and closed her eyes to hide her tears. Though she wouldn't dare say it, Freddie wondered if Cleveland thought it should've been him trapped in that warehouse with people standing in the hospital mourning him. And she couldn't help but wonder if he blamed her.

Cleveland patted her thigh. "I don't regret coming to find you," he said.

"But . . ."

"No buts," he said. "We put our lives on the line every day, but you never want to see anyone go down."

"Is there anything I can do?"

Cleveland looked up at her, his eyes damp with unshed tears. "Just be here."

Darren and Jill walked over to the couple and Darren looked just as emotional as his brother. Jill seemed to be supporting her husband as they stood.

"Cleveland," she said quietly. "I'm so sorry."

Sniffing, he weakly smiled at his sister-in-law. "Thanks, J."

Jill stroked Darren's arm. "Remember the first time I met Roland?"

Both Darren and Cleveland chuckled, then said at the same time, "Halftime entertainment."

Freddie furrowed her brows. "Halftime entertainment?" she questioned.

Jill smiled. "These cavemen weren't used to having a woman come over and watch the game. Roland and Louis went on and on about how women didn't know anything about football."

"And let's not forget how you schooled him on those stats," Darren said. "He had a newfound respect for women who actually knew what a first down was."

Silence enveloped them as they had individual memories of Roland. "I've got to get out of here," Cleveland said, breaking the quiet. He rose to his feet and Freddie followed his lead.

"Cleveland," she called out as she rushed to catch up with him.

"Freddie, I need some air and I need to be alone for a minute, all right?" he said.

She stepped back and nodded. As he walked away from her, Freddie wondered if Cleveland was blaming himself or worse yet, her, for his friend's death.

Chapter 25

That night, Cleveland crawled into bed without saying a word to Freddie. She glanced at his somber frame, not knowing what to say to him or if she should say anything. Inching closer to him, she wrapped her arms around his waist.

"Cleveland," she whispered.

"Hum?"

"Are you all right?"

"Just tired," he said as he patted her hand.

"Is that all?" Freddie probed.

"Isn't that enough?" he said as he shrugged out of her embrace. "I just need to get some sleep, all right?"

Freddie dropped her hands from his waist and turned her back to him. She couldn't be angry with him because she knew that he was going through some difficult emotions with the loss of his friend. Still, she wanted to help, to do something to make him feel a little better. Right now, she just felt as if she was in the way. When she heard the slight sound of Cleveland snoring, Freddie crept from the bed and headed downstairs. She didn't know what she should do, should she leave him alone and let him deal with this on his own?

What if he thinks this is all my fault? Freddie opened the refrigerator and pulled out a bottle of water and nervously took a sip. It had been her insecurities and irrational dash to New Orleans that caused Cleveland to follow her and give up his shift. What if he'd been at that fire, would things have been different? Would Cleveland be dead or would he have been able to save Roland?

"Stop it," she whispered to herself. "The man is grieving." Setting the bottle of water on the bar, Freddie decided that she needed to be there for Cleveland in any way that he needed her, even if that meant giving him the space he needed to cope with his friend's death.

She crept back upstairs to the bedroom. Cleveland was still sleeping, seemingly unaware that Freddie had even left the bed. She gazed down at his slumbering frame and her heart swelled. She felt helpless to assist him or understand what he was going through. She pushed a stray loc from his forehead with a gentle touch so as not to wake him. Cleveland shifted in the bed, but didn't wake up. She walked over to the other side of the bed and eased back into place.

"Where did you go?" Cleveland asked as soon as her head hit the pillow.

"To get some water. I can't sleep."

"I hope you don't think I'm trying to shut you out or that I'm being an asshole, this is just hard for me."

Freddie inched closer to him as he turned around and faced her. "You know," he said, "Darren and I were there when my father died. It was bring your child to work day at our school and the call that came in was supposed to be routine. It was a small house fire that turned out to be more extensive when we got there. The men in my Dad's battalion secured me and Darren on the truck and they went to do their business. Then the explosion happened."

She stroked his cheek. "My goodness."

"It was the worst thing that a kid could ever see. But what made it worse was waiting in the hospital for the doctors to state the obvious. Darren and I knew Dad was dead the minute he was loaded into the ambulance." A lone tear trickled down Cleveland's cheek. "Anytime we go to a call, in the back of my mind, I'm thinking about that day."

"Why do you keep doing it?"

"Because there have been so many lives saved because of what we do. I wish that we could save everybody. But who saves the hero?" Cleveland wrapped his arms around Freddie and held her tightly.

"No one expects you to save the world," she whispered. "Your father and Roland died doing what they loved. I know it doesn't make it any easier."

He shook his head. "It's never easy. You think about things you said to him or stupid little arguments that you had that didn't make any sense in the grand scheme of things."

Freddie leaned in and kissed the tip of his nose. "People know that they are loved," she said. "Even when you argue with them."

"I know that, but it's still . . ." Cleveland became choked up with emotion. "Some times you say things that you want to take back and the sad thing is I can't even remember the last thing that I said to Roland."

Freddie held him tighter. "It's going to be all right," she whispered as she felt his warm tears on her shoulder.

It was hours before Freddie and Cleveland drifted off to sleep. But Cleveland didn't sleep soundly as he tossed and turned, waking Freddie up just as she'd drift off to sleep. Freddie wondered what was going on in his mind and what, if anything, she could do to help him through these trying times. Freddie slipped out of the bed again, heading into the bathroom to splash some water on her face. Maybe after the memorial service, Cleveland would come to terms with Roland's death and find some peace. Still, Freddie had a gnawing feeling that Cleveland blamed himself and her for Roland's death.

Morning came and Cleveland left the bed without Freddie knowing it. When she smelled coffee wafting though the air and felt the coolness of the cotton sheets where Cleveland had slept, she rose from the bed and headed down to the kitchen.

"Good morning," she said as Cleveland poured coffee into a mug.

"Did I wake you?" he asked as he pulled another mug out of the cupboard. "I noticed that you didn't get a lot of sleep last night."

"Neither did you," she said as she crossed over to him and took the mug of java that he offered.

"Well, it was either lie in bed and keep you up or come down here and make coffee."

Freddie dumped a few teaspoons of sugar in her coffee cup and looked up at Cleveland as he pulled down a box of bran flakes. "I can cook something, if you want," she offered.

"That's all right," he replied. "I'm going to eat a quick bite and head to the station to see what the plans are for Roland's memorial service."

"Do you want me to drive you?"

Cleveland clanked a bowl against the counter. "Freddie, I'm not an invalid. I don't need you babysitting me, I don't need you feeding me, and I don't need you driving me around."

She shrank away from the counter, tears welling up in her eyes. "Look, I'm just trying to be supportive and I don't know what to do," Freddie said, struggling to hold her emotions in check.

Cleveland closed his eyes and dropped his spoon in his bowl. "Freddie," he said. "I'm sorry." He crossed over to her and pulled her into his arms. "I'm not good at dealing with this. And lashing out at you is wrong."

She pushed out of his embrace. "I understand," she said, though she didn't.

"I'm glad you do, because I don't."

She flashed him a weak smile. "Everyone grieves differently, but I don't want to be your whipping boy."

"You won't be, but I need some space," he said. "If I'm quiet, let me be. I'm not shutting you out, but I have to deal with this my way."

Freddie nodded and fought back the urge to ask him if he was blaming her for what happened. "I'm going back to bed," she said.

"I'll be at the station," he said as she headed upstairs.

Cleveland drove aimlessly, not really wanting to go to the fire station. His thoughts were a muddled mess. What if he had waited a few days to go after Freddie? Would Roland still be alive? It was his shift that Roland had been called in to work. He knew the station had been facing a manpower shortage. He should've put the needs of the department ahead of his own selfish desires.

But you love her, you love Freddie and if you had been at that fire, you would've been distracted with thoughts of her. Still, you would've been there. You could've made a difference, couldn't you?

After an hour of riding up and down the Interstate, Cleveland finally headed for the station house. He wasn't surprised to see a couple of grief counselors talking to a number of the firefighters. Walking in, he headed directly for Darren's office and was surprised to see Jill and Darren embracing each other passionately. He started to back out of the office, when his brother spotted him.

"Cleveland," Darren said as he and Jill broke off their kiss. "What are you doing here?"

"Hey, man, I didn't mean to interrupt."

Jill crossed over to Cleveland and gave him a tight sisterly hug. "How are you doing, Cleveland?" she asked.

He shrugged, wishing that people would stop asking him how he was doing. What did they expect that he was going to say? *"My friend just died, but I'm doing great?"*

"You're here to talk to somebody?" Darren asked.

Cleveland frowned and shook his head. "I'm tired of talking."

Jill looked from Cleveland to Darren. "Babe," she said. "I'll see you at home."

"Kiss Kayla for me," he called as his wife walked out the door. Cleveland sat down across from his brother's desk and waited for Darren to close the door. When he turned to his brother, Darren had questions dancing in his eyes. "What's the real deal, man?"

"Meaning?"

"You're not scheduled to be here for six hours and you've never been one to hang out around the station. Is ever . . ."

"Don't finish that statement. Everything is not all right and it may never be again."

"No, I know what you're thinking," Darren said. "I've struggled with the same thing. Maybe I worked you all too hard and maybe I shouldn't have allowed you to go to New Orleans. But you know what, every call is a risk."

"Yeah, but what if I had been there that night? Roland would still be here . . ."

Darren placed his hands on his desk. "No, you can't say that. That could have been any one of us. We don't have a crystal ball and we can't see into the future."

"So, that's why you're jumping ship?"

"Here we go," Darren said. "I knew you had an issue

with me moving on. Do you think I want Kayla growing up like we did?"

"Ma did a hell of a job."

"I'm not saying she didn't, but I miss Dad every day and I don't want her to feel that."

Cleveland rolled his eyes, but he knew that what his brother said was true, because he'd had the same thoughts and feelings that Darren had about not having a father growing up.

"You're going to be leading this station," Darren said. "And you're going to lose men. How are you going to deal with it?"

"Maybe I'm not cut out to lead," Cleveland mumbled.

"What's that?" Darren asked.

"Nothing."

Darren leaned in toward his brother. "You need to speak with a counselor."

"Is that an order? Because I really don't feel like . . ."

"It is an order. I've even talked to a counselor. Trust me, it's going to help because no one on the outside really understands what we're going through."

Cleveland rose from his chair, not wanting to admit that he needed to get some things off his chest so that he could process his grief.

"How's Freddie?" Darren asked.

"What?"

"Your girlfriend. Please tell me that you haven't run her away with your attitude."

Not yet, he thought. "She's at home."

"That's another reason you need to talk to someone. Our women are great, but they don't understand what we're going through, no matter how much we explain it to them. That doesn't mean that we can shut them out," Darren said wisely.

"Maybe I will talk to someone," he said, replaying the

row with Freddie in his mind. Rising to his feet, Cleveland headed for the door, then he turned to his brother. "Do you wonder what would've happened if I had been here that night?"

Darren shook his head. "No, because I don't want to think that I could've lost two men that night. Louis and I only got out of there seconds before everything went to hell. Roland was right behind us, at least I thought he was. If you had been there, there would have been nothing I could've done to stop you from going back in that building to look for him. Just as I tried to get Roland on the radio, the warehouse collapsed and the flames rose even higher."

Cleveland closed his eyes and imagined the wooden beams falling on top of Roland. "He didn't have a chance, did he?"

Darren somberly shook his head. "We tried to save him, digging through the rubble, but then there was another collapse and . . ." His voice trailed off and his eyes watered.

Cleveland nodded and walked out the door to find a grief counselor to talk to.

It was a little after noon when Freddie pulled herself out of the bed. The silence in the house was deafening and she didn't want to be in there alone. She wondered if Lillian and Louis were going through the same thing. Cleveland was so cold to her, and his apology didn't make things better. She bounded down the stairs and headed for the kitchen, dressed in her thigh-skimming night gown. She opened the refrigerator and searched for something to eat. As she decided on a salad, grabbing a head of lettuce, an overly ripe tomato and an onion, a pair of hands snaked around her waist causing her to drop the vegetables.

"What the . . ." she said as she turned around and

looked into Cleveland's smiling face. "You scared the living daylights out of me."

"I'm sorry," he said, kissing her cheek. "This morning I was a complete ass."

Freddie nodded but remained silent. Cleveland continued, "I can't expect you to understand what I'm going through because I haven't really given you a chance to."

"True," she said. "And I do want to understand. I thought that last night we'd made some headway, but this morning . . ."

"I was wrong. I keep thinking that if I had been there, I could've made a difference or I could've saved him."

"Do you blame me?" she asked and grimaced as she waited for the answer.

"No," Cleveland said. "Freddie, I was blaming myself. But when Darren told me what happened, I realized that whether I'd been there or not, Roland would've died. It was one of those things that happen."

"Still, it's not any easier to deal with, huh?" she said quietly.

"No, especially when in a few months, I'm going to be the guy that has to keep it together and help others get through losing a brother," he said.

Freddie bent over and picked up the produce that she'd dropped. Cleveland stepped back and watched her as she moved. "You know," she said as she felt his eyes watching her every move, "you could help me clean up the mess you made me make."

"I want you to get to know my mother," he blurted out.

"What?" she said as she scooped up the busted tomato.

"I don't usually bring a lot of women around my mother and I normally wouldn't want my mother to get to know a woman, because she can be brutal. Let me tell you right now, she's going to grill you relentlessly."

"Okay," Freddie said.

"Tomorrow night, dinner, right here."

"Just the three of us?" Freddie asked.

Cleveland laughed. "I wouldn't do that to you. I'm going to invite Jill and Darren too."

"What's with this change in attitude?" Freddie questioned with her eyebrow raised.

"I spoke to a grief counselor and she told me that I can't live my life waiting for bad things to happen when I have so much to live for," Cleveland admitted.

Freddie's smile belied the fiery nervousness in her stomach. What if his mother didn't like her? This was one time when she wished that she could take a page from Lillian's book and put on a charming front. Then again, that's not who she was and she knew that people, especially a mother, would see right through that.

"What's going to be on the menu?" Freddie asked.

"I'm going to order something Cajun," he said. "And you're not going to lift a finger." Cleveland leaned in and kissed Freddie's cheek.

"I appreciate that, but I want to cook," she said. "Remember, I'm a New Orleans chick. I love to cook."

"No, I don't want that kind of pressure on you," he said. "This is just a relaxing inquisition."

The fiery nervousness had turned into a raging inferno as she dumped the mess in the trash can.

Chapter 26

The next day, Cleveland felt as if he were a renewed man. His talk with the grief counselor had put a lot of things into perspective. Though he was good at his job, because of the death of his father, he had a hard time processing death. He wanted to save everybody because he couldn't save his father. The counselor told him that he needed to live his life and not think about losing it and the people he loved so much.

When he told her about Freddie and their romance, she told him the way he went after her was the way he should look at other things in his life. And, she told him that he shouldn't blame himself for Roland's death. Had he been there, what could he have done differently?

Cleveland was still sad that Roland was gone, but life had to go on and if he was going to be the new battalion chief, he was going to have to figure out how to help others deal with grief if they lost a man in the future.

"What's with that smile on your face?" Freddie asked when she walked out of the bathroom.

"Well, I was thinking about what's underneath that

towel," he said as he rose from the bed and crossed over to her.

She opened the towel and let it fall to the floor. "Here you go," she said.

Cleveland pulled her damp body against his chest. "Well, anything that I was thinking doesn't match up to the real thing." He gently kissed her neck, inhaling the peach scent of her body wash. "Umm, do you taste as good as you smell?"

"You tell me," she moaned as Cleveland slipped his hand between her bare thighs. His fingers found their way to the moist folds of flesh that hid her throbbing bud of desire. Her breathing was staccato as his finger explored her womanhood and her knees shook when he touched her bud. "Cleveland," she called out when his hot mouth covered her breast, suckling at her erect nipple.

He removed his hand because he needed both of them to scoop Freddie up into his arms. She wrapped her legs around his waist, feeling his full manhood against her middle. Nibbling at his ear, Freddie heated Cleveland's body like a match. He fell back on the bed with Freddie on top of him. She took control of his body, kissing his neck as she roamed her hands across his broad chest. His ripped body was like a topography map underneath her fingers and though she knew every nook and crevice of it, she reveled in the feel of him. He throbbed against her thighs as she spread her legs and teased him with the heat from her core. With her tongue, Freddie made a path down the center of his chest. Cleveland buried his hands in her hair as her mouth covered his manhood. Cleveland closed his eyes as intense waves of pleasure flowed through his body as she bobbed up and down, taking him deeper into her mouth. He writhed underneath Freddie's touch and when her tongue crawled up the length of him, it was all he could do to keep from exploding. He reached down and grabbed her around the waist. "Umm," he moaned as he pulled her to the center of his chest and assailed her breasts with kisses. Freddie arched her back as her nipples hardened like precious diamonds. With his free hand, Cleveland reached over to his nightstand and grabbed a condom. Gently, he flipped Freddie on her back and continued stroking her breasts. He made short work of opening the latex sheath and slipping it on his rigid desire. Licking his lips, he rolled over on his side and looked at Freddie. Lying against his white cotton sheets, she looked like a goddess. Cleveland spread her legs apart, exploring her creamy core with his finger.

Freddie moaned as he found her blossoming bud of desire. She pressed his hand deeper, pleading with him for more. Cleveland knew she was primed and ready to take him inside, so he removed his finger and buried himself inside her wetness. Freddie cried out in bliss.

They matched each other stroke for stroke. Freddie's nails bit into Cleveland's shoulder as he pressed deeper, faster and harder into her awaiting body. She wrapped her legs around his waist and ground against him until she exploded from the inside out. But Cleveland wasn't done with her as he pulled her on top of him, gripping her hips as she rode him like he was a mechanical bull. She went slow, then fast, slow again and faster. Now it was Cleveland's turn to explode. Holding her against his chest, Cleveland climaxed and released a satisfied moan. Freddie kissed his shoulder and glanced at the clock on the nightstand.

"My God," she exclaimed. "Do you know what time it is?"

"Um, I don't care," he said as he snuggled against her.

"Dinner, Cleveland, we have to get the food for dinner.

What's your family going to think if they come here and there's no food?"

He smiled wickedly. "That we spend the morning and the afternoon in bed."

She swatted his hands away from her waist. "Like that's the image I want your mother to have of me."

Cleveland tweaked her nipple. "Come on, they know what's going on already."

Freddie hopped off the bed. "I'm going to take another shower and go to the grocery store and you're coming with me."

"To the shower, all right," he said, following her into the bathroom. When Cleveland reached the door, she pressed her hand against his chest.

"Uh-uh, Mr. Man. You're not coming in here with me." Before he could respond, Freddie slammed the door in his face and locked it.

"Oooh, you're not fair," he said. "I'm going downstairs to take a shower myself and I'm going to use all the hot water."

"Not if I use it first," she shot back.

About thirty minutes later, Cleveland and Freddie were dressed and on their way out the door heading to Kroger's. When they arrived at the grocery store, Freddie and Cleveland behaved like two schoolchildren, skipping down the aisle as they picked up ingredients for blackened catfish, jambalaya and smothered okra and tomatoes. They also stuck in their cart a Mrs. Smith Apple Pie and vanilla ice cream for dessert. When they passed the produce department, Freddie grabbed a container of strawberries. "This is for when your mother leaves," she said wickedly.

"Keep this up and I'm cancelling dinner," he replied with a gleam in his eye.

"And have your mother thinking that I'm some harlot.

I don't think so," she said as she placed the berries in the loaded shopping cart.

"Let me get some wine and whipped cream and we can go," Cleveland said as he glanced at his watch. "Because it looks like you have a lot of work to do."

"Oh, I have a lot of work to do?" she teased. "And what do you plan on doing while I'm cooking?"

"Watching."

Freddie rolled her eyes as Cleveland dashed off to the wine aisle. Though she and Cleveland were laughing and joking, she was extremely nervous about officially meeting Cleveland's mother and cooking for her.

I should've just let him order takeout, but no, I had to open my mouth and insert my entire foot. What if this woman doesn't like my cooking or God forbid something goes wrong, she thought as she made her way to the register. Cleveland walked up behind her and placed the wine and whipped cream on the counter. Then he kissed Freddie on the cheek. "Are you sure you can handle all of this?" he asked.

"Well, I'm certainly going to try," Freddie replied as the cashier began to ring up the groceries.

"I was joking before, I'll help you cook," he said.

"There was never a doubt."

After paying for the groceries, Cleveland and Freddie headed back to his place to begin preparing the feast.

By six o'clock, Freddie had prepared a perfect meal. The catfish was cooked to perfection and the rice in the jambalaya was fluffy and tender. She'd even cooked the okra and tomatoes so that they weren't too soupy. Cleveland was impressed.

"Ever considered a career as a chef?" he asked as she set the table in the dining room.

"No, but do you think we should've gotten some flowers for the table?" she asked, her voice peppered with nervousness.

"Calm down, Martha Stewart isn't going to be grading the table," he said with a chuckle.

"But your mother might," she mumbled.

"Babe, calm down. She's going to love you and if she doesn't, I love you enough for both of us."

"Was that supposed to be reassuring?"

He shrugged his shoulders. "Was it?"

"No." She smacked him on the shoulder just as the doorbell rang.

Cleveland opened the door, leaving Freddie to fidget with the place settings some more.

"Well, what's the occasion?" Margaret asked as she embraced her younger son.

"I can't invite my mother over for dinner?" he asked.

She raised her eyebrow at Cleveland. "Where is she?"

"Who?"

"The woman who's brought this change in you. She is the same one who came to Darren's house after the baby was born, right?"

"Yes, Mother."

Margaret walked into the foyer and smiled. "I never can tell with you," she said. "You change them like most people change socks. Are Darren and Jill bringing Kayla?"

Cleveland shrugged his shoulders. "Freddie is in the dining room," he said.

"Freddie? What kind of name is that for a woman?" she asked as they headed into the dining room.

"Be nice," he cautioned respectfully.

"Um," Margaret said.

They entered the dining room, catching Freddie changing a place setting.

"Winfred Barker," Cleveland said. "This is my mother, Margaret Alexander."

Freddie walked over to the older woman and extended her hand. "It's nice to see you again," she said demurely.

"Winfred, you're very pretty," Margaret said as she shook hands with Freddie. "Did you cook all of this?"

"Yes, ma'am. I hope you like it."

"Me too. I don't know why my son didn't just order take-out from Houston's like he usually does, instead of chaining you to the stove all day."

Freddie opened her mouth to tell her that she wanted to cook, but they were interrupted by the doorbell.

"That must be Darren and Jill," Cleveland said, then headed for the front door. Seconds later, Jill, Darren and Cleveland entered the dining room.

"Hey Freddie," Darren said. "Ma." He kissed his mother on the cheek.

"Wow," Jill said as she surveyed the spread on the table. "No Houston's takeout tonight. I'm already impressed." She then hugged her mother-in-law. "You look nice tonight."

"Thank you, Jill," Margaret said as she smoothed her purple pants.

"Well," Freddie said. "Let's eat."

The group sat down at the table and Freddie smiled as Margaret said, "Let's bless the table."

Freddie couldn't remember the last time she'd sat down for a family meal that didn't end in an argument between her and her mother. Hell, she couldn't remember the last time that she'd sat down and ate with her family.

As they said, "Amen," Cleveland got up to get the wine from the fridge and Margaret turned to Freddie.

"So, Winfred, where are you from?" she asked as Jill passed her the platter with the catfish.

"New Orleans."

"You and Lillian grew up together, right?" Darren said.

Freddie took the platter from Margaret's hands and placed fish on her plate and Cleveland's. "We did, until her family moved to Georgia. My mother and I had a hotel to run and . . ."

"Hey," Cleveland said when he reappeared in the dining room with an open bottle of wine, "can we hold off the interrogation until after dessert?"

His mother shot him a look that said, "Shut up, boy."

Jill cleared her throat and reached for the okra and tomatoes. "Freddie, everything looks great."

"Thank you," she replied, grateful that Cleveland's mother hadn't continued her inquiry. She didn't want to have to get into everything about her father and her mother and how if they were in New Orleans right now, none of them would want to be seen in public with her. "I love to cook."

"Is that what you did in New Orleans?" Margaret asked as she sliced into her catfish.

"No, I ran a hotel with my mother," Freddie said. "It was the family business."

"Katrina destroyed it? That was such a sad time," Margaret said. "You know, Jill and her company got there before the government. What kind of sense does that make?"

"None," Darren said. "And after all this time you still have neighborhoods that haven't been rebuilt."

Freddie shook her head. "I know. Everyone down there wants to pass the blame, but that doesn't help people rebuild. I was lucky to have someplace else to go. But not everyone was."

Cleveland reached out and grabbed Freddie's hand. Margaret looked at the two of them and smiled. "So, are you relocating to Atlanta and into my son's home?" she asked, still smiling sweetly.

Darren nearly choked on a fork full of jambalaya and Jill, who was in mid-sip of a glass of wine, almost spit back into her glass. Cleveland sat in his chair mortified.

"I, uh, do plan to start over in Atlanta," Freddie said, her hand trembling a bit.

"Here with my son or are you going to find your own place?"

"Ma," Darren and Cleveland said in unison.

"What? Don't you two sit there and pretend that I'm acting out of character," she said. "I'm only asking because I'm concerned about what's going on here." Margaret turned to Freddie. "Well? What are your intentions with my son?"

Freddie dropped her fork and stared at Margaret. "Is this really the time to . . . Um, I love-love your son."

Cleveland's mouth fell open and a flustered Freddie quickly filled her mouth with food. She'd never told Cleveland that she loved him, never said those words to him in their private moments, but she blurted it out in front of his entire family.

"Love him? So, you two plan on getting married?" Margaret pressed.

"Ma, come on," Darren said. Jill squeezed her husband's knee.

"You know how your mother is," she whispered.

"Can we just eat?" Cleveland said with a smile on his face.

A tense silence fell over the table as everyone ate. Freddie gulped down her wine, still feeling the heat of Margaret's gaze.

"This is really good," Jill said, breaking the silence.

"Uh-huh," Darren said.

"Thanks," Freddie replied, almost afraid to speak.

"I have to admit, it puts Houston's to shame," Margaret

said. "Winfred, dear, I'm not big on small talk. I speak my mind and I don't believe in pulling punches. My sons and my daughter-in-law know that." She picked up her wine glass and took a sip.

"I understand," Freddie said, seeing that Margaret Alexander wasn't being difficult, but just looking out for her son. She wondered what it would have been like to grow up with a mother who put her child's needs first. Loraine never did that and Jacques was never around at all because of his crime.

"And," Margaret said, turning to Cleveland, "I can't remember the last time you were serious about a woman. So, do you love her?"

Darren and Jill shook their heads as they watched the scene unfold. Margaret lifted her glass and took another sip of wine.

"Well," she asked her son again, "do you love her?"

"With everything in me," Cleveland replied without hesitation.

Darren leaned over to Jill. "We have officially stepped into the twilight zone," he whispered.

Freddie released a sigh of relief. "Coffee and pie, anyone?" she asked as she rose to her feet.

"Let me help you with that," Cleveland said as he followed Freddie into the kitchen. Once they were out of earshot of the rest of the family, he asked, "Are you all right?"

"That was pretty intense," she said as she fell into Cleveland's open arms. "Your mother doesn't hold back, does she?"

"That means she likes you. Otherwise, she wouldn't have asked you a thing."

Freddie exhaled and pulled back from Cleveland.

"You'd better start the coffee." She opened the refrigerator and pulled out the pie. "You really think she liked me?"

Cleveland chuckled as he poured coffee grinds in the maker's basket. "Do you really think she would've had a problem telling you if she didn't?"

"No," Freddie said with a laugh. "Not at all."

"Excuse me," Margaret called out from the dining room, "are you two getting the pie or doing something else?"

Cleveland winked as he took the pie off the counter and headed back into the dining room.

Chapter 27

After dinner and dessert, the group headed into the den with coffee in tow, except for Jill, who said Kayla was all the caffeine she needed.

"That little girl wakes up the moment she hears me typing," Jill said as she sat down on the sofa beside her husband.

"She's just telling her mother that she works too much," Darren said.

"Whatever," she said as she playfully slapped her husband's cheek.

"Leave that woman alone," Margaret said. "Some men would be glad for their woman to work."

"Thank you," Jill said. "And I'm not necessarily working, remember, Malik is in charge these days."

"Yeah, right," Cleveland said as he took a seat on the arm of the chair where Freddie was sitting. "I can't believe you have given up control of your first baby."

"I have," Jill protested. "To a point."

They all laughed. "Well, I think it's time for this old lady to go home," Margaret said as she rose to her feet. "It was a lovely dinner."

"I'll walk you to the door," Cleveland said as he stood and wrapped his arm around his mother's shoulders. Once they were out of earshot of the others, Margaret turned to her son and kissed his cheek.

"I like that girl," she said.

"I'm glad."

"She can cook and she has a lot of spunk and brain cells unlike those other women that you've dated in the past."

"Freddie's not like any woman I've ever known," he said.

Margaret nodded. "And that's a good thing, too. I always figured that when you decided to settle down that you'd pick the right girl." She poked her index finger in his chest. "Don't mess this up."

"Ma!"

"I'm not playing boy, that woman is a keeper and you'd better not let her get away." Margaret opened the door and said good-bye. "Remember what I said."

"Yes, ma'am." As Cleveland headed back to the den, he couldn't wipe his smile off his face. Freddie loved him. Though he would've preferred hearing it while they were alone and naked, she still said it.

He walked into the den and winked at Freddie. "It's official, she likes you."

"What?" Freddie said with a nervous giggle.

"My mother said she likes you," Cleveland said.

Jill turned to Darren. "Did your mother like me when we first met?" she asked.

"Yeah," he said. "It was later when she stopped liking you. But you delivered her first grandchild so I think she's over it."

Jill tweaked the end of Darren's nose. "Whatever."

Darren glanced at Cleveland and Freddie, who were

talking in hushed tones and holding hands. "I think we ought to follow Ma's lead," he said.

Jill glanced at the couple. "You're right. They're so cute."

"We can hear you," Cleveland said. "Good night."

Darren walked over to his brother and punched him on the arm. "We're leaving already. See you at the station tomorrow?"

"Yeah, yeah," he said.

Darren extended his hand to Freddie. "Good seeing you again."

"Thanks," she said as she shook his hand.

Jill gave Freddie a hug. "Welcome to the family," she said. "Next time we're going to have to do this at my place."

"As long as you don't cook," Darren and Cleveland said.

Jill rolled her eyes. "You know what? My cooking has gotten better," she protested.

"Not much," Darren said. "But I didn't marry you for your cooking."

"Do tell, Mr. Alexander," Jill said as he scooped her up into his arms.

"Let me get you home so that I can show you," he said.

Cleveland and Freddie waved to them as they left. Leaning against Cleveland, she said, "That went well."

"You say that as if you were expecting trouble," Cleveland said as he nestled closer to her.

"I've watched enough family dramas to know that most dinners with families don't end without a fight or someone revealing some big secret," Freddie said.

"Can I tell you that you watch too much TV?" Cleveland said with a laugh. "And you're wrong about our dinner party tonight."

"How so?" she asked.

"There was one secret revealed," he said.

"And just what might that be?" she asked, smiling as if she already knew.

Cleveland held her tighter. "I mean, it's not like I didn't already know, but to hear you say it was great. No, phenomenal."

She offered him a slick smile. "What if I was just trying to impress your mother?"

"Nah, that's why you cooked. Say it again."

"Um, Cleveland Alexander, I love you."

He began unbuttoning her shirt. "What are you doing?" she asked.

Cleveland leaned in and kissed her collarbone. "See, I had a different idea about how I would hear those words," he said as he continued to kiss her exposed flesh. Freddie melted against his taut body. "You were supposed to be totally naked and lying in my arms." He unzipped her pants and slid them down her ample hips, then he made short work of removing her black-lace thong. "This is more like it."

"You have me at an unfair disadvantage," Freddie moaned as Cleveland took one of her breasts into his mouth. His tongue flicked across her hardened nipple, sending a shiver down her spine.

"What would that be?" he asked as he pulled back from her succulent breast.

Freddie reached for Cleveland's shirt. "You're still fully dressed."

She pulled his shirt over his head and worked her way down to the waistband of his pants. Cleveland stepped out of his pants and his desire spilled from the confines of his boxers as he lifted Freddie from the easy chair and carried her to the sofa. He planted her on the sofa, then spread her legs apart.

Cleveland dove in between her thighs, kissing the wet folds of flesh that hid her throbbing bud. Freddie's leg shivered in anticipation of feeling him deep inside her. Gently, he nibbled and sucked her tender bud until Freddie cried out and dug her nails into his shoulder. "Cleveland, Cleveland," she repeated like a mantra as he deepened his kiss, intensifying the pleasure she felt.

He slid her hips closer to his lips, still sipping the sweetness of her essence. His manhood grew as Freddie moaned and licked her lips. Though he wanted to take her right there, he pulled back from her and exhaled. He held his finger up and dashed up the stairs to the bedroom and grabbed a condom. When he returned downstairs, Freddie was lying on the floor on an afghan with the package of strawberries and the whipped cream at her side.

"It would've been a shame to let this go to waste," Freddie said as she slathered some cream across her breasts. Smiling, as if he had been offered the finest chocolate in the world, Cleveland pounced on top of Freddie and proceeded to lick the sweet cream from her breasts. She grabbed the back of his head as his tongue flicked across her nipple. Every muscle in her stomach clenched as she felt him against her thighs. She parted her legs and wrapped them around Cleveland's waist. She had to have him inside her because she was burning with a desire that only he could quell. Ripping the condom package open, Cleveland slid the sheath in place and slipped between Freddie's thighs.

Her heat and wetness enveloped him and Cleveland shuddered with delight. She ground against him, with her head thrown back in ecstasy. He buried his head in her breasts, kissing and licking them, sending Freddie's body into overdrive. She tightened herself around him, sending the same intense feelings of pleasure through his nervous system.

"Umm," he moaned as Freddie arched her back and placed her hands on his chest and gyrated her hips like a belly dancer. He cupped her bottom and rolled over so that she was on top of him. She leaned into him and kissed him slowly, matching the rhythm of her hip movements. Cleveland felt as if he was about to explode from the inside out as her tongue danced in his mouth. She was sweeter than sugar, more addictive than any illegal drug.

"I love you," Freddie whispered as if she were in a trance. "I love you, I love you."

Cleveland was unable to speak, unable to breathe as his body throbbed and he felt himself release inside her. Clutching her back, he released a guttural moan. "I love you too," he said breathlessly as she collapsed on his chest. He kissed her on the top of her head. "But you already knew that."

Freddie sighed with satisfaction. "I guess I didn't believe it," she said. "But now I do."

Cleveland stared into her eyes and smiled. "What's changed?"

"I guess me. It's time that I start believing that every man isn't my father. My screwed up father." Freddie pulled away from Cleveland. "Before we can go any further, I have to go back to New Orleans."

"Why?" he asked, propping up on his elbows.

"Because we can't start over if I don't tie up some loose ends in the Big Easy," she said.

"I'll go with you," he said.

Freddie shook her head. "I don't think so," she said. "You have a promotion to get, remember."

"But if you need me . . ."

"When I return, I know that I'm going to need you," she said. "But I have to do this on my own."

"All right," he said. "But you know part of being in love is letting the person you love have your back."

She stroked his cheek. "I know. Still, this I have to do on my own. My family is a huge mess, and I don't want to drag you into it right now."

"I'm already all up in it," he joked as he thrust his hip forward.

"You're bad."

"And you love it." Cleveland picked up a berry from the bowl next to them and traced her lips with it. "Freddie, I can see myself spending my life with you."

"Don't say it if you don't mean it because I'm going to hold you to it."

He put the berry between his lips and bit into it. "That's what I want you to do." Cleveland brushed his lips against Freddie's. "Before you go, let me give you something to think about on that long trip to Louisiana."

The next morning, Freddie reluctantly peeled herself out of Cleveland's arms and began preparing herself to head back to New Orleans. As she walked in the bathroom, Freddie thought about what was waiting for her. *Drama.* Turning the faucet on, she splashed water on her face and sighed. "I wish I didn't have to leave," she mumbled.

"Then don't," Cleveland said as he wrapped his arms around her waist.

"Where did you come from?"

"That bed over there." Cleveland leaned in and kissed her on the back of her neck. "Want to get back in it?"

Freddie turned around and pushed him away. "No, because if I do, I won't leave—ever."

"And the problem with that would be?"

Freddie placed her hand on her hip and stomped her foot. "Because there's an old saying that goes, you can't move forward if you're always looking back. One or both of my parents are probably in jail. I have to know how this all pans out. This thing with my family has been going on for a long time and I have to see how it ends."

"How it ends?"

She nodded. "Last night when I met your family, I realized that as much as I'd like to forget mine ever existed, I need closure with them. I need to know how this is going to turn out."

Cleveland agreed, though the last thing he wanted was to see Freddie walk out the door.

"I'm coming back," she said as if she was reading his mind. "Because trust me, I believe my life is here with you."

Cleveland crossed over to her and pulled her into his arms. "You don't know what that does to me to hear that." He brushed his lips against hers. "Don't go right now."

Freddie moaned as she stepped back from him. "I have to take a shower, call Amtrak and . . ."

"How about we save water and take a shower together and instead of you taking a train, why not take my car?"

She placed her hands flat on his bare chest. "Because, I'm bringing my Mustang back. I changed my mind about leaving it down there."

"All right," he said. "I'll call the train station and get you on the next thing smoking to New Orleans and you take your shower."

Freddie blew him a kiss as he headed out of the bathroom. Moments later, she emerged from the bathroom, showered and dressed in a black-and-gold sweat suit and her hair pulled back in a ponytail. When she headed downstairs to the kitchen, Cleveland, now dressed in a pair of cotton boxers and an Atlanta Falcons T-shirt, handed her a cup of coffee.

"Your train leaves at eight," he said. "So, that means drink this and grab a banana so we can get downtown."

Freddie took the mug from his hand and smiled. "Let's just leave, because there's no telling how bad traffic is going to be."

Cleveland nodded then headed upstairs to get dressed. Freddie leaned against the counter and exhaled. As she peeled her banana, Freddie's mind wandered to New Orleans and what was waiting for her down there. The fallout from her father's return and his allegations against her mother was going to be substantial. She knew the hotel, which was barely making a profit following Katrina, probably would recover from the Babineaux storm. *It's not my problem any more,* she thought as she chewed her fruit.

Looking around the kitchen as she sipped her coffee, Freddie smiled thinking of the previous night and the dinner that she and Cleveland cooked for his family. She wished that her family was like his. Instead, she had two criminals to call Mom and Dad.

Maybe I should've listened to Loraine and left the past alone, she thought as she downed her coffee. It was too late to turn back.

"You ready?" Cleveland asked, breaking into Freddie's thoughts.

"As I'll ever be," she said as she set her coffee mug on the counter.

Cleveland took her hand in his. "Everything is going

to work out just fine and when you come back, I'll be right here waiting for you—naked."

Freddie playfully slapped him on the shoulder. "What am I going to do with you?"

Cleveland kissed her hand. "Love me," he said. "That's all I need you to do."

Chapter 28

Freddie opened her eyes as the train jerked then came to a stop. No way they were in New Orleans already. She looked down at her watch and saw that she was only three hours into her trek. A conductor walked by and she reached out and touched his arm. "What's going on?" Freddie asked.

"There's a freight train crossing," he said. "We're just going to be stopped for a short while."

She smiled sweetly and thanked the man for stopping. Freddie was about to close her eyes again when her cell phone rang. "Hello," she said.

"I miss you already."

"Cleveland, I've only been gone for a couple of hours," she replied with a big smile on her face.

"That's a few hours too long. I'm starting to sound like Darren, all mushy and . . ."

"Don't go changing on me too much," she said. "I might not be able to recognize you."

Cleveland chuckled. "And I thought you didn't like it when I was all stuck on myself. What did you call me when we first met?"

"Let me think," she said. "Probably a pompous jerk. An arrogant jackass. There were so many things I said to you, I just can't remember."

"Well, that sounds about right," Cleveland said. "Is everything going all right on the train?"

"Yeah, luckily I have the row to myself. I've just been sleeping and thinking about you."

"Umm, what have you been thinking?" Cleveland's voice was low. "Because I have been thinking about you and me on a beach somewhere."

"Really, keep talking," she said, grinning like the cat that swallowed the canary.

"That body in a yellow bikini and I'm going to have to save your skin, so that means I have to rub your body down in some coconut oil and sunscreen. And you know that I don't follow the rules, so I'm going to slip my fingers underneath your top and run them across your breasts until your nipples are hard and ready for my lips. I'd have to make sure no one is looking before I take your top off completely and give your nipples the kisses they need."

"Don't do this to me," Freddie said, "these people on this train are going to wonder why I keep smiling and moaning."

"The only reason I'm stopping is because my nosy brother just walked in and I don't want to be interrupted when I tell you what I'm going to do once I have that shirt off."

"You are so bad," she said, her voice in a low whisper as the conductor passed her seat.

"And you love it. Make sure you call me when you get to New Orleans. I need to know that you made it safely and so I can finish telling you this story."

"Bye, Cleveland," Freddie said as she snapped her phone closed. Now she wished that she had taken his car because after that heated conversation, she wanted to turn around and make him do all of those things that he'd been describing on the phone.

Focus, Freddie, focus, she told herself. The train started moving again and Freddie closed her eyes, trying to think about her parents, but her mind kept drifting to Cleveland as she fell asleep again.

Darren shook his head as Cleveland hung up his cell phone with a smile a mile wide on his face. "I never thought I'd see the day," he said.

"What?" Cleveland asked.

"You, Mr. Bachelor, acting like a lovesick puppy."

"I can't be any worse than you were when you decided that you couldn't live without Jill."

"I never called my woman up and had phone sex," he said.

"Damn, you were eavesdropping?" Cleveland laughed. "Don't knock it until you try it."

"I'm really happy for you," Darren said. "You've finally found someone that you can open yourself up to and you know she has your back and you can trust her."

Cleveland nodded and sighed thoughtfully. "Still, I feel like there is a part of her past that she doesn't want to open up to me about."

Darren placed his hand underneath his chin. "That's not good, because the past can come back to bite you."

"I don't think it's like what went down with you and Jill," he said. "It has something to do with her family. It's like she's trying to shield me from something."

"You know, if she feels that way, maybe you ought to just let it be. When she's ready to open up to you about her family, she will. I hope that's all that it is."

"What do you mean?"

"Look, I'm happy for you and all of that, but you'd better make sure the secret she's hiding isn't more than what she's telling you."

Cleveland looked at his brother and shook his head. "Freddie's not that type of woman."

"Are you sure? Don't get me wrong, I do like her and think she's a nice woman, but I've been on the other side of a lie more than once. Just make sure that . . ."

"Whatever, man," Cleveland interrupted. "I know what's going on with her and there won't be any newspaper exposes or letters in the mail to expose her secrets."

"Don't bite my damned head off because I'm trying to look out for you. It was hard enough for you to open up to a woman to begin with. I don't want to see you hurt. Because if this doesn't work out for you, I pity the next woman who comes into your life."

Cleveland stood up with a scowl on his face. Though he knew his brother was trying to look out for him, he didn't need him feeding his insecurities.

"I'm going to write up some incident reports," Cleveland said, leaving Darren in the break room alone.

When Cleveland got into Darren's office, he thought about what his brother had said. Was there something more in New Orleans that Freddie had to tie up? How well did he really know her?

This is crazy, he thought. *Freddie has been up front with me. I can understand why she's a little wary about opening up. Her family's past would scare off anyone. But I accept all of her, crazy parents and all. I just hope that is all there is.*

Cleveland returned to his reports, but his mind was in New Orleans.

* * *

When Freddie stepped off the train, she had an over-whelming urge to turn around and leave. She'd never been afraid to face anything. If her mother had taught her one thing it was to stand tall and face adversity. But this was different. Her life, her family's freedom were at stake. What was waiting for her at the hotel? Would the media be camped out waiting for someone connected with her family to show up? She didn't want to deal with that, so she hailed a cab and headed for St. Vincents, a hotel on Magazine Street. Freddie hoped that no one would recognize her as Loraine's daughter. In the morning, she would try and find out where her mother was and what the status of her case was. Had her mother even been arraigned? She was curious as to whether or not the courts believed her father's allegations about her mother being involved in the murder of the Rev. Nolan Watson. A cab stopped and Freddie got in, telling the driver where she wanted to go.

"You know, chere, The French Garden Inn is a much better place to stay," he suggested.

"Thanks, but I have a reservation," she lied. Freddie hoped that the hotel did have some rooms.

The taxi stopped in front of the hotel and Freddie gave the driver the fare and a hefty tip. She was happy that the cab company was living up to their end of an agreement that she and the owner had brokered a few months before Mardi Gras to send visitors to her hotel.

Walking into the hotel, Freddie glanced over her shoulder to make sure no one had followed her.

"Welcome to St. Vincents. Do you have a reservation?" the young desk clerk asked.

"No," she said. "But please tell me you have some vacancies."

The woman leaned across the desk and peered at Freddie. "Are you a reporter too?"

"Please, I just came to . . . No."

"I have a single room, non smoking with a queen sized bed," she said.

"That's fine," Freddie replied with a yawn. "I just need the room for one night."

The clerk typed Freddie's information into the computer and handed her a room key. "Enjoy your stay," she said.

Freddie took the elevator to her second floor room, ready to get into bed and go to sleep. As soon as she stepped in the room, she missed her suite at her hotel. The bed wasn't exactly queen sized, it was more like a full sized bed. The blanket looked as if it were a hold over from the 1970s. She took off her hotel owner cap as she collapsed on the bed. It wasn't her job to critique the room, she just needed to sleep.

It was a little before eleven when Freddie woke up from her nap. She turned on the television to watch the late news, because she knew the top story would be about her parents.

"The police and the district attorney's office have re-opened the case on the murder of Reverend Nolan Watson. The man convicted of the crime, Jacques Babineaux, who had escaped from federal prison, turned himself in, but was granted a conditional release when evidence surfaced that Babineaux isn't the real killer. In fact, the court heard evidence in a hearing this morning that points the finger at Loraine Barker, Babineaux's ex-wife. She was arrested and charged with Watson's murder. In a shocking turn of events, she was granted bail because of her ties to the community. She is expected in court in the morning for a preliminary hearing at eight A.M."

Freddie snapped the television off. "This is too much," she muttered. Too wired to sleep, Freddie took a long shower and decided that she would go to her mother's arraignment in the morning because she figured that might be the only way she'd get the truth about what was going on.

When she finally went to bed, Freddie's sleep was hampered by thoughts of facing her mother in court.

The next morning, Freddie woke up about five after eight, late for her mother's hearing. She dressed quickly, rushed downstairs to pay for her room and had the front desk clerk call her a cab. As she waited out front for her car, Freddie massaged her temples. She prayed that after today, the answers she'd been searching for would be revealed and she could move on with her life, even though to do that she had to leave behind everything she knew.

"It's going to be fine," she said aloud as she pulled out her cell phone and called the hotel.

"French Garden Inn, this is Celeste."

"Celeste, it's Freddie."

"Hey, I am so glad you called, your mother has been raising hell around here. Three people quit and she said you'd never come back. We've been losing business because her face has been all over the news and reporters are always calling and coming by here. She's out on bail now. Are you really going to stay in Atlanta?"

"I guess she told you all everything," Freddie said.

"And then some. She walks around muttering about you throwing everything away for a damn man. Is it that sexy guy who was here for Mardi Gras? I knew something was going on between you two." Freddie could almost see Celeste's smile through the phone. "Shoot," she continued. "I would've left with him too."

"Celeste," Freddie said. "I'm going to come to the hotel and get a few of my things, but I'm not coming to come back to work. There's just too much baggage here."

"I hear you," Celeste said. "If I had the means to leave

New Orleans, I would. This place just hasn't been the same since Katrina."

"But it's still New Orleans," Freddie said. "Still home."

"Having second thoughts, maybe?"

Freddie thought for a moment, with her eyes closed and images of Cleveland flashing in her mind. "Nah."

Celeste laughed. "I'll bet not."

"Is my mother there now?" she asked.

"No, thank God. She's in court."

"Then I'll see you after the hearing. I need to get some things out of my room," she said.

"Okay," Celeste said.

"My cab is here, I have to go," said Freddie as the car stopped in front of her.

"Where to, chere?" the driver asked.

Before Freddie knew it, she was telling the driver to take her to the Orleans Parish courthouse. The scene outside the courthouse reminded Freddie of something she'd seen on television. Satellite trucks lined the streets, a few reporters were on the steps smoking and chewing the fat about the case. Freddie paid the cabbie and got out of the car. She walked up the steps of the courthouse slowly, paying little attention to the conversations going on around her. Though it did sting that these people just thought of her mother as another headline. As angry as she wanted to be with her mother, Freddie thought about all the years when she and Loraine jokingly called themselves Thelma and Louise.

She walked into the courthouse and had no trouble finding the room where her mother was, because there were more reporters and observers standing outside the door. Freddie pushed through the crowd.

"There are no more seats in there," a woman said.

"I don't care, that's my mother in there," Freddie said as

she wedged her body between the crowd and the door. It was standing room only inside the courtroom and she could only see the back of her mother's head. The judge banged his gavel.

"Bailiff, make sure that door doesn't open again. There will be order in this courtroom." His voice was angry and boomed like thunder. All of the movement and chatter in the courtroom stopped. "Now," the judge said. "Mr. Sparks, continue."

"Your honor, the DA is wasting the tax payers' time and money on the word of a convicted killer. Ms. Barker is in no way connected with this murder and I move that these charges be dropped."

"Your honor," the district attorney interrupted. "If we reopen the murder case, we wouldn't just be going on Jacques Babineaux's word. There is new evidence . . ."

"Where was this evidence during Babineaux's trial?" the judge questioned.

The DA faltered for a moment. "Well, his attorney and a private investigator presented our office with the evidence and it was authenticated by the police department," the DA said.

"I'm not comfortable with this," the judge said. "We're talking about a twenty-year-old murder. Evidence could've been tampered with and this doesn't smell right to me."

"But your honor," the DA protested, openly showing his frustration.

The judge held up his hand. "I'm dismissing the charges against Ms. Barker with prejudice."

Freddie shook her head. Her mother had gotten away with murder. So, what did this ruling mean for her father?

The courtroom began to clear out, but Freddie stood her ground and waited for her mother to walk across the room.

What would she say to her? It took about five minutes for Loraine to make it to where Freddie was.

"Winfred," she said happily when she saw her daughter. "I'm happy to see you."

"Really?"

"Now do you see why I've never encouraged a relationship with your father?"

She shook her head and leaned into her mother as if she was going to give her a hug. "I guess you're proud of yourself since you've just gotten away with murder."

Loraine shook her head. "This is over. Your father made a mess of my life and you're going to stand here and defend him?"

"Both of you are sick and I'm washing my hands of you." Freddie stormed out of the courtroom, ignoring the flashing light bulbs of the photographers' cameras.

Once she made it outside, Freddie ran into her father, who was standing away from the crowd and watching the door. She shook her head when she saw him.

He crossed over to her and tried to embrace her, but Freddie put her hands up. "Are you happy?" she asked.

"Is she going to jail?"

"No, so, all you did was bring a lot of undue attention to us."

Babineaux frowned at his daughter. "I was only trying to clear my name. I didn't kill that man. Now, it's on the record."

"Well, no one is going to be punished for it. In the eyes of this city, you're going to be O.J."

"What about you? How do you see me?"

"The same way I see your ex-wife, you're sick. This family is a circus and I'm bowing out."

He shrugged his shoulders and extended his arms to Freddie. "I love you and I'm sorry."

"Empty words that are way too late," she snapped, side stepping her father so that he couldn't reach out to her.

"I'm sorry you feel that way, but you know the truth now. One day, I guess you'll be able to forgive me."

Freddie turned her back to her father. There were so many things she wanted to say and needed to get off her chest. When she turned around, Jacques was gone. Freddie was sure that she'd never see him again. As she turned around and watched her mother hold court with the reporters, she was sure she never wanted to see her again. Freddie started walking, wanting to get far away from the scene at the courthouse. She didn't know who she was most angry at, her mother, her father or herself. *Neither one of them think that they're wrong,* she thought bitterly. Before she knew it, she found herself on Bourbon Street. Shaking her head, she hopped on a streetcar to get to the French Quarter.

Riding on the car, listening to the clang and beat of the city, she almost forgot that she was there because her father and mother just exchanged accusations of murder. As the smell of crawfish jambalaya and Po-Boys mixed with the wind, Freddie wondered if she was really ready to let go of New Orleans and what it meant to her. The success of the hotel was because of her. This was her home and despite all that happened, New Orleans was special to her. *But does this city mean more than Cleveland?*

"No," she said quietly to herself as the streetcar stopped at her destination. Freddie walked up to the hotel and smiled because this was the last time she'd ever see the place. Her emotions swirled like a hurricane wind. The French Garden Inn was a big part of her, much of who she was resided in that hotel. She framed that place to be a great getaway for guests at a time when she wanted to get away from the pain and heartbreak in her life. It was the place where Cleveland Alexander opened her mind and body to the possibility of love and untold passion that she'd never dared to dream about.

She took a deep breath and walked in the door, finding Celeste sitting behind the desk with her eyes glued to the overhead TV that wasn't there when Freddie left for Atlanta.

"This is some bull," Celeste muttered.

"I know I taught you how to properly greet guests when they walk through the door," Freddie said.

Celeste quickly turned the TV off and rose to her feet. "You coulda told me you were coming back here today. Please, please don't leave us to face the wrath of your mother."

"Sorry, the only thing I can do is suggest you find a new job if you don't want to deal with Loraine. Can you hand me a key to my suite, please?" Freddie asked.

"Sure, but your mother has moved into that suite as well. I guess you two were going to be roommates if you ever did decide to come back."

Freddie's right eyebrow and blood pressure shot up at the thought of being Loraine's roommate. Knowing her mother, she'd probably tossed Freddie's things aside as if they were garbage. That was Loraine's way and now that she'd gotten away with murder, she'd be intolerable. In a way, Freddie felt sorry for her staff and what they were going to face working for Loraine.

When she entered the suite, her suspicions were right. Her belongings were flung in a corner as if Goodwill needed to come and get them out of Loraine's way. Freddie went through her clothes, picking out the things that she wanted to take with her and what she would leave for her mother to do away with. After sorting out the things that she wanted, Freddie went to the closet to retrieve a suitcase. That's when she heard the door open.

"Winfred," Loraine called out.

Freddie stepped out of the closet and faced her mother. "What?"

"Don't leave. Please, I need you here to help me . . ."

"No," Freddie said as she tossed the empty case on the bed. "You don't get to do this."

"Do what? I have been through one of the most harrowing ordeals of my life while you were in some man's bed in Atlanta. It's not going to last. He's going to disappoint you just like every man in my life let me down."

"That's your life, not mine. Cleveland and I love each other. Your history with men is not going to be my future. You set all of this in motion, so now you're at the wheel. Enjoy the drive, Mother," Freddie spat, then began stuffing her clothes into her suitcase.

"You're wrong and you're going to get your heart broken because . . ."

"No," she snapped. "You've been bitter for years and I'm not following in your footsteps. I can recognize a good man, too bad you couldn't." Freddie zipped up her suitcase and yanked it off the bed. "Good-bye, Mother." Loraine grabbed her daughter's arm.

"Freddie, don't be like me, don't . . ."

"I'm nothing like you and any second thoughts that I may have had about going back to Atlanta, you've crushed them." She pushed past her mother and headed out the door.

Chapter 29

Cleveland used to enjoy being alone at home. After all, he spent days in a firehouse surrounded by loud dudes with dispatchers always calling, so his time at home meant solitude. But tonight, he was missing the touch of Freddie's fingers on the back of his neck. He was missing the sound of her voice as they talked about what to eat for dinner.

Cleveland entered the kitchen and poured himself a glass of water, wondering when Freddie was going to return. She'd been gone for two days. Was she safe? Did she find the closure that she needed?

He grabbed his phone and dialed Freddie's number. It was nearly eleven P.M. and he was beyond worried about her. *She said she was going to get her car and come back. What if she got into an accident or worse?*

"Hello," Freddie said, immediately putting Cleveland's mind at ease.

"I was worried about you," he said. "It's getting pretty late."

"I know and I should've called. When I got into town, I found out that my mother had a court date and against my better judgment, I went over to the courthouse and watched my mother skate away scot-free."

Cleveland furrowed his brows in confusion. "You wanted your mother to go to prison?"

Freddie sighed into the phone. "It's a long ugly story and I don't want to drive and talk about it."

"Are you sure you're all right to drive back tonight because I don't want you to be fuming about your mother and run off the road."

"Baby, I'm fine and if I don't get home and see you ASAP, I'm really going to lose it. I really want your arms around me when I go to sleep," she said.

"Then call me Motel 6 because I'm leaving the light on for you."

"I'll see you in a few hours," she said.

Cleveland hung up the phone and started a pot of coffee so that he would be fully awake when Freddie arrived at his place. Despite his best efforts, Cleveland fell asleep after his second cup. He'd had a taxing day training to be the new battalion chief. There were tests that he had to take, training exercises and countless other tasks that had to be completed before he was installed as the new leader.

Still, part of him wondered if he would be able to lead the station as well as Darren had over the years. He was still mourning the loss of Roland and how would he rally his men if he lost someone on his watch?

But as an Alexander, he knew this was in his blood. He wanted to save lives and he wanted to keep people safe. It was a calling that all of the men in his family had answered and when he needed to be strong, he would be.

Shifting in the recliner, Cleveland inhaled and could've sworn that he smelled Freddie's rose perfume. His eyes fluttered open and he smiled when he saw her standing over him. Had he really slept that long?

"Leaving the light on for me, huh?" she ribbed as she kissed him on the cheek.

"It was a long day," he said then pulled her onto his lap in a quick motion. "Glad you made it back in one piece, though."

Freddie wrapped her arms around his neck and nestled against him. "This feels so good," she said.

"What happened in New Orleans?"

She sighed and began to tell him the entire story of her family's history. "This all started a long time ago, even before I was born. My father had some vendetta against Nolan Watson because he cheated my grandmother out of an insurance policy payment. My mother was dating Nolan and Jacques made it his mission to woo her and steal her away from him. She ended up getting pregnant with me after all of the wooing," she said.

Cleveland watched her incredulously as she told the story. "Wow," he said. "That's something."

She shook her head and sighed. "It gets worse," Freddie said. "My parents got married, but I'm not sure how much love was between them. But they started the hotel and for a little while, we seemed like a normal family. But Nolan ended up dead because he attacked my mother."

"Your father did the right thing by protecting his woman," Cleveland interjected.

Freddie dropped her arms from around his neck. "My father didn't kill him. It was my mother. She saw an opportunity to get back at my father and Nolan because she was tired of being a pawn in their game."

"So, all of this time that your father has been on the run, your mother was keeping this secret from you?" Cleveland asked.

"She flat-out lied," Freddie corrected. "She lied to the police, the courts, and me. The worst thing about all of this is that she got away with it. My dad is gone again, even though his conviction was vacated because of the new evidence his investigator found. He knows he's not going to get any peace in New Orleans. Then again, it's not like he's innocent in all of this either."

Cleveland didn't know what to say. He couldn't imagine what it must have been like for Freddie growing up and not being able to depend on either one of her parents. This explained a lot about Freddie and why she had a tough time trusting people.

"This has to be hard for you," Cleveland said.

She didn't say anything, but Cleveland felt her warm tears drop on his shoulder. He stroked her back and rocked her back and forth as she cried silently.

"Are you all right?" Cleveland asked after a few moments passed.

She faced him, dried tears on her cheeks. "Yeah," she said. "I'm tired. This whole thing has been overwhelming." She rose from his lap and wiped her face.

Cleveland stood up and closed the space between them and gave Freddie a tight hug. "What do you say to a nice warm bubble bath and candles?" he asked as he kissed her on the top of her head.

"That sounds beautiful, but I'd probably go to sleep on you," she said. "That ride back took a lot out of me. Besides, it's almost morning."

"That's why I want to help you relax," Cleveland said with a slow smile spreading across his face.

"Umm, rain check, baby? I just want to lie down and close my eyes."

"All right," he said as they headed upstairs.

As soon as Cleveland and Freddie undressed and got into bed, they both fell fast asleep. He held Freddie close to his chest and had the best night of sleep that he'd had in months.

The next morning, Freddie woke up with a start. All night she pretended to sleep soundly, but she couldn't shut off her mind. Lying in Cleveland's arms, she should've been happy and content. He loved her unconditionally and even though he knew her family had demons, he didn't look at her any differently. She knew that the Alexanders were a close-knit family and there was no way he could understand what she was going though. Hell, she didn't understand it herself. It wasn't as if she and her family had ever been close. But knowing that she would never see her parents again made her feel some kind of way. She couldn't explain the feeling. Peeling herself out of Cleveland's arms, she walked into the bathroom and splashed some cold water on her face. Had she made the right decision, leaving her family behind and coming back to Atlanta? She was so sure when she told her mother that she never wanted to see her again that it wouldn't affect her. But here she was in the bathroom when the man she loved was lying in bed.

Freddie knew if she was going to move on with her life that eventually it wouldn't matter what her mother or father did because she'd have a family of her own.

I would never do to my child what my mother and father did to me, she thought as she wiped her face. She headed back to the bed and snuggled up beside Cleveland. This was her future.

"Where did you go?" he asked as she wrapped her arms around his waist.

"Bathroom."

"You all right?"

"Yes," she said. "I'm going to be just fine." Freddie looked into Cleveland's sleepy eyes. "I love you."

"I love you more," he said then sought out her lips.

She responded to his gentle kiss by pressing her body against his.

Cleveland slipped his hands between her thighs as her kiss became deeper, wetter and hotter. Freddie moaned as he entered her with his finger, finding her throbbing bud of desire. Closing her eyes, Freddie sighed. If this was her future, then she was looking forward to it.

"I need you," she cried as Cleveland eased a second finger inside her hot body. She didn't know if he understood the meaning of what she was saying. Not only did she need him physically, but she needed Cleveland more than she ever thought she would.

Would their love last? Would their love be enough? Could she trust that he would never hurt her or leave her?

He reached for a condom and slid the latex in place then turned to Freddie. Her eyes were wet with unshed tears. "What's wrong?" he asked.

"Tell me this is going to last," she whispered. "Tell me that I can depend on you no matter what."

Cleveland pulled her against his chest. "Of course you can. Baby, I love you and I never thought I'd love someone the way that I love you. I've never allowed anyone to get this close to me."

"Why am I special?" she asked.

Cleveland groaned. "Are we really going to do this, now?"

Freddie cocked her head to the side and simply said, "Yes."

He pulled her on top of him and she shifted her hips away from his swelling manhood. "Well," he said with a sigh. "No woman has ever challenged me the way you do. No other woman has ever turned me on the way you do."

"So it's just physical?" she asked. "Because you haven't said one thing . . ."

Cleveland placed his finger to her lips. "Will you let me finish?" He struggled to breathe as he felt the heat from Freddie's body. "When you're gone, I worry about you. I wonder what you're doing and if you're thinking about me. When I look at you, I want to know what you're thinking, even if it's just about what you want for dinner. This has never happened before. I've never cared about a woman deeply enough to have these feelings. So I should be asking you if you're going to leave me."

Freddie spread her legs and straddled his body. "I'm not going anywhere," she said as she mounted him. "Cleveland." Her voice was like a breeze as he filled her. "I love you."

He gripped her hips, unable to speak as she tightened her grip around his manhood. He pressed his mouth against her neck as she leaned forward, pushing her breasts against his chest. Cleveland seemed to set her body on fire with his lips. Closing her eyes, she rode him faster, crying out in ecstasy as she neared climax. But Cleveland wasn't finished with her. Flipping her over, it was his turn to control the passion. Wrapping her legs around his waist like two silk ribbons, he rotated his hips, touching every spot that made her moan. Freddie dug her nails into his back as he pressed deeper and deeper into her wetness.

"Damn," Cleveland moaned as Freddie ran her tongue up and down the side of his neck, sending his body into overdrive. "Marry me."

Freddie closed her eyes, because she knew he didn't say what she thought he'd said. *He said marry me, I know that he did, but he can't mean it.*

Cleveland rolled over on his side and faced Freddie. Sweat rolled down his face and he closed his eyes. "Umm, Cleveland," she said, stroking his cheek.

"Yeah, baby?"

"Did you just say what I think you said?"

He opened his eyes and smiled. "And just what do you think I said?"

She shook her head. "It doesn't matter," she said and pinched his shoulder. "Don't you have to go to work today?"

Cleveland snuggled closer to Freddie. "No, I don't. And that's not how I meant it to come out, but I meant what I said. I want to marry you."

"Wha-what?"

Cleveland kissed her on the lips and pulled her even closer to his chest. "I want to marry you. I want to spend the rest of my life with you."

"This is so sudden," she said. "I don't know what to say."

"All you have to do is say yes," Cleveland said. "Say yes to our future."

"I don't know," she said, gently pushing away from him. "I don't have anything to offer you. I don't have a job, I don't have . . ."

Cleveland shushed her with a gentle kiss. "Do you think I care about any of that? We're going to work all of that out."

"Cleveland, this is . . ."

"Baby," he said. "You're going to be Mrs. Cleveland Alexander whether you like it or not."

Throwing her head back, Freddie was filled with happiness and dread. Could she marry him with all of the turmoil that she had going on in her life?

Chapter 30

Two days after Cleveland's impromptu proposal, Freddie had hoped that he wouldn't bring it up again. There was no way that she could accept his proposal. Yes, she loved him. But she didn't know how to make love last. While Cleveland was at work, Freddie headed to Lillian's house to talk to her friend. She hoped that Lillian had some pointers about marriage.

"Well, you are still in Atlanta," Lillian said when she opened the door. "I haven't seen my best friend in weeks."

"Shut up," Freddie said as she walked in and gave Lillian a hug. "I've been busy trying to settle in and then there was my trip to New Orleans."

Lillian ushered Freddie to the sofa. "What happened? Did you see your parents? Are they both going to jail?"

Freddie raised her eyebrow. "You know a lot about this case," she said.

Lillian nodded, "My mother has been checking the Internet for any updates on it. She wanted to call your mother, but they haven't spoken to each other in years."

"She got away with it."

"Huh?"

"My mother killed a man and she's just walking around scot-free, just like she didn't take a man's life and ruin my father's life." Freddie pulled at her hair in frustration. "And you know what else? I walked away from everything."

"You mean your hotel?"

She nodded solemnly. "Since Loraine claims that she did everything that she did for the good of the business, she can have it."

"No offense, but your mom has never been good at business and you basically built that hotel into what it is now."

Freddie didn't want to think about what she'd given up and how much of her blood, sweat, and tears she'd poured into The French Garden Inn. "Cleveland asked me to marry him," she blurted out.

"What? Are you kidding me?" Lillian asked, her eyes stretched to the size of silver dollars. "But you haven't known him that long and . . . Did you say yes?"

Freddie closed her eyes and dropped her head. "As much as I love him, I don't know if I'm ready. What do I have to offer him?"

Lillian didn't say anything as she rose from the sofa and headed to the kitchen. Freddie followed her. "Lil, how are you just going to walk away?"

"Because I'm just blown away that Cleveland would want to get married. What do you two really know about each other?"

"Here we go. You still don't like him, do you?" Freddie asked.

"I don't have to like him, but you can't seriously be considering marrying him?"

"Why not?" Freddie said as she sat down on a bar stool and grabbed an apple from the fruit bowl on the center of the bar. "I love him."

"And love isn't going to pay the bills, love isn't going to get you through the hard times . . ."

"Are you and Louis having problems?" Freddie asked.

Lillian grabbed an apple of her own and sat beside Freddie. "No, we're not. But marriage isn't easy and look at how long Louis and I knew each other before we got married."

Freddie bit into the apple, wishing that she could write off what Lillian was saying, but she knew marriage was hard. She knew that she and Cleveland had a lot of things to work out before they could start a life together. But she wanted to be with him and she did love him, but did she know how to love him and be a wife? Then there was the whole thing with her finding a job. There was no way she could be a housewife. She had to do something. But did that mean she had to accept his proposal?

"Lillian," Freddie said. "I need a job."

"Uh-huh. Why don't you just talk to your future sister-in-law? Do you want me to cook some lunch?" Lillian looked at her watch. "Or I guess it would be brunch."

Freddie rolled her eyes. "Look," Lillian said. "The last time I gave you advice it nearly ruined our friendship, so I'm not going to say anything."

"Lil," Freddie said. "I was wrong before and I'm sorry that I took things so personally when I told you about Cleveland."

"And I shouldn't have gotten on my high horse about him. I don't really know him the way you do and I could be wrong about him. I've seen a change in Cleveland. The other day when I took Louis lunch to the fire station, Cleveland was talking about you."

A slow smile spread across Freddie's face. "Really?"

Lillian nodded as she walked over to the stove. "I've heard Cleveland talk about women in the past and it was all about her ass, her breasts or what she did or didn't do in bed. Of course, these were conversations that I wasn't supposed to hear," she said as she pulled a pan from underneath the stove.

"So, how did you hear these conversations?"

Lillian turned around and smirked at her friend. "Hello, I know where to sit and wait for my man without being seen or heard."

"Okay, you're scary," Freddie said with a laugh.

"It's no secret that I'm nosy. But anyway, Cleveland and Louis were sitting in the break room, drinking Coca Colas and talking about us. Cleveland was gushing about how special you are to him. He said that he'd never met a woman like you. Basically, he said that you're on his level. You're smart and witty and it doesn't hurt that you have a banging body. That's when I made my presence known. The last thing I wanted to hear were any details about what you two do when you're naked."

Freddie smiled, imagining the look on their faces when Lillian walked in the room. "Maybe I was wrong about Cleveland," Lillian said as she opened the refrigerator and searched for something to cook.

"All right," Freddie said. "Let me write this down because you just admitted that you were wrong about something."

Lillian pulled out a carton of eggs and a roll of turkey sausage. "Whatever, Winnie."

Freddie tossed her apple core at Lillian. "There you go with that Winnie crap!"

"Just kidding with you. I know you hate that nickname."

Freddie walked over to Lillian and started helping her cook the eggs and sausage. Lillian looked at her friend as she cracked some eggs into a bowl.

"You know all that stuff I said about love?" Lillian

began as Freddie sprinkled paprika in the eggs. "I was wrong. Love changes people, and if you love Cleveland Alexander, then you should marry him."

Freddie stopped sprinkling the seasoning. "What?"

"Marry that man. If you want to marry him, then do it."

"I'm scared," she whispered as she began to stir the eggs. "I really don't know if I can be the wife that he deserves."

Lillian turned the stove on and smiled. "Yes, you can. Even though I would've never admitted it on my wedding day, I don't think I was ready to get married. And then when we began living together as husband and wife, I thought that I wasn't good enough for Louis. I was afraid for him to see that I'm not perfect."

"No one expects you to be perfect," Freddie said. "You put those restrictions on yourself."

"That's not true. When people come to my house, everyone expects me to have the perfect dinner, a spotless house and . . ."

"Once again, no one expects you to be perfect, you just want us to think that you are perfect. We know the truth, and even with your flaws, we love you," Freddie said.

"I learned that when Louis woke up one morning before I did and he was just staring at me. So, I'm thinking, my God, I must look a mess. But he gently kissed me on the lips and said 'Good morning, beautiful.'"

"What's so special about that?" she asked.

"Because, I used to get up and pull a Whitley."

"A what?"

"Remember on *A Different World* when Whitley would get up and put makeup on and brush her teeth before Dwayne Wayne would wake up? That's how I spent the first month of our marriage."

Freddie poured the eggs into a heated pan and laughed uncontrollably at her friend. "You have got to be kidding me."

Lillian tossed in the crumbled sausage. "No."

Freddie shook her head and thought that Cleveland was going to have to love her just for who she was because there was no way that she'd do what Lillian did.

Cleveland and Darren stood at the counter in Ross-Simons looking at diamonds. Shaking his head, Cleveland expelled a curse. "This is too much," he said.

"What?"

"Shopping for a diamond ring," he said.

Darren laughed and slapped his brother on his back. "This is what you get for asking a woman to marry you. So, tell me again, you blurted out that you wanted to marry her while you two were having sex?"

The clerk, who was about to open the case to show Cleveland a group of rings, arched her eyebrow at Darren's comment. She put back the rings that she'd initially reached for and pulled out a group of rings that were about two carats bigger.

"Something tells me that she deserves more than a half karat," she said.

Darren turned his head away and laughed. "Damn," he said.

Cleveland punched his brother in the arm. "Maybe I want to do something different. Because Freddie is just that special," Cleveland said. "How about a ruby?"

The clerk nodded. "That is different. Do you think that's wise? What if she wants a diamond?"

Cleveland smiled. "I think she'll like it. Our love is fiery just like that stone."

The clerk put the diamonds away and excused herself to find some ruby rings, which were in a different display case. Darren closed his hand around Cleveland's shoulder. "Are you sure you're ready to do this?"

"Yeah, if she doesn't like the ring then . . ."

"I'm not talking about buying a ring. I'm talking about marriage. This isn't something that you should enter into lightly."

"Now you sound like a preacher," Cleveland said. "Do you think I would've asked her to marry me if I wasn't ready?"

Darren nodded. "Yes, I do. I don't understand how you go from Mr. Bachelor to Mr. I'm-Ready-to-Make-a-Commitment."

"Freddie has shown me what it's like to be with someone worth risking it all for. When I wake up in the morning, she's my first thought."

"I guess so since she's living in your house, sleeping in your bed, and she doesn't have a job. Are you sure this woman isn't just using you as a means to start her life over after Katrina."

Cleveland fought the urge to deck his brother. "When did you become Mr. Cynical? How can you even say that about her? You've met Freddie and . . ."

The clerk returned with a tray of ruby rings. "Here we go. These are some of the most beautiful rings that we have with ruby stones."

Cleveland glared at Darren before he turned back to the clerk. He couldn't understand where his brother's attitude came from.

Darren remained silent as the clerk presented Cleveland with a princess-cut ruby ring in a white gold setting.

Cleveland picked up the ring, held it up to the light and smiled. "Perfect."

"This is wrong," Darren blurted out.

"What?" Cleveland said, nearly dropping the ring.

"There are other rings," the clerk said. "I can grab some of the other ones and . . ."

Cleveland reached out and touched her shoulder. "No, this is fine." Then he turned to Darren. "You need to chill the hell out."

"Excuse me," the clerk said, pushing her raven hair behind her ears. "I'm going to wrap this up." She couldn't get away from the brothers fast enough.

"Listen, this thing has happened too fast. If you really love her, then take a little more time to get to know her," Darren said. "What if she sees you as a pay day?"

"Bullshit," Cleveland said. "Just because you have made bad choices, don't try and put that off on me."

"Didn't you warn me about Rita?"

"And didn't you ignore me?"

"Look how well that turned out."

Cleveland shook his head and glowered at his brother. "You know what? I have faith in what Freddie and I have. I don't give a damn what you or anyone else thinks about us."

"Whatever, but I don't want to see you get hurt because if that happens, you're going to shut yourself down to any other woman that you come across," Darren said.

"And when Freddie and I live happily ever after? Then how many times do I get to say 'I told you so'?"

Darren ran his hand over his face. "I pray that I'm wrong. But be realistic, bro. What you're doing only happens in the movies and in fairy tales."

"And how often does the fireman end up with the billionaire?" Cleveland snapped before stomping off to the cash register. He didn't give a damn what Darren thought, he loved Freddie and she was going to be his wife.

Cleveland decided to take the MARTA back to his place because he was too pissed off at his brother to ride in the same car with him. But part of him wondered if Darren was right. Was he rushing into marriage with Freddie? They'd fallen in love so quickly. But he and Darren knew that tomorrow was never promised.

His cell phone rang. "Yeah," he said.

"All right, bro," Darren said. "I'm sorry, I was out of line and I shouldn't have said those things in the store."

"You're damned right."

"I know you're pissed," he said. "But marriage is serious business and you don't want to do it more than once."

"I know this, but she is the love of my life."

"Well, I hope she says yes when you ask her again," Darren said. "Properly."

"All right. Maybe I'll invite you to the wedding when she says yes," Cleveland ribbed. "I'll call you later." After hanging up the phone, he smiled and prayed that the train would grow wings so that he could get home and pop the question again.

Chapter 31

After Freddie left Lillian's, she didn't go straight home. She wandered around downtown Atlanta, for once not cursing the slow flow of the traffic and clogged streets. As she drove, with her windows down and the wind blowing her hair, Freddie went back and forth on saying yes to Cleveland's marriage proposal. *What if I say yes? Will his family think I'm trying to take advantage of him because I don't have a job and my savings aren't going to last much longer? And if I say no, I could miss out on the best thing that's ever happened to me,* she thought as she slowed her car for a red light. Looking to her left, she glanced at the DVA building where Cleveland's sister-in-law worked. Though she didn't know Jill that well, Freddie decided that she needed to swallow her pride and pay her a visit. Maybe Jill could help her find a job, because Freddie didn't want to enter into a marriage where she was totally dependent on Cleveland.

Pulling into the vast parking garage, she wondered if Jill was in the office or if she would even see her. This woman was the CEO of the company and it was highly doubtful that she'd just open her door to Freddie as if they were two girlfriends about to have a chat. Still, Freddie got out of the car and headed into the building. As she entered, she saw Jill and a tall, brown-skinned man who wasn't Darren. The way they laughed with one another, she sensed they were familiar with one another, but not romantically.

"Freddie," Jill said when she spotted her. "What are you doing here?"

"I'm sorry to just show up like this, I'm sure you're really busy," Freddie said.

"Malik and I were just going to grab some lunch. How rude of me, Malik Greene, this is Freddie Barker, Cleveland's girlfriend."

Malik extended his hand to Freddie. "Nice to meet you." He suavely kissed her hand as if they were meeting on a street in Paris. Jill rolled her eyes and shook her head.

"Down boy," she ribbed. "Remember who's waiting for us at the restaurant."

"My beautiful wife," he said. "I'm married, not blind."

Freddie laughed nervously. "I don't mean to interrupt your lunch, I just . . ."

"Why don't you join us?" Jill suggested. Freddie looked down at her jeans and simple white oxford shirt.

"I don't know, I'm not properly dressed and . . ."

"We're going to a casual place and you're basically family, so it's cool," Jill said as they headed outside. "It's just two blocks down."

Freddie nodded and fell in step with Jill and Malik. "So, you're another Alexander?" Malik asked.

"Not yet," Freddie replied with a smile. "That's something we're working on."

"It's the season of the bride," Malik said then turned to Jill. "My lawyer's getting married next week."

Jill smiled. "You started all of this," she said. "You and Shari make marriage look so easy and breezy."

"You know that isn't true," Malik said. "And you of all people should know that Shari and I have had a time of it."

Jill nodded, then turned to Freddie. "Don't listen to us. It's all worth it in the end. Having someone who you love and who loves you back is an indescribable feeling."

Malik nodded. "And don't tell my wife, because I don't like to get mushy, but I can't sleep unless I feel her arms around me."

"I feel the same way about Cleveland," Freddie said.

"So, when's the wedding?" Jill asked. "I hate that I missed Louis's wedding. But that's where you two got your start, huh?"

Freddie blushed as she recalled the wedding and how she spent the wedding night. "Yes," she said. "Here's the thing, though, I can't marry Cleveland the way I am now."

Jill furrowed her eyebrows and looked at Freddie. "What do you mean?"

She sighed and ran her hand over her windblown hair. "I walked away from everything that I built in New Orleans and I don't want to be dependant on Cleveland or not be able to contribute to our marriage."

Malik tapped Jill on the shoulder. "I'm going to go inside and wait for you guys."

She nodded and then led Freddie to a bench near the entrance of the restaurant. The women took a seat and Jill faced Freddie. "I understand what you mean. But Cleveland loves you and I'm sure he doesn't think you're leeching off him or anything like that."

"I know, still, I've been working all of my adult life. I'm not wired to be a housewife."

"What were you doing in New Orleans?"

"Running a hotel," she said. "My mother and I own The

French Garden Inn in the French Quarter. I was in charge of the day-to-day business and she spent the profits."

"I have some friends in hospitality around here, I can put some calls out there and see what's available," Jill said.

"I really appreciate that." Freddie extended her hand to Jill, but Jill hugged her tightly.

"We're practically family. Come on, let's go eat."

Freddie released a sigh of relief, happy that Jill was willing to help her.

"Freddie," Cleveland called out when he walked into the house. "Freddie?" When he didn't get a reply, Cleveland knew that he had time to set the mood. He dashed upstairs and prepared the bathroom by setting candles around the tub. Then he went downstairs to the kitchen and filled a bowl with strawberries and took them into the bathroom as well.

Cleveland grabbed a pair of plush brown towels from the linen closet and hung them on the towel bar. Then he opened the bathroom cabinet and searched for some bath oil. As he began to run the water, he heard the front door open.

"Cleveland," Freddie called out as she headed upstairs.

"In the bathroom," he said. "Come join me."

She appeared in the doorway and smiled as he lit the last candle. "What's all of this?"

"Something special for you because you deserve it," he said as he began taking his shirt off. "Why are you standing over there with all of those clothes on?"

Freddie placed her hands on her hips. "You are something else."

Cleveland crossed over to her and brushed his lips against hers. "You think?" With nimble fingers, he unbuttoned her shirt. "Where have you been?" Before Freddie could answer him, he closed his lips on her neck, making her shiver.

"Umm, I had lunch with Jill and—ah—I was looking for a job and . . ." She stopped talking as his fingers slipped inside her bra.

"Come on, let's get in the tub," he said as he pushed her shirt off her shoulders. Freddie stepped out of her pants and followed Cleveland to the bathtub. The water smelled of sweet jasmine and was warm to the touch. Freddie stepped in the water and Cleveland took his clothes off then joined her. They lay in the water, Freddie's back against Cleveland's chest. He took the bath sponge and ran it down the center of her chest.

"You don't have to find a job right away, I know you need to get settled in," he said as he made small circles around her nipples with the sponge.

"Umm, I need a job. Sitting at home all day isn't my idea of fun," she said.

Cleveland dipped the sponge between her legs and toyed with her inner thighs. "I hear you. But I can take care of you."

Freddie turned around and kissed the center on his chest. "I know you can," she said. "But it's not always all about me and what I need."

"It is if I say it is," he said as he tweaked the end of her nose.

She slapped his hand away, sloshing water over the side of the tub. "Seriously, Cleveland. I'm unemployed right now and other than the best sex of your life, what do I have to bring into this relationship?"

Though he was highly aroused, Cleveland found the voice to say, "What we have is about more than sex. Hell, the sex is good because we connect on so many other levels. Look, you haven't been in town that long and you've been through a lot. If you want to regroup before you get back on your feet, I'm fine with that."

"But I don't want you to feel like you're carrying me," she said. "That's why I went to Jill to ask her for help finding a job."

Cleveland pulled her against his chest, so close to his face that their lips brushed against one another's. "You're important to me and if you feel like you have to work, that's fine. I never expected you to be a housewife, besides, I couldn't afford to keep you at home anyway."

"And I wouldn't want you to," she said, thrusting her hips into his.

"Don't do that. I'm trying to prove to you that what we have is more than sex and you do *that*."

She gyrated against him, sloshing water with every sensual move. "Who said sex was a bad thing?"

Wrapping his arms around her hips, Cleveland blew out the candles, then slowly lifted her from the tub. "Then let me get some of this good thing," he said with a grin on his face.

Later after they were spent from lovemaking, Cleveland and Freddie layed in bed wrapped in each other's arms. While she slept soundly, he drank in the beauty of her silky skin, her thick lips that were pressed against his moments ago. Freddie looked like an angel as she slept. Gently he ran his index finger down her cheek, careful not to wake her up. He inched closer to her and brushed his lips softly against her cheek. With his free hand, he reached into the nightstand drawer and pulled out the ruby ring that he'd bought earlier that day. He placed the box on her pillow then kissed the back of her neck. Freddie's eyes fluttered open.

"Wake up, Sleeping Beauty," he said.

"Umm," she moaned. "Do I have to?"

"Yes," he said.

Freddie stretched her arms above her head and her hand brushed against the box. "What's this?" She took the velvet box into her hand then opened it. "Cleveland."

"Do you like it?"

"I love it."

"Do you love me?"

"You know it."

He took the ring from the box and reached for her left hand. "What do you say we get married?"

Freddie's smile spread from ear to ear. "I say yes."

He slipped the ring in place and it fit perfectly, just as he knew it would. "I can't wait to spend the rest of my life with you."

Freddie looked at the ring. "How did you know that I loved rubies?"

He shrugged. "It was just a hunch and I wanted something different for you. Because we have a different type of relationship, you know."

"Do you think we ought to pull ourselves out of the bed and share our news?" she asked.

Cleveland took her left hand and placed it over his arousal. "Getting out of bed isn't an option right now." He covered her body with his, kissing her with a fiery passion that was hot enough to make her melt. Freddie wrapped her arms around his neck, pulling him closer and deeper. Her legs quivered as his hand dipped between her thighs and anticipation coursed through her body like the blood that flowed through her veins.

"Cleveland," she moaned as his finger found his way between the moist folds of flesh hiding her throbbing bud of desire. Inching down her body, Cleveland buried his face between her thighs and lapped her womanly juices like they were the sweetest nectar he'd ever tasted. Freddie grasped the sheets as he circled her most tender spot with his tongue. Her breasts heaved as she panted while his lips covered her flesh.

Freddie released the sheets as she exploded under his kiss. Intense feelings of pleasure filled her senses and all she could do was let Cleveland control her body as he had been. He traveled up her body until he reached her breasts. Freddie's nipples were rock hard, waiting for his lips and tongue to tease them. She placed her hand on Cleveland's manhood, stroking him as he kissed and licked her breasts and then her neck.

He moaned with a sound that came from the depths of his soul. "I need to be inside," Cleveland groaned.

"Need. You. Inside." Her voice was staccato. Cleveland retrieved a condom from underneath his pillow and with the quickness and skill of a magician, he slid the sheath in place and melted with her. As he pumped his hips in, Freddie matched him stroke for stroke. The heat between them was enough to build a forest fire in the middle of the bed. He lifted her from the sheets and folded her legs around his waist. They danced a sensual dance of passion until sweat dripped from their bodies like falling rain.

"Cleveland, Cleveland, Cleveland," she repeated as if she was in a trance. The hot wetness that surrounded him rendered Cleveland unable to speak. Unable to say how much he loved her, unable to tell her that he wanted every moment of their lives to be this way.

Collapsing against the sheets, Freddie and Cleveland held each other and silently basked in the afterglow of their desire.

"Promise me that after we walk down the aisle that

you're going to continue to blow my mind like this," he said when he caught his breath.

"Are you sure you can handle this for the rest of your life?" she teased.

"Umm, you've been more than I can handle since the day we met, but somehow I've managed." He kissed her passionately, arousing himself again. When she felt him throbbing against her thighs, Freddie knew that she was in for the ride of her life.

Epilogue

When Freddie and Cleveland got married, it wasn't a fancy affair. They'd had their fill of wedding drama after standing up for Lillian and Louis. Instead, the Grand Hilton hotel in downtown Atlanta, where Freddie was the General Manager, served as the venue for the wedding. The ballroom was aglow with the flickering light of a hundred candles (Lillian's idea) and a few hand-tied bouquets of white-and-pink roses circled the altar, even though Lillian thought the pink roses were mauve. Freddie told her friend that she needed to get her eyes checked.

As the couple stood in front of the reverend, Freddie stared deep into Cleveland's gray eyes. This wasn't a dream, she was going to be happy and spend her life with a man that matched her passion and intensity. A man who loved her above all else and someone who would never let her down. Just as the minister was about to pronounce the couple man and wife, Freddie could've sworn she saw her father tipping out the back of the ballroom. Smiling, she said, "I do."

Before the reverend got the words, "You may kiss the bride," out of his mouth, Cleveland had Freddie in his arms, kissing her as if they were the only two in the room. Catcalls and cheers came from the small audience of family and firefighters. Most of the guests at the wedding had to see Cleveland tell this woman "I do," because they just couldn't believe that he was getting married. Though it was the happiest day of his life, Cleveland did miss Roland. He could only imagine what his friend would've said when he announced his engagement.

"Are you kidding me?" Roland would've said. "First of all, I can't even imagine that she gave you the time of day. Now you two are getting married? Damn, another player gone."

"You can have my player card, man," Cleveland would have told him as they kicked back over some beers and hot wings.

Roland would shake his head. "I don't get it man, first Darren, which I can understand. Then Louis, which I'm sure he was given a timetable to get married, but not you, man!"

"What did Teddy Pendergrass say? It feels so good when someone loves you back."

Grunting, Roland would grab another wing. "What time do I need to be there?"

Cleveland smiled and squeezed Freddie's hand. Roland would've loved Freddie, eventually.

"Are we really supposed to be this happy?" she whispered as they posed for pictures with the wedding party, which was comprised of Jill, Lillian, Louis and Darren.

"Yes, we are," Cleveland said. "And trust me, the best is yet to come."

Look For These Other
Dafina Novels

If I Could
0-7582-0131-1
by Donna Hill
$6.99US/**$9.99**CAN

Thunderland
0-7582-0247-4
by Brandon Massey
$6.99US/**$9.99**CAN

June In Winter
0-7582-0375-6
by Pat Phillips
$6.99US/**$9.99**CAN

Yo Yo Love
0-7582-0239-3
by Daaimah S. Poole
$6.99US/**$9.99**CAN

When Twilight Comes
0-7582-0033-1
by Gwynne Forster
$6.99US/**$9.99**CAN

It's A Thin Line
0-7582-0354-3
by Kimberla Lawson Roby
$6.99US/**$9.99**CAN

Perfect Timing
0-7582-0029-3
by Brenda Jackson
$6.99US/**$9.99**CAN

Never Again Once More
0-7582-0021-8
by Mary B. Morrison
$6.99US/**$8.99**CAN

Available Wherever Books Are Sold!

Check out our website at www.kensingtonbooks.com.

More of the Hottest
African-American Fiction from
Dafina Books

Come With Me J.S. Hawley	0-7582-1935-0	$6.99/$9.99
Golden Night Candice Poarch	0-7582-1977-6	$6.99/$9.99
No More Lies Rachel Skerritt	0-7582-1601-7	$6.99/$9.99
Perfect For You Sylvia Lett	0-7582-1979-2	$6.99/$9.99
Risk Ann Christopher	0-7582-1434-0	$6.99/$9.99

Available Wherever Books Are Sold!